THE NEIGHBOR

LET EVERYONE GUARD AGAINST HIS NEIGHBOR...

MARK DAVID ABBOTT

Copyright © 2023 by Mark David Abbott

All rights reserved.

No part of this book may be reproduced in any form or by any electronic or mechanical means, including information storage and retrieval systems, without written permission from the author, except for the use of brief quotations in a book review.

❦ Created with Vellum

For Tiamo
The best kind of neighbors

DO YOU WANT ADVANCE NOTICE OF THE NEXT ADVENTURE?

The next book is currently being written, but if you sign up for my VIP newsletter I will let you know as soon as it is released.

Your email will be kept 100% private and you can unsubscribe at any time.

If you are interested, please join here:

www.markdavidabbott.com
(No Spam. Ever.)

1

The elderly man tucked the tail of his wife's coat inside, then pushed the passenger door closed. He straightened up as best he could, trying to ignore the protests from his ageing body.

Getting old was a pain in the... well, the whole body.

David Hayes grimaced, finding no mirth in his own joke.

He hobbled around the back of the car, nodding a greeting to a young mother pushing a shopping trolley laden with groceries. Her young son sat facing her in the trolley's child seat, chewing on a carrot stick, and as they passed the rear of the car, he held out a chubby little hand, offering David a bite of the carrot.

Despite his aches and pains, David smiled and shook his head. That was the best age, but sadly, it didn't last long enough. Cute little kids became moody, cranky teenagers who then left home, only to be heard from at Christmas and on birthdays.

David took a deep breath, then opened the driver's door of the car and eased himself into the seat.

"Alright, dear?" he asked, more out of habit than

anything else, as he fumbled in the pocket of his tweed jacket for the car keys.

"Can't complain."

Carole never complained. She was always grateful, no matter what happened... and they had plenty to complain about.

The car engine grumbled and coughed before reluctantly settling into an uneven idle. He selected reverse, then checked the mirrors and backed the car out of the parking space.

There was a loud honk, and he jumped in his seat, instinctively jamming his foot on the brake pedal. With difficulty, he turned stiffly and looked over his shoulder to see a dark blue BMW flashing its lights. The driver gave him the middle finger before revving the engine and accelerating past.

"Bloody impatient bugger," he muttered, then checked his mirrors again before reversing. Why was everyone in such a hurry?

Exiting the supermarket carpark, he took a left turn, taking the route that led through the outer suburbs on the northern edge of Winchester toward their home just outside the village of Stockbridge. Once out of the city, it was a pleasant drive along country lanes lined with hedgerows and stone walls. It was one of those beautiful spring days where the sun held warmth, and the clouds that punctuated the deep blue sky were for decoration rather than threatening rain. The rolling green fields of Hampshire spread out on either side and bunches of daffodils and buttercups dotted the roadside.

The scenery lifted David's mood and he and Carole settled into a comfortable silence as they drove deeper into the countryside. They loved their part of the world and couldn't imagine living anywhere else.

After twenty-five minutes, David indicated left, then pulled into the narrow lane leading toward their cottage. The road surface was pitted and broken and he guided the car carefully around the worst of the potholes, as the edges of the road tapered in, and the ancient hedgerows on each side towered over the car, creating a tunnel effect. The road curved to the right as it narrowed further, and he honked a warning before continuing cautiously around the corner.

As the road straightened, he saw two vehicles heading towards him at speed. He braked instinctively, but in his panic stalled, and the little hatchback jerked to a halt.

The oncoming vehicles, a black SUV and a sleek black sedan, flashed their lights and honked, showing no sign of giving way.

David's heart raced and his hand trembled as he reached for the ignition key and twisted it. The car lurched forward, but didn't start. He tried again, this time putting his foot on the clutch and the car started, but he had nowhere to go, the two black vehicles filling the lane in front of him. Engaging reverse, he glanced at his wife. Her face was pale, her eyes wide, and her hands gripped the seat belt across her chest.

The SUV honked and flashed its lights again.

"Okay, okay," he grumbled. "I'm moving."

He backed up as best as he could, but the high banks and hedgerows lining both sides of the lane gave him no option to get out of the way. He glanced toward the front again, hoping the convoy had moved over a little so he could squeeze past, but the grill of the SUV loomed in his windshield as if pushing him along.

Gritting his teeth, he looked back, and reversed around

the corner until the lane widened slightly and moved the car closer to the edge of the road. There was a loud thud, and the car lurched at an angle as the left rear wheel entered a ditch.

"Dammit."

He pressed his right foot on the accelerator, but the car struggled to move, the little engine whining in protest. The black SUV honked again, then pushed through the gap between the hatchback and the hedgerow on the other side of the lane, followed closely by the large sedan.

The heavily tinted windows prevented them from seeing inside, but they didn't have to. They knew who it was.

It was the new neighbour.

2

John slipped the clutch, easing the car forward, then turned left down the ramp leading off the Eurotunnel Shuttle and onto the platform. He blipped the throttle of his 1970 Porsche 911S, the 180 horsepower flat-six engine giving a satisfying bark from the exhaust, earning a grin and a thumbs up from one of the Eurotunnel workers standing beside the train.

John waved back, then searched for the exit signs while a growing nervousness churned away in the pit of his stomach.

He had left Lisbon three days earlier, taking a leisurely drive north, stopping for the night in northern Spain, then once again in a small town in the French countryside before boarding *Le Shuttle* in Calais. He'd avoided the toll routes, taking instead the country roads, a slower, less direct route, but in the car that was his pride and joy, much more fun. It served another purpose, too. Delaying his arrival.

He climbed slowly through the gears, short-shifting, keeping the revs low, until the engine temperatures warmed up. He'd had the car stripped back to bare paint and then restored, but it was still over fifty years old, and needed to be handled with respect.

Ignoring the signs for the M20, he followed the directions he had programmed into the sat-nav. Directions leading to the minor roads heading west toward the city of Winchester. It would take him longer, almost doubling the journey time, but he was in no hurry.

The truth was, England was almost like a new country to him. He had turned his back on the country of his birth since Charlotte's funeral[1]. There were memories he didn't want to relive, but they only accounted for some of the nerves. It was the thought of seeing his parents after so long that was causing the most apprehension. But John had made a promise to the parents of Trevor Hughes,[2] the young man killed by Atman. A promise he hadn't meant to keep until Adriana convinced him otherwise... and she was usually right.

John slowed for a junction, downshifting with a blip on the throttle to match the revs, and cast a quick glance at the oil temperature. Warm enough. He checked to his right for oncoming traffic, then accelerated out of the junction, changing gear only when the needle on the rev counter was just below the red line. The growl of the flat-six boxer engine made the hair on his arms stand up, and he grinned. He never tired of it. The car wasn't powerful by modern standards, but the rawness, the way it involved him as a driver, the constant feedback from the steering and the suspension, more than made up for the lack of modern technology. He concentrated on the road for the next few minutes, a huge grin on his face, the winding 'B' road giving plenty of opportunity to work the gears, then when it joined a wider 'A' road he allowed his thoughts to wander back to his parents.

His father had always been distant, even while growing up, and he'd had little to do with his parents once he finished school and left home. Birthdays, Christmas, and the occasional call in between, had been the extent of the contact. But when Charlotte was murdered, John had struggled with grief for a long time, and he had shut himself off. Getting his revenge on her killers had helped somewhat, but even then, he had no desire to revisit his old life in England. Memories from the past were better left buried. The wounds were still too raw, and he could feel himself tensing up, his heart rate increasing.

He stamped hard on the accelerator, flashed his lights and pulled out to pass a slow-moving hatchback. His knuckles turned white as he gripped the steering wheel, still accelerating well past the car, until a sharp bend forced him to brake heavily. John took a deep, slow breath, calming himself, and continued at a more sensible speed. Wrapping himself around a tree wouldn't help anyone.

John checked the journey time on the GPS. There was still plenty of time left before he would see them. He might as well enjoy the drive.

3

John downshifted, made the turn, then immediately slammed on the brakes.

The lane ahead was rutted and pitted with holes, the tarred surface in desperate need of repair.

John frowned. Granted, he hadn't been back in years, but he had never seen it this bad. Slipping the car into first, he moved slowly forward, scanning the road ahead for the best route, trying to avoid the worst of the potholes. But the narrow lane provided little room to manoeuvre, and he winced at the sound of metal on stone as something underneath the car ground along the broken road surface. The joy from the last couple of hours' cross-country drive evaporated as he crawled up the lane toward the cottage. John couldn't understand how it had fallen into such disrepair.

A few painful minutes later, John pulled up outside the cottage and turned the engine off.

Willow Cottage looked shabbier than he remembered. The paint on the window frames was peeling, the lawn looked like it hadn't been mown in months, and the garden, his mother's pride and joy, was filled with weeds.

The Neighbor

John hadn't told his parents that he was coming. He'd wanted to leave a way out in case he changed his mind, and even now he was hoping they weren't home. But their car was in the driveway and the net curtains in the living room window twitched as someone peered out.

Taking another deep breath, he opened the door and stepped out. He twisted from side to side, easing out the kinks from the long drive, and inhaled a deep lungful of fresh country air while gazing out over the fields. A pheasant crowed from a nearby copse, and John sighed.

Now he was here, he might as well make the most of it. Turning back toward the house, he opened the wooden gate and walked up the brick pathway toward the house. He was halfway along the pathway when the door opened and his heart skipped a beat.

His father stood in the doorway, his eyes narrowed as he peered over the top of his reading glasses. His gaze moved past John and lingered on the red Porsche for a moment, then back to John.

"John," he nodded, his moustache twitching as he pursed his lips. "You'd best be coming in then."

4

"Who is it, dear?"

"John."

John heard a squeal of delight, and he smiled for the first time. *He shouldn't have left it so long.* Stepping inside, he pulled the door closed behind him, taking a moment for his eyes to adjust to the dim light. There was something about the air inside that was instantly familiar.

John saw his mother struggling to rise from an armchair near the window and he rushed over and eased her back into her chair. She threw her arms around him and he closed his eyes and leaned forward, then after a moment wrapped his arms around her.

"Hi, Mum," he murmured into her shoulder, as a lump formed in his throat.

"Oh, John, John." She released her embrace and held him at arm's length, studying his face with moist eyes. "It's been so long."

John swallowed and looked away, unable to maintain eye contact.

She let go, and he straightened up, looking over his

shoulder for his father, who stood in the hallway that led toward the kitchen.

"Dad," John nodded a greeting.

"I'll get you some tea," he replied gruffly, and disappeared down the hallway.

"Don't mind him. He's become a grump."

John turned back to his mother and smiled. "He always was."

His mother giggled, the sound at once comforting, and filling John with warmth. He looked around for somewhere to sit, then grabbed one of the dining chairs and placed it beside her armchair.

"How have you been?" he asked, as he sat down beside her.

"I can't complain, John." She reached out and took his hand. "I'm getting older, that's all… but tell me about you. It's been so long."

"Yeah," John sighed. "I… I'm sorry." He shrugged and gazed around the living room of the cottage. "After… you know… I couldn't come back."

He felt his mother squeeze his hand and recognised his own sorrow mirrored in her eyes. But then she smiled. "We loved her too, John."

John looked away, his eyes welling with tears, just as his father walked into the room carrying a tray. He stopped, looked over at John, frowned, then placed the tray on the dining table.

John let go of his mother's hand, blinked the tears from his eyes, stood up, and crossed the room. He stood next to his father and looked down at the tray holding a teapot and three cups. Beside them was a side plate with several chocolate biscuits, a small bowl of sugar cubes, and a jug of milk.

"Give it a minute. It needs to brew."

John nodded, not knowing what to say. He had been close to his mum, but his father had always been distant and reserved. It seemed now, as if the distance had increased, but then John felt a hand on his shoulder.

"Welcome home," his father muttered, then let go, and reached for a cup. "Sugar?"

"No. Thank you."

His father nodded, and set up the other two cups, placing a cube of sugar in his own. John watched him pour the milk — he always put the milk first — then pick up the teapot and give it a swirl, before topping up the cups with tea.

John carried a cup over to his mother, who winked as she took it from him. John went back for his own and then stood awkwardly beside his father, both holding their teacups and staring at nothing in particular.

David Hayes cleared his throat. "Will you be staying?"

"Yes... if that's okay."

"Of course," Carole piped up from the other side of the room. "Stay as long as you like."

John smiled at her, then glanced at his father, who nodded and took a sip of his tea.

He wiped his moustache with the back of his hand and said, "Your mother insisted on keeping your room as you left it. She said you would come back."

John looked away and took a large gulp of tea so he didn't have to say anything.

5

John reached behind the seat for his bag. He was travelling light, just one leather holdall enough to carry what he needed. There wasn't much room in the little sports car for anything else.

"Is that all?"

John jumped, not expecting the voice behind him, and he turned to see his father looking at the bag in his hand.

"Yup. I travel light."

"Not planning to stay long?"

"I told you, I travel light."

"Hmm," his father replied, his attention moving to the car. His face visibly softened as his eyes roamed the interior.

John moved aside and held the door open. "Take a look."

David stepped forward, bending down to look inside. "You've kept it original."

"Almost. I've upgraded the brakes, suspension, sound system, and had a bit of work done to the engine. Mainly for reliability and safety, but the rest is stock."

"She's beautiful."

John dangled the car keys in front of his father's face. "Start her up."

David hesitated, a twitch of his moustache hinting at a smile, then took the keys from John and lowered himself into the driver's seat.

A moment later, he actually smiled as the Porsche engine burst into life. He turned his head slightly, so his left ear could hear the engine at the rear, and he blipped the throttle.

"She's a beauty. Early 70s?"

"1970."

His father nodded. "I saw one once, in the High Street. Beautiful. But expensive even then." He looked up at John. "It must cost an arm and a leg now."

John shrugged. "In some ways I've been fortunate, Dad."

His father's eyes roamed John's face, as if looking for something, then he nodded. Reaching out, he switched off the engine, then sat silently looking out the windshield. After several moments, he said, "We miss her too, John."

John couldn't think of anything to say, so he straightened up and gazed across the fields. Fields he had walked across with Charlotte. He forced the memory back into the box and mentally closed the lid, as he felt a hand on his arm.

His father was smiling for the second time since John's arrival. "Perhaps we can go for a drive later?"

"Definitely." John stepped back, then reached down and helped his father out of the car, David grunting with the effort, his knees cracking and popping as he stood up.

"What happened to the road?" John nodded toward the lane behind the car. "It was never this bad."

"No." David shook his head, his smile fading rapidly.

John waited for him to say more, but when he didn't, John probed further. "Has Lord Atwell run out of money?"

The Neighbor

The access to Willow Cottage, technically a 'byway,' crossed the Atwell Estate and had been maintained by Lord Atwell and his family for generations.

"Lord Atwell has gone. Lost all his money to the bookies, then put a shotgun in his mouth and blew a hole in his head."

"What? No!"

"Yes." His father exhaled loudly. "There's a new owner now. A foreigner. Bought the Estate for a song. But he doesn't like to spend money on the road."

John frowned. "But he has to. It's a legal requirement."

"Huh," David snorted and closed the car door.

John looked back down the road, at the water-filled potholes and the encroaching branches from the overgrown hedgerow. "Have you spoken to the council?"

"I've tried, but why will they listen to me? I'm an old man."

John turned back and looked at his father, who suddenly looked very frail. His shoulders were slumped, his head hung low, and there was a slight tremor in his hand as he handed John the keys. John hefted the bag in his left hand, taking his father's arm in his right. "I'll speak to them for you."

"Good luck with that," his father harrumphed. "You haven't met the new owner yet."

6

The knuckles of Xie Longwei's hand turned white as he dug his fingertips into the leather covered centre console of his Mercedes Maybach S600.

Who the hell did Philip Symonds think he was? The stupid little man in his badly cut tweed suit and his tiny office stuffed full of files. He probably lived alone in a semi-detached house with a cat and ate microwaved meals in front of his TV.

The Atwell Estate was Xie's property, and Xie alone decided what he did with it. He had spent a considerable fortune repairing and updating the property after the previous owner had let it fall into disrepair. How on earth did the man think he had the right to tell Xie what to do? No-one told Xie what to do.

The West had a lot of things going for it, but the democracy they crowed about was highly overrated. Back in China, if he wanted something done, it was done. No questions asked.

He ground his teeth together and clenched his fist as the Maybach slowed, the black Range Rover in front turning

The Neighbor

into the entranceway of his estate. The large wrought-iron gates swung open, and the Range Rover accelerated through and up the long curving driveway toward the house. The Maybach followed smoothly after, Xie ignoring the salute from the guard at the entrance. He paid no attention to the expansive parkland, or the herds of grazing deer sheltering in the shade of the oak and sycamore trees. Today it gave him no pleasure. He could only think about his meeting with the irritating councillor.

And the racism... he saw it in the eyes of the man when he walked into his office. What did these white devils think of themselves? The Chinese were a superior race, and always had been. China had been a civilised empire for thousands of years while the West had been bickering over turnips and cabbages.

The two vehicles pulled up in front of Atwell Manor, and Xie waited impatiently as his two Chinese bodyguards fanned out from the Range Rover, their eyes hidden behind dark glasses, their suit jackets unbuttoned, allowing rapid access to their shoulder holstered weapons if necessary. Phillip Symonds had no idea of who he was dealing with.

His door opened, and the driver stood to attention, holding the door as Xie climbed out. Xie grunted a curt thank you, then made his way up the steps toward the front door of the house, grimacing at the complaints from his knees. The weather here didn't suit him either; the constant dampness seeping into his joints.

"Soup," he barked at the Chinese cook waiting at the top of the steps. Xie didn't have to explain which soup. The cook had been with him long enough to know when his *chi* was blocked.

7

John slowed to a walking pace, his breath visible as clouds of vapour in the chilly morning air. It was much cooler than in Portugal, and at first he'd found the run difficult until he had warmed up.

The sun stood just above the horizon and the sky was a crisp blue, with not a cloud in sight. Stopping, he stood with his hands on his hips, gazing around at the landscape falling away on each side of the bridle-path. A distant fox barked, and a rabbit halted in the middle of the ploughed field, raising its head in search of danger. John grinned. The English countryside on a clear day was beautiful... but he certainly didn't miss the winters.

He had slept well, surprisingly well. Three days of driving had taken its toll, but it was being home with his parents that had finally relaxed him. The guilt he had carried for so long had fallen away, leaving him feeling lighter and free.

The delight in his mother's eyes melted his heart, and even his father had warmed up, bringing out a bottle of his prized single malt to share with John after dinner. John wasn't a whisky guy—had never developed a taste for it—but he wasn't about to turn down the opportunity to reconnect with his father.

There were many things that were the same, as if he had never left, although they were older and frailer than he remembered, which was to be expected. Time waited for no-one.

His parents interacted with the comfort of years of marriage. They grumbled and teased, but beneath it all lay a genuine care for each other. John didn't have that kind of relationship—at least not yet. Charlotte hadn't lived long enough, and his relationship with Adriana, although filled with love, was still only a few years old.

Filling his lungs with the crisp, cold morning air, he smiled. Adriana had been right. If she hadn't pushed him, he wouldn't have come back. He checked his watch, but it was still a little early to call her. Shaking his arms out, he rotated his head, loosening his neck, and rolled his shoulders, before setting off again.

He was still a couple of miles from home, and was cutting across the Estate on a bridle-path, part of the network of ancient public pathways that criss-crossed the countryside. Nearing the edge of the field, he slowed to climb a stile set in the hedgerow. There was a sign next to it, and John frowned.

Private Property. No Entry.

Strange. Had he taken a wrong turn? He looked back the way he had come to make sure, then climbed onto the bottom step of the stile and looked across the next field. He could just make out the roof of his parents' cottage several fields away. He was in the right place. Shrugging, he vaulted over the stile, landing easily on the other side, and continued on his run. Whatever the new owner thought, bridle-ways were a public right of way, and no amount of signs on them could stop the public using them.

8

"Good morning, Mum," John leaned in and kissed his mother on the cheek. "That smells good."

"I hope you still like black pudding?"

His stomach growled, even though he rarely had more than coffee for breakfast. But he didn't want to disappoint his mother. "Yes, and how can I turn down yours?"

Carole chuckled.

"Can I make some coffee?"

"Oh, John," his mother turned away from the stove. "We don't have any. Your father and I only drink tea."

"That's okay. I'll pop out and get some later."

"I've made a fresh pot of tea, if you want some."

John smiled. "Thanks. Where's Dad?"

"He's in the bathroom. He takes a little longer these days."

"Still shaving every day?"

"What do you think?"

John chuckled and rubbed his chin. "He must hate seeing my stubble."

Carole wiped her hands on her apron, then placed both

hands on John's arms and gazed up at him. "He's thrilled to see you, John. I know he doesn't say much, but he loves you."

John nodded and looked away, embarrassed. Changing the subject, he asked, "Hey, what's with all the 'No Entry' signs on the Estate? I ran across it this morning."

A shadow passed across his mother's face. She looked down, then back up at John. "There's been a lot of changes since Lord Atwell... passed." Her eyes flicked over John's shoulder, and she lowered her voice. "Try not to talk about it in front of your father. He gets very angry, and it's not good for him."

"What's not good for me?"

John felt his mother's hands let go, and he fixed a smile on his face, before turning to see his father enter the kitchen. He was freshly shaved, his hair slicked down in an arrow-straight side parting, and a tightly knotted tie jutted proudly from the neck of his crisp checked shirt.

"Black pudding," John replied hurriedly. "Too much oil."

"What nonsense," his father grumbled. "Don't fill your mother's head with these new-fangled health fads. I'm as strong as an ox."

"And as stubborn as a mule," Carole retorted, with a wink at John. "Now, John, have a shower and change. Your breakfast is ready."

9

John walked slowly down the High Street. He could have gone anywhere, but he was drawn to one place in particular.

He stopped, stepping back into an empty doorway to avoid blocking the footpath and gazed across the street at the café where he had first met Charlotte. His heart was doing a dance in the middle of his chest, and there was a tingling in the tips of his fingers. He clenched his hands into fists and released them, then did it again. It was almost as if something in his subconscious took a perverse pleasure in digging up old memories.

He remembered that day like it was yesterday. He was sitting at a table in the window; the same table occupied now by a young couple who sat ignoring each other, staring at their phones. The café had been full, just like today. He smiled, as the memory of her walking in played like a movie in his mind. It had felt as if the breath had been sucked from his lungs, and he couldn't take his eyes off her. When she sat at the next table, the only seat available, time had stood still.

Charlotte had been the first to speak, asking him to pass

the sugar, and after a nervous start, the conversation flowed so well that an hour passed without them realising.

His smile broadened as he remembered her laugh, the sparkle in her eyes, her golden hair catching the sunlight from the window. He had felt guilty about the fading of her memory, but now he saw her smiling, almost as if she was standing in front of him. He saw her lips move, and although he couldn't hear anything, it felt as if she was saying, 'everything is okay.'

"Excuse me."

He flinched, startled by a voice behind him. John stepped out of the doorway and smiled at the young man, trying to get past. "I'm sorry."

The man grunted a reply, then walked away up the street as the door banged shut behind him.

John took a deep breath, then crossed the street and entered the café. It buzzed with animated conversation, and the air was filled with the promise of freshly roasted coffee. At the checkout he picked up a bag of coffee powder and a small French press, ordered a coffee to go, then leaned against the counter while it was being made, and watched the customers.

The young couple in the window were still staring at their phones, and John smiled. If only they could interact with each other, or the people around them. There was a whole magnificent world waiting to be experienced, a world far more fulfilling than they could ever experience through the screens of their phones.

His own life had truly begun at that table simply by engaging with the person next to him. Yes, there had been sorrow, heartbreak, and loss, but there had also been love, laughter, and adventure. If he could rewind to the day when he saw Charlotte for the first time, he would do it all over again.

"Black coffee for John Hayes?"

John turned back to the counter, flashed a big smile at the barista, and took his coffee.

"Have a great day, sir."

"Thank you." John's smile widened. "I intend to."

10

John took an indirect route back to his car, through the grounds of Winchester Cathedral. Students lounged on the grass, some studying, others giggling, flirting, and laughing with the carefree spirit of youth.

Little seemed to have changed since he was last there. Some shops were different, and people spent most of their time engrossed in their phones, but the atmosphere was the same. It was still the quaint little city he had left, but he couldn't imagine living there again. The city hadn't changed much, but he had. Significantly.

Once back at the car, he placed his shopping in the passenger footwell and climbed in. Two young boys stood on the footpath, watching, their eyes widening as he started the engine and gave it a rev. They looked up at their father, and said something John couldn't hear, but the expression on their faces was enough. Grinning, John gave them a wave, then pulled out of the parking space and headed home.

He drove slowly and, once out in the countryside,

wound down the windows, making the most of the crisp air and sunshine of spring.

His phone vibrated in his pocket and, shifting position with one eye on the road, he retrieved it and took a quick glance at the screen.

Adriana.

The phone rang off before he could answer and he drove on for a little while until he found a lay-by and pulled over. Switching the engine off, he stared out the windshield for a moment, confused by the emotions doing battle inside his head.

John loved Adriana with all of his heart, so why was he hesitating to call her back?

He was excited, of course, but there was guilt, too. He'd never made a secret of his feelings for Charlotte and how he had struggled with her loss, and to be fair, Adriana had accepted everything without question. But now Charlotte's memory had been rekindled, he almost felt like he was betraying Adriana. His thumb lingered over her number for a long moment, then he tapped the screen.

"Hey."

The nervousness evaporated as soon as he heard her voice, and he grinned. "*Bom dia.*"

"Did I disturb you?"

John shook his head as if she could see him. "No, no. I was driving so I couldn't take the call. I'd gone into town to get some coffee. My parents only drink tea."

"How... how are they? Happy to see you?"

"Yes, thrilled." John's tone became serious. "I shouldn't have left it so long. Thank you."

"For what?"

"For insisting I come."

"They're your parents, John. They're important."

John swallowed. "I know. You're right. It was just..." he trailed off.

Adriana waited for him to finish, then, when he didn't, filled in the silence with a question of her own. "How are you feeling? Being back?"

John took a deep breath and exhaled loudly. How did he feel? "Well... at first I was... apprehensive, yes that's the word I would use..."

"Apprehensive?" Adriana interrupted.

"Yeah." John sighed again. "I was scared. About the memories. About how I would feel... I've suppressed it for so long, baby." He felt a tear forming in his eye and he blinked it away, frowning, annoyed with himself. He took another deep breath and continued. "But to be honest, it's like a weight has been lifted from my shoulders. That's a cliché, I know, but that's what it feels like. I didn't even know I'd been carrying it around. The memories are still there... the sorrow also... but somehow I feel lighter." John made a face and glanced out the window as a car drove past. "I don't know if any of that makes sense, but..." he shrugged.

"I think... I think you still needed closure, John. I know you've always put a brave face on things, but I saw you suffering. You don't realise it, but when you're alone, when you think no-one's watching, your face is full of sadness."

"I'm sorry."

"Why should you be sorry? Those things happened to you. It's not your fault. You're a good man, John Hayes. A wonderful man, and I wouldn't want to share my life with anyone else. I just want you to be happy. Truly happy."

"I am when I'm with you."

"Good."

John could almost sense Adriana smiling at the other end of the line.

"Hey, I think..." John paused, putting his thoughts into words. Thoughts he hadn't had until this moment. "I think I'll stay longer. Spend more time with them... do you mind?"

"Mind? Why would I mind? It's good. Take all the time you need. It's important, John."

"Yeah, thanks." John smiled. "I love you, don't forget that."

"I know you do, John. Do what you have to do. I'm here for you."

"Obrigado, meu querido."

Adriana giggled. "You smooth talker. But don't take too long. I miss you."

John smiled and felt another tear in his eye, for a different reason this time. "I miss you too. I'll let you know when I'm heading back."

"Okay, please pass on my best wishes. Bye, John."

"Tchau-tchau." John ended the call and stared blankly at the dashboard of the Porsche. He'd been away a lot recently, first India, and then his trip to Australia, but he'd make up for it when he got back. He'd force her to take time off and they would go somewhere nice.

John smiled and turned the key in the ignition. Life wasn't so bad after all.

11

"Philip?"

Philip Symonds looked up from his desk and asked the question with his eyebrows.

"There's a Peter Noble here to see you."

Philip frowned and glanced over at the open diary on his desk. He didn't have any scheduled appointments. Looking back at his secretary, he asked, "Do you know what it's about, Helen?"

Helen shook her head, glanced over her shoulder, then stepped inside the office. "He looks important," she whispered.

Philip sighed and closed the file, setting it to one side. "Okay, show him inside, please... But Helen?"

"Yes?"

"After this, no more interruptions." He had two more planning applications to review before lunch and was running out of time.

"Yes, of course."

Philip sat back in his chair and listened to the voices outside. Helen's voice and a deeper, well-educated voice.

The Neighbor

Helen appeared in the doorway, smiling nervously, then stepped aside and gestured for Philip's visitor to enter.

A tall man in an expensive-looking navy suit with thick chalk-stripes entered the room. He smiled back at Helen, then approached Philip's desk.

"Mr Symonds?" His voice was deep, confident, and suggested a public school education. What looked like a regimental tie was knotted immaculately at his throat, and when he held out his hand, the suit sleeve rode up, revealing a French cuff and engraved gold cufflinks.

All this Philip registered in an instant as he stood and shook the man's hand.

Behind the visitor, Helen hovered in the doorway, one hand on the door handle, her expression asking if she should close it. Philip gave a shake of his head, then switched his attention back to the visitor.

"How can I help you, Mr...?"

"Noble, Peter Noble. Of Carruthers, Watson, and Smythe."

Philip blinked at the mention of the expensive law firm and gestured toward the seat in front of his desk.

Peter Noble smiled, placed his black leather briefcase on the floor beside the chair, then glanced back toward the open door. He took an easy stride across the office, closed the door, then returned to the seat, unbuttoned his jacket and sat down, crossing his legs and brushing an imaginary speck of fluff from his trouser leg.

Philip watched from his side of the desk, suddenly self-conscious about his off-the-rack tweed suit from Marks and Spencers. He cleared his throat, waiting for Peter Noble to explain the reason for his visit. Whatever it was, he had a gut feeling it would not be good. It never was when a high-priced lawyer turned up un-announced.

Peter Noble smiled broadly, as if he was meeting an old friend. "I have been retained by the owner of the Atwell Estate."

Philip clenched his jaw. His gut was correct. He took a breath. "Mr Xie was in here yesterday. I was under the impression I had dealt with all his concerns."

"Hmmm," Peter nodded slowly, still smiling. He held up his right hand and examined his fingernails. "Well, here's the thing. My client..." he nodded at Philip, "... Mr Xie, feels that you are not appreciating his... ahhh... unique position."

Philip blinked his surprise. "Unique? What's unique about his position? Has he explained to you what he wants to do?"

Peter nodded, his mouth still smiling, but his eyes were cold.

"So you understand your client wants to close public access to his land, shutting down bridle-ways and byways that have been open to the public for as far back as records go?"

Peter made a dismissive gesture with his hands.

Philip continued, "Did he tell you he has failed to maintain a byway which forms the only access to a property he doesn't own? A duty he is bound to by law? Or perhaps he told you about the illegal alterations he has made on the property, without permits and with complete disregard to planning regulations. I shudder to think what he has done to the main house, Atwell Manor, a heritage building that dates back over four hundred years."

The smile had left Peter's face, and he stared back at Philip with narrowed eyes. His face had gone hard, and a muscle pulsed in his jaw. There was a heavy silence which lasted longer than it should, then he adjusted his position in the chair. "I have been fully briefed on the current state of affairs regarding Atwell Estate. My client is a very busy man, and he unfortunately cannot devote more of his personal time to this matter, as I'm sure you will understand."

Philip remained silent.

"So from this moment on, he requests that all correspondence now goes through me."

Philip dipped his head in acknowledgement.

"He has also instructed me to see if there is some way we can find a solution to the current issues."

"Well, the solution is simple. Stop blocking access to the public, uphold his responsibility to maintain the byways that cross his property, and..." Philip paused for effect, fixing the lawyer in his gaze. He wasn't about to be intimidated by an old Etonian in a fancy suit. "In the interests of cordiality, I am prepared to consider a retrospective planning application for the illegal alterations. There may, of course, be some changes that need to be done to adhere to planning norms, but we won't know that until he makes an application. As for any alterations done to the main house, that's a matter he needs to take up with the people at English Heritage."

Peter was now frowning, and his index finger tapped an irritated rhythm on his thigh. "My client is hoping for a solution, that's more..." he looked around the office as if he would find the words amongst the filing cabinets, "beneficial to both parties."

Philip bit his tongue.

Peter Noble reached down for his briefcase and lifted it onto his lap. He clicked open the clasps, opened it up, and removed a single manila folder before closing the case and placing it back on the floor. Opening the folder, he examined the contents as if studying a menu in an expensive restaurant. Finally he looked, made sure he had Philip's attention, then began reading from the file. "I understand you still have ten years left on your mortgage, and your car is now fifteen years old." He paused and looked up.

Beneath the desk, Philip's hands gripped the edge of his chair, but he said nothing.

"I also understand you haven't been on an overseas holiday for several years. In addition..."

"Enough!" Philip knew where it was heading, and couldn't hold his tongue any longer. "I don't know how things are done in China, and quite frankly Mr Noble, I am shocked that a firm like yours would even be involved in something like this." Philip released his grip on his chair and stood up. He leaned forward, placing his hands on the desktop. "I suggest you go back to your client and tell him that in England," he raised a hand and pointed his index finger at the lawyer, "your country, we do things according to the law. As a lawyer, and I am sure a highly paid one at that, you should be able to educate your client on the current laws regarding public access, land rights, and building regulations. Once you've done so, I might..." he jabbed his finger at the lawyer again, "might consider another meeting with you. Until then, please get out of my office."

Peter Noble stared back, the muscle pulsing in his jaw again, then he closed the file and tossed it onto Philip's desk. He reached down for his briefcase and stood up, buttoning his jacket with his free hand. He paused, as if he was about to say something, then apparently thought better of it and turned toward the door.

"Leave the door open." Philip watched the man leave, then sat back in his chair and exhaled loudly. He rubbed his face with both hands, his fingers trembling with anger. He took another deep breath and let his hands fall to his lap.

If there was only one thing he did properly in his life, it

was his job. The city of Winchester and the Hampshire countryside attracted thousands of visitors a year, and it was because of the natural beauty and the historic architecture. Philip's job was to make sure it stayed that way. He had spent his entire career ensuring planning laws were adhered to, preserving the unique history that attracted people from all over the country and even the world. He'd be damned rather than let some rich foreigner come in and stomp his way all over the county's history.

He checked his watch. Forget the two applications he was supposed to review before lunch. He needed a drink.

He was about to stand when he spotted the file the lawyer had left behind. Pulling it closer, he opened it and scanned the contents. His latest mortgage statement lay on top. He slid it aside. Underneath was a copy of his car registration. He ground his teeth together and slid that aside, too. It was what he saw next that made his heart pound.

Several large glossy prints taken with a zoom lens outside his house. Taking out the trash, feeding his cat, and even a couple of photos of him moving around inside the house.

"You dirty bastard," he cursed under his breath. He tossed the file into the bin, pushed back his chair, and stood up. "Helen," he growled. "I'm going for lunch."

12

John slowed as the wall marking the front boundary of the Atwell Estate came into view on his left-hand side. Constructed of brick and flint and standing almost eight feet high, the wall stretched for over a mile and John marvelled at the work and the expense that must have gone into constructing it several hundred years ago. There would be few with the wealth to replicate the same thing now, let alone the craftsmen with the skill to do it.

The Atwells had lived on the property for centuries and had been popular custodians of the land. They had been fair landlords for the tenant farmers and always ensured the public rights-of-way across the land were kept open and well maintained. The family had donated generously to local charities and, once a year, held a fair for the local population on the grounds of the Estate. John remembered it fondly—the candy floss, the livestock and cooking competitions, and the fairground rides run by the gypsies. He wondered if the new owner would maintain the tradition.

John downshifted, reducing his speed even more, and as

he cruised slowly along the boundary, his thoughts wandered to his parents' house. The story was that Willow Cottage had been gifted almost a hundred years ago to a loyal servant, a butler who had been with the Atwell family for all his adult life. Unfortunately, he had left no heirs, and the cottage eventually, after several owners, ended up in the hands of John's parents.

It was unusual in that, although it was a freehold property, it was surrounded by the Atwell Estate and the only access to it was along a byway across the Atwell land. It had never been an issue while the Atwells were in residence, and legally, it shouldn't be an issue now.

John neared the large ornate wrought-iron gates that marked the entrance to the Estate and slowed even further. The gates were closed and John frowned. In all his years growing up in the area, he had never seen them closed. He rolled to a stop outside the gates and spotted the security cameras looking down on him from each of the gateposts. Those hadn't been there before either.

The door of the gatehouse opened, and a man stepped out. He was well built, his hair cropped close to his head, and dark wraparound sunglasses hid his eyes. He stood just outside the door and stared at John, as if waiting for John to do something.

John stared back. There was something intimidating about the man's posture and the way he was dressed. He wore black cargo pants over black combat boots, but incongruously wore a waxed green Barbour jacket over the top, as if he was some sort of para-military farmer. John watched the man raise his wrist to his mouth and saw his lips move. John couldn't help but grin. It was like he had strayed onto a movie set. Who the hell was the new owner?

John gave the engine a rev, slotted the gear stick into first, nodded at the guard, then accelerated away.

13

John left the car at the beginning of the lane. There had been too many scrapes and grinds on the chassis when he had driven out, and he loved his car too much to put it through that again. He grabbed his shopping, locked the door and walked around the other side to make sure the passenger door was locked too, then made his way back to the cottage.

On foot, the terrible state of the road was even more obvious. John dodged from one broken section to another and winced at the sight of a long metallic scrape along the edge of one of the potholes. It had definitely been a wise idea not to drive the Porsche back in.

Reaching the cottage, he saw his mother sitting in a canvas deck-chair on the front lawn, a blanket over her legs. Her eyes were closed, her face angled toward the sun, and she didn't hear John approach until he was standing next to her. He placed a gentle hand on her shoulder, and she jumped.

"Sorry, Mum, I didn't mean to startle you."

She giggled, and John couldn't resist a smile.

"Naughty boy, sneaking up on an old lady like that."

John grinned. "I'm hardly a boy, Mum."

"You'll always be a boy to me." Carole looked at the shopping bag in John's hand. "Did you get your coffee?"

John nodded, reached into the bag and pulled out the French press. "I even bought one of these. I assumed you don't have one."

Carole shook her head.

John looked around. "Where's Dad?"

"He's in the shed."

John chuckled. "He still spends all his time in there?"

"I think he has a girlfriend in there."

John burst out laughing, and his mother joined in.

"Dad? Girlfriend? That'll be the day."

"Whoever she is, she should get a medal. Putting up with his grumbling," Carole quipped.

"You need a medal then, Mum."

"Yes..." she shrugged. "But he's not so bad."

John smiled. His parents, for all their good natured grumbling and teasing, obviously still loved each other. In a world where relationships seemed to end at a blink of an eye, it was refreshing and heartwarming to see.

John nodded down at the shopping bag. "I'll just put these inside. Can I get you anything?"

"No. Your Dad will bring me some tea in a while."

John smiled and then walked toward the house. The grass on the lawn was long and the flower beds unkempt. He looked across at the peeling paint on the window frames. The house needed a good spruce up and he doubted his parents could do any of it themselves. His Mum certainly not. John had watched her moving around. Her mobility wasn't good and although she didn't mention it, he could see she was often in pain.

The Neighbor

He stowed the coffee powder and French press in one of the overhead cupboards in the kitchen, then walked back outside and sat down on the grass in front of his mother.

"Who does the garden for you now, Mum?"

"One of Lord Atwell's men used to come and cut the grass every month, but now he's gone..." Carole trailed off, her smile fading away.

"I'll do it. I'm going to stay for a while, if that's okay?"

"Of course," a broad smile returned. "Stay as long as you like, John. I know your dad will be happy, too."

"Hmmm." John half smiled. If his dad was happy, he wouldn't show it.

"Now, tell me more about this young lady of yours. Why didn't you bring her with you?"

John grinned. "You'd love her, Mum. And I know she'll love you."

"Then where is she?"

"She'll come, Mum. But this trip... was unplanned." John fell silent. He didn't want to go into his reasons for turning up out of the blue after so many years.

"But she makes you happy?"

John nodded.

"And you love her?"

John smiled and looked away over the fields. "With all my heart, Mum."

He felt a hand on his arm. Carole had leaned forward, and she smiled. "Then that's all that's important. We just want you to be happy, John."

John smiled back. "I am." He reached up and took his mother's hand in his. "I'm sorry it took me so long to come back. I should have come sooner." His smile faded, and he looked away. "It was... hard for me. Too many memories."

Looking back at his mother, he smiled again, "but I'm okay now."

Carole nodded, still studying John, her eyes searching his face. "I'm happy you came, John. Don't leave it so long next time."

John shook his head, then, embarrassed, changed the subject. "Tell me more about the new owner of the Estate. There's a guard at the front gate."

His mother slipped her hand free and sat back in her chair. Her eyes darted toward the house, then looked back at John. Her smile from earlier had disappeared. "Don't talk to your dad about him. He gets very worked up."

John frowned. "You said that before. Why?"

His mother sighed and looked down at the grass. "The new owner wants to buy this house and your dad refuses to sell."

"How about you?"

Carole shrugged. "We love this place. So many memories... you grew up here. But... we aren't getting any younger. It needs a lot of maintenance and your dad, despite what he says, can't cope."

John nodded slowly and glanced back toward the house, at the weeds growing around the front step, and the sagging guttering on the front left corner. It would be sad to think that his parents no longer lived in the house he grew up in, but John had moved around so much, he knew there was little point in being sentimental over property.

Turning back to his mum, he asked, "So what's Dad's objection? Is the offer not high enough?"

Carole sighed loudly. "Not at first. He's increased it twice since then, but there's more to it."

John's frown deepened, and he waited for her to continue.

The Neighbor

"You know what he's like about foreigners..."

John was shaking his head. "Oh, come on. You can't seriously tell me he won't sell because he's a foreigner? What does he think about Adriana then? She's a foreigner."

"Well... we'll deal with that when he meets her... but it's more than that now. He says it's a matter of principle."

"Principle?"

"He's a bully."

His dad's voice caught them both by surprise. John turned and saw his father standing behind him, a teapot and teacups on a tray in his hands. He glared down at John.

"I will not stand for bullying."

14

"Dad, why don't I get you a chair and you can explain everything to me?"

David Hayes muttered under his breath while looking around for somewhere to put the tray. John reached up and took it off him, placing it on the lawn, and then got to his feet.

"There's another chair like this in the shed," Carole added helpfully.

"Thanks, Mum." He glanced at his father. "Am I allowed in your shed, Dad?" John gave his mother a wink.

David muttered something inaudible, which John took as a yes, walking away and heading down the side of the house toward the rear garden. The grass at the back of the house was even longer and the flower beds were a tangled mass of weeds. John could see he had a lot of work to do before he left.

The shed was at the foot of the garden and was just as John remembered it. Unpainted wooden walls under a corrugated tin roof. The roof was rusted in places, but from the outside looked watertight and the cedar panelling of the walls looked like it would last another couple of decades.

John pushed the door open, the hinges complaining as the door swung open—he'd oil them later—and paused in the doorway. The shed had always been out-of-bounds for John when he was growing up, and he only knew it as the place his dad retreated to whenever he wanted to get away from the house. But now John was finally allowed inside, he was disappointed. It had been much more mysterious in his imagination.

Unlike the garden, the interior of the shed was immaculate. Tools hung on hooks on the walls, a black outline drawn around each tool showing its correct place, and the floor was spotless, as if freshly swept.

There was something on a workbench under the window, and John walked over for a closer look. A partially built scale model of an aircraft lay on a vinyl cutting mat, together with a set of tweezers, a craft knife, and a pot of modelling glue. A magnifying glass on a stand with a flexible arm sat to the right of it, and a cardboard box filled with plastic parts sat on the left. John pulled a set of instructions out of the box and leafed through it. A World War II Spitfire.

John put the instructions back and took another look around the shed. How long had his dad been making models? Was this a new hobby? If he had made others, where on earth did he keep them once they were finished? John shrugged. Yet another thing he didn't know about his father.

Spotting the deckchair leaning against the wall just behind the door, John picked it up and exited the shed, pulling the door closed behind him.

He carried the chair around to the front lawn, opening it up as he approached his parents.

"Here you go, Dad."

"Thank you."

John knelt on the grass and poured two cups of tea, passing one to his mother, and then held the second one out for his father.

"Since when have you been making model aircraft, Dad?"

His father took the proffered cup, the cup jingling in the saucer as his hand shook.

"A couple of years."

John raised his eyebrows, but then realised it shouldn't be surprising. It had been years since he had been home, so how would he know? "What do you do with them once you complete them?"

"He donates them to the Youth Club in Winchester."

David glared at his wife, but she dismissed him with a wave and a chuckle. "What? It's not a secret. You don't want your son to know you have a heart?"

David grumbled and made a show of stirring his tea noisily.

John exchanged a look with his mum, and she grinned.

John settled back onto the grass and waited for his father to finish sipping his tea before asking, "So, Dad, tell me what's going on with the neighbour."

David Hayes scowled and lowered the cup, placing it back onto the saucer. He muttered something that sounded like, "Dirty foreigner."

"Dad," John admonished.

His father looked up in surprise, then took a breath. "The new owner wants to buy our house, but I won't sell it to him."

"Okay." John nodded slowly. "I'm not suggesting you sell it, but why the animosity? You said he's a bully?"

The Neighbor

"He is."

John waited for him to say more and when he didn't, he pressed him, "Start from the beginning, Dad. Who is he and what's going on? Maybe I can help."

David looked over at his son, studying him for a while as if trying to decide how much to tell him. Eventually, he leaned forward and placed the teacup and saucer on the grass near his feet.

"Your mother and I didn't accept his first offer. We had no intention of selling—we still don't—and anyway, it was a low offer. Insulting, in fact. He made another higher offer. We turned it down again. So he offered even more. What I don't understand is if he was prepared to pay that much, why didn't he offer that at the beginning?"

John shrugged, "No-one offers their final price first, Dad."

"Huh. Anyway. After we turned that offer down, he showed his true colours."

"What do you mean?"

"Lots of things. He stopped the workers from cutting our grass. He doesn't maintain the road. His convoy has even run us off the road several times."

John frowned. "And how long has this been going on?"

"About six months."

John thought for a moment. "But the road can't have got that bad in just six months."

His father was shaking his head. "No. He's made it like that."

"How?"

"By driving heavy machinery up and down the road. Tractors, bulldozers, he even had a tractor drag a plough down the road."

"You're kidding?"

His father shot John a stern look. "And he does it early in the morning. Woken your mother and I up, many a time."

John gave his mother a questioning look, and she nodded agreement.

"Have you complained to him about it?"

"I tried. But it's not like the old days. Lord Atwell was ready to see everyone. Now you can't even get past the front gate."

John nodded. "I saw the gates were closed. They have cameras and a guard, too."

"Lots of guards. Sometimes we see them walking the fields. With guns."

John blinked in surprise. "Who is this guy? Where's he from?"

"Xie something. Chinese. He has plenty of money. I'm sure he's doing something illegal."

"Why?"

David looked at him sternly. "I know you think I'm saying that because he's foreign. But no. An honest man does not need armed guards and cameras over his gate."

John nodded in partial agreement. A thought struck him. "How did you receive the offers for the house? Did he come to you?"

"No," David shook his head. "He hides behind some high-priced lawyers in Winchester. I don't remember the name."

"Hmmm." John leaned back on his hands and gazed out across the lawn. He too didn't like bullies, but he wasn't sure how much of the story was his father's inbuilt dislike of anyone different, and how much was fact. "Do you still have the offers here?"

"I told you we're not selling. This is our home and some dirty yellow Chinaman will not force us out."

Ignoring the racism, John sat up and held up both hands. "No, no, I'm not suggesting that at all. It's your home and your decision. I just want to know who this guy is and what he wants. And then I'm going to pay him a visit."

"You what?"

"John, no," Carole protested.

John shrugged and grinned. "Why not?"

"You'll never get past the gate."

"I won't if I don't try, Dad."

15

Peter was nervous. It was an unfamiliar feeling. He had built a successful career representing the rich and powerful of Southern England and had frequently faced down formidable barristers and judges in court. It took a lot to unsettle him, but right now he felt uncomfortable.

He took a deep breath and crossed his legs, settling back into the overstuffed leather armchair, and looked around the room. A large picture window looked out onto the Estate lawns, and the other walls were lined with floor to ceiling shelves filled with books. Peter doubted the current owner had read any of them, and assumed they had come with the house. An expensive looking but well-worn carpet covered the polished wooden floor and the leather sofas and antique occasional tables lent the room the air of a private club—a bit like Peter's club in London. Not that the current owner would ever get to see it. His club viewed foreigners with suspicion, unless, of course, they had been educated at Eton or somewhere similar.

He shrugged off the thought. It wasn't his problem. The

man was paying him well, even though some of his requests were, how should he say it... sailing close to the wind. But Peter had learnt in his career, there were few problems money couldn't fix and if his client had deep enough pockets, and it looked like he did, then Peter would use his skills and legal flexibility to find solutions.

He glanced over toward the door where a large man in a black shirt and combat pants stood staring at an unseen point outside the window, his hands clasped in front of his groin as if protecting himself from attack. He had spoken only two words since Peter arrived, 'Vait here.' But it was enough for Peter to place his accent somewhere in eastern Europe, the Slavic features reinforcing his opinion.

As if he could read Peter's thoughts, the man's eyes flicked toward him as he raised one hand to his ear. He nodded to someone unseen, then spoke for only the second time.

"He vill see you now."

"About time," Peter muttered. He'd been waiting for the best part of twenty minutes, but he fixed a smile on his face, stood up, re-buttoned his suit jacket, then followed the guard.

The Slav led him down the wide hallway and stopped outside another door. He waited for Peter to join him, then opened it and stepped aside.

Peter nodded a thank you, then widening his smile, entered the room.

Xie Longwei sat behind an expansive oak desk, watching him approach with piercing eyes set in a fleshy round face.

"Mr Xie." Peter strode forward and held out his hand. "A pleasure to see you again."

Xie ignored his hand and pointed at one of two leather chairs in front of the desk.

Peter ignored the slight, keeping his smile fixed, and turned to sit down, noticing for the first time a middle-aged Chinese woman sitting at the rear of the room. He nodded in her direction, but she looked right through him, and he sat down, unbuttoned his jacket and smoothed the creases from his suit pants.

"Well?"

Peter cleared his throat. He knew what he was about to say would not be well received. "I did as you asked. However..." Peter hesitated, "Mr Symonds of the Hampshire County Council has turned down your very generous offer of... ahem... financial assistance."

Xie stared back, his expression giving nothing away.

Peter continued, "We have, of course, the normal legal route to pursue. My team is putting together the documentation for the appeal process..."

Xie held up his hand, stopping Peter in mid-flow. He glanced over Peter's shoulder toward the woman at the back of the room, gave an almost imperceptible nod, then looked back at Peter. His voice when he spoke was low but firm in tone. "You have failed to perform a simple task. I'm wondering why your firm deserves the exorbitant fees you are charging."

He spoke perfect English with a slight American accent... what Peter thought of as 'the international school accent.' He'd heard it before in some children of his wealthier clients.

"No, I haven't failed." Peter smiled the broad smile he used when addressing a jury in court, but inside he was thinking fast. *This horrible little man fails to realise that all the money in the world won't buy class.* But he paid very well and Peter needed to stay on his good side. "This is just a temporary setback. I assure you, we will succeed. We just need a little more time."

Xie's face changed for the first time, a frown briefly creasing his forehead. "You have had enough time. It's been six months and we are no further forward. People are still wandering across my land. I am still receiving enforcement notices from English Heritage, and that house on the eastern boundary remains in private hands. I'm paying you to make these problems go away, and you haven't."

"Mr Xie," Peter spread his hands wide, the smile on his face belying his irritation. "I understand your frustration, but as I have previously explained to you, these things take time. Laws can be circumvented, but it takes time, money, and certain skills. It's those skills for which you have retained me, but even with my... ah... considerable experience, it's not a simple process."

He paused for emphasis. "I know you have experience of business in Africa and parts of Asia, but this is England. These rights-of-way and rights-of-public-access have been around for centuries. We have an established legal system that has served this country well for hundreds of years. We can't remove the laws overnight." Peter stopped speaking, aware his irritation might get the better of him. But this man had to know. England was a civilised country.

Xie said nothing. He just stared at Peter.

Peter tried matching his gaze but had to look away. There was something unnerving about the way the man looked at him. Peter considered himself an expert in body language, and usually, there were signs that gave away what a man was thinking. The movement of the eyes, a facial tic, the pulsing of a jaw muscle, but here there was nothing, and it unsettled him. After a moment, he forced himself to look back at Xie.

"We..." Xie's eyes flicked past Peter again, "... will deal with this from now on."

Peter turned and looked back over his shoulder. Who is that woman? She returned his stare with the same lack of expression Xie maintained. Is she his wife? She was about the same age as Xie, but then again, you could never tell with these Asians. And surely a man with Xie's money and power would have a younger, much more attractive woman hanging around than this frumpy old hag in her shapeless grey suit and sensible shoes.

Peter turned back and asked, "What do you mean?"

"For an expensive lawyer, your comprehension of simple matters seems to be lacking."

Peter bit his tongue. He needed to regain control of the conversation. He forced a smile, "Mr Xie..."

Xie held up his hand, stopping Peter in mid-flow. "You can leave now. If... and I mean if, you are needed again, I will send for you." Xie ended the sentence with a dismissive flick of his hand, then turned his attention to the large flat-screen monitor on the side of his desk, the meeting obviously over.

Peter sat still, his mouth hanging open, then took a deep breath and exhaled slowly. He stood up, buttoned his jacket and smiled. "Of course, Mr Xie. Consider me to be always at your disposal."

He waited for an answer and when it wasn't forthcoming, he turned and walked toward the door. He glanced at the woman in the corner but couldn't be bothered to smile, and neither did she.

His brain played back the conversation. What could he have done differently? He should have said this... should have said that... would he still get his retainer?

The door opened as if by magic, the Slav standing outside.

Peter paused in the doorway and looked back into the room. The woman was walking toward the desk and Xie still had his attention on the computer monitor, as if neither Peter nor the woman existed.

Peter opened his mouth to say something, then changed his mind. There was no point.

16

"Are you comfortable?"

"Yes. It feels strange to be sitting on this side, though."

John grinned at his father in the passenger seat. "Well, I do live in Portugal. We drive on the other side of the road there. Only the former British colonies drive on the right."

"Hmmm."

John chuckled. His father still mourned the decline of the British Empire. He twisted the key in the ignition and the engine burbled into life. Giving the throttle pedal a blip, he watched his father's reaction out of the corner of his eye. There was almost a smile.

John looked over his shoulder, checked the lane was clear, then pulled out onto the road. He didn't wait for the engine to warm up, but mashed his foot immediately on the accelerator and felt himself pushed back into his seat as the car leaped up the road. He climbed the gears, then braked heavily for the corner, glancing over at his father.

He was smiling.

"What do you think?"

"Wonderful, absolutely wonderful, son."

John felt a warmth fill his body and a smile spread across his face.. Praise like that, even though it wasn't for John, was a rare thing.

"Hey," David pointed out the side window. "You've missed the Estate entrance."

John nodded as he sped up the road. "Let's enjoy the drive first."

Twenty minutes of fast driving later, John slowed for the entrance to the Atwell Estate and glanced across at his dad. A broad grin was fixed firmly across his face, something John hadn't seen for as long as he could remember.

"Okay?"

"Yes. Very."

John chuckled, downshifted, and pulled to a stop just as the gates swung open. A dark blue Bentley Continental appeared from inside the Estate, pausing as the driver looked both ways before pulling out onto the road. The driver, a middle-aged Caucasian in a dark suit, looked across at John's father, frowned, then his eyes moved to John as the car rolled past.

"I'm guessing that's not the owner?"

"No," his father growled, his smile vanishing. "That's the fancy lawyer."

"Really?" John nodded slowly, returning the lawyer's stare. He waited until the car had moved past, then turned into the Estate, stopping immediately, the way blocked by the security guard he had seen earlier. He stood in the middle of the entrance with his hand held up, leaving no room for misunderstanding. John slipped the car into neutral and wound down the window as the guard moved around to the side of the vehicle.

"Can I help you, sir?" He spoke with a slight accent. Definitely not English.

John fixed a smile and nodded. "Yes, we are here to see the owner."

"Mr Xie?"

John nodded. "Yes, Mr Xie."

"Do you have an appointment?"

"Do I need one?"

"Yes, sir." The guard nodded, bending down to look inside. He peered at John's father, then turned his attention back to John. "I can't let you in unless you have an appointment, sir."

John continued smiling, keeping his tone friendly. "Can you call ahead and check if he is free now? We are neighbors."

The guard frowned. "Neighbors, sir?"

"Yes."

"Your name, sir?"

"Hayes, John Hayes."

"Wait one moment, sir."

John nodded and watched the guard step away from the car and walk around until he was standing in front of it. He raised his wrist to his mouth and started speaking, but he was too far away for John to make out what he was saying.

"He won't let you in," John's father grumbled.

"Let's see," John replied, not taking his eyes off the guard. The guard continued speaking, then nodded. He looked back at John, then down at the vehicle registration, and raised his wrist to his lips again.

John watched his lips move. It looked as though he was reading the vehicle registration out to whoever was on the other end of the radio. The man stopped speaking, nodded once more, then walked around to the side of the car. As he rounded the front corner of the car, his jacket swung open, giving John a brief glimpse of a shoulder holster.

The guard bent down and placed one hand on the door. "I'm sorry, sir, but Mr Xie is busy today. I suggest you call ahead next time."

"Okay." John studied the guard's face, then turned and looked up the long curving driveway that led into the Estate. He contemplated ignoring the man and accelerating past, but with his father in the car, and knowing the guard was armed, erred on the side of caution.

He turned back to the guard and flashed him a smile. "Thank you for your help. I will take your advice."

The guard, visibly relaxing, returned John's smile. "Thank you, sir. Do you have the number?"

John glanced at his father, who nodded.

"We do, thank you."

"Good." The guard straightened up and added, "That's a beautiful car you've got there, sir."

"Thank you. Have a good day." John selected reverse and twisted in his seat to look out the rear window while his father continued scowling at the guard.

John reversed out onto the road, gave the guard a nod, then as he slipped the car into first, a movement on top of the gatepost caught his eye. The security camera was moving to match the car's movement. John put his arm out the window, waved at the camera, then accelerated away up the road.

"I told you so," David grumbled.

"Yes. You did."

17

Philip Symonds burped loudly, and he glanced toward the open doorway of his office, hoping the sound hadn't carried outside to his assistant. Reaching for his water bottle, he took a sip, rinsing out the taste of regurgitated Guinness and beef stew.

Taking a breath, he then rubbed his face. He'd had a couple of pints too many. His anger at the lawyer's visit prompted him to break his strict rule of one pint of beer at lunchtime. The second pint had calmed him down and the third made him feel good about the world again. But now he was paying for it.

Glancing down at the file in front of him, he tried to focus on the typewritten lines, but they blurred into a tangled mess as a wave of drowsiness swept over him.

"Helen, can you please bring me a coffee?" Another rule he was breaking—no coffee after midday—but he doubted he would last the afternoon without one.

He waited for a reply, but it wasn't forthcoming, although he heard voices in the outer office. A moment later, Helen stood in the doorway.

"A Mr. Hayes is here to see you."

Philip stifled a groan. The last thing he felt like doing was meeting a member of the public.

Hayes, Hayes, the name sounded familiar. He frowned at Helen while he racked his brain. Oh yes. The owner of Willow Cottage on the Atwell Estate. He groaned again. It was bad enough having two meetings about the same matter in the one day, but old Hayes was a grumpy old git.

The buzz from his boozy lunch faded away, and he made a face at Helen. She was supposed to run interference for him, but once again she'd failed in her duty. She shrugged, glancing nervously back into her office.

Philip sighed. "Okay, show him in, and bring me a coffee... please."

Helen dipped her head in acknowledgment, then disappeared from sight.

Philip closed the file, dropped it back into his in-tray, then shuffled through the pile for the Atwell file. It was rapidly becoming the thickest one on his desk.

"Thank you for seeing me without an appointment."

It wasn't the voice he was expecting, and Philip looked up in surprise.

Standing just inside his office was a lean, fit looking man, much younger and more tanned than the owner of Willow Cottage.

"Mr Hayes?"

The man stepped forward and held out his hand. "John."

His grip was firm, his gaze intense. He had an aura of confidence, as if little could faze him.

"Philip Symonds." He let go of John's hand and gestured toward the chair in front of him. "Please take a seat. What can I do for you?"

John Hayes sat down, crossed his legs and smiled. "My

father tells me you are the person to speak to regarding Willow Cottage."

"Your father?" Philip frowned briefly. "Ah yes." Now he could see the resemblance, although the man in front of him was better looking than the father ever was. He must have got his looks from his mother's side. "He never mentioned you."

"No?" John's smile slipped for the briefest of moments before it returned. "I don't live here. I live overseas."

"Oh." Philip waited for him to continue.

"I wanted to find out what's happening regarding my parents' property and the new owner of the Atwell Estate, a Mr…"

"Xie. Xie Longwei."

"Yes. And particularly what my parents' rights are."

Philip sighed loudly, gesturing at the bulky file lying on the desk in front of him. "Where do I start?"

At that moment, Helen walked in with his coffee and placed it on his desk. She turned to John, who gave her a big smile.

"Mr Hayes, can I get you something?"

"Please, call me John," he replied. "I would love a coffee too, please. Black, no sugar."

"Of course."

Philip watched the exchange. Was she blushing?

He waited until Helen left the room, then picked up his coffee cup, blew the steam from the top and took a sip. He made a face. Too much sugar. Sighing again, he placed the cup back on the desk and turned his attention back to his guest. "As you can see, I have a rather extensive file on the Atwell Estate. There are several issues that you need not concern yourself with, but as it pertains to your parent's property, the issue is the access."

The Neighbor

John nodded, no longer smiling, his eyes narrowing slightly.

"The lane leading toward Willow Cottage is a byway. Are you familiar with public rights-of-access in England, Mr Hayes?"

"John. I have a vague knowledge, but perhaps you can make things clear for me."

Philip cleared his throat. "Of course. There are two types of byway. One is a byway open to all traffic, and the other is a restricted byway, limited to traffic on foot, horseback, or bicycle."

"So I assume my parents' access is a byway open to all traffic?"

"That is correct." Philip paused while Helen placed a cup of coffee in front of John. She almost curtseyed when he smiled again, and Philip arched an eyebrow.

Again, he waited until she was out of the room before continuing. "The issue your father has raised is that Mr Xie is not maintaining his responsibility as landowner and ensuring the right of way is maintained and open at all times."

John nodded but said nothing, reaching forward for his coffee and taking a sip.

"Is that okay?"

"Yes," John smiled. "Thank you."

"Good." Philip wished his own coffee was okay.

He opened the file and shuffled through the papers. Finding the one he wanted, he looked up, "Your father has reported frequent instances of the lane being blocked by agricultural equipment, and even..." he raised his eyebrows and looked up at John, "a plough being dragged along it."

"Yes. So I believe. Have you seen the surface of the lane recently?"

Philip shook his head.

John put down his coffee cup, retrieved a phone from his pocket, and swiped the screen. "Here, look at the photos I've taken today."

Philip took the phone and looked at the screen.

"Swipe left, there's more."

He did, then handed the phone back. "That's much worse than the last time I visited."

"Yes." John put the phone back into his pocket. "I believe there is a deliberate campaign to degrade the access and to harass my parents who are the legal owners of the cottage."

Philip nodded. He agreed.

"Did you know he's offered to buy my parent's house?"

Philip nodded again. "Your father mentioned it."

"Did he mention there have been multiple offers, and he's turned all of them down?"

"No, he didn't mention that."

John reached forward and adjusted the position of the coffee cup, then leaned back in his chair. "Mr Xie wants them out of there, and since his offers to purchase the place have not worked, he is making it difficult for them to have access to their home."

"It does seem that way, yes." Philip sighed and spread his hands. "Look, I don't know what you want from me, but this is where we stand. We are aware of what he is doing, although," he pointed toward John's phone, "I wasn't aware how bad it's become." He opened the side drawer of his desk and removed a business card and passed it to John. "Can you send me those photos? The number is on the card."

"Sure."

"We can issue a notice. It's actually a criminal offence to obstruct a public byway, but to be honest..." he sighed again. "I don't think it will achieve much."

"Why do you say that?"

Philip studied John's face for a moment. There was something about him, a quiet confidence that made Philip feel comfortable about telling the truth. "Because I've already issued notices against him for other matters, and they have been ignored or contested by his lawyers."

"I see."

"His lawyers are expensive and can tie this up for years."

"Mr Noble of Carruthers and something?"

Philip nodded slowly. "You know him."

"No. But the offers for the house came from him. And I saw him earlier. Leaving the Atwell Estate in a Bentley."

"Huh. Visiting his paymaster."

John tilted his head and frowned. "I get the impression you don't think much of him."

Philip pursed his lips and drummed his fingers on the desktop. He then leaned forward and lowered his voice. "Peter Noble, a man who definitely does not live up to his name, tried to bribe me in this office today."

18

For some reason, John didn't look shocked. Instead, he looked back at Philip with a slight smile, as if he was expecting the news.

"Really? That's interesting. Does that happen often?"

"No."

"I didn't think so. Tell me what you know about Mr Xie."

Philip sat back again in his chair and crossed his arms. "I don't know a lot. Chinese, obviously, um... apparently he's in construction. Infrastructure, not so much buildings, but bridges, ports, airports, that sort of thing. Seemingly very wealthy. He bought the Estate sight unseen after Lord Atwell's... unfortunate demise."

"Yes, I heard about Lord Atwell. A great pity. He was a good man."

Philip nodded agreement. "He was. The complete opposite of the current owner. I've spent most of my career in these offices, coming up to twenty years, and we've never had a problem with the Atwell Estate." He grimaced. "That's all changed now."

"Yes, so it seems. I went for a run across the Estate and there are 'No Entry' signs everywhere."

Philip gestured at the file. "It's all in there."

"And I tried to meet the man today. Was stopped at the gate by an armed guard."

Philip shrugged and spread his hands. "Now you know what I'm up against."

John nodded and chewed his lip while staring at a spot just above Philip's head.

Philip reached for his coffee cup and made another attempt at drinking it. Cold and sweet. He screwed up his face, put the cup back down, and wiped his mouth with the back of his hand. When he looked up, he noticed John watching with amusement.

"That bad?"

"Awful."

John chuckled. "If you come by the house in the next few days, I'll make you a good one. I'm a bit of a coffee... snob, you could say."

Philip nodded and steepled his fingertips in front of him. "You said you live overseas?"

"Yes. Lisbon."

"Oh, nice... I think. Is it?"

"Very nice."

"If you don't mind me asking, John, what do you do? I've not met anyone who lives in Lisbon before. At least not an Englishman."

John half smiled and looked away, finding something outside the window very interesting.

Philip was puzzled. What did he do that meant he couldn't reply immediately?

"I was in banking, a long time ago... but now you could say I'm retired."

"Retired?" Philip asked in surprise. "But you are..."

"Too young to retire? Yes, it's a long story. Maybe I'll tell you one day." John turned back and shrugged. "Now, I suppose you could say I solve problems."

"As a business?"

John laughed. "No. Not really. It just happens. Keeps me busy."

Philip was more confused than before he asked and it must have shown on his face.

John held up his hand, still smiling. "Don't worry about it. I'm not a criminal. That's all you need to know."

"That's a relief." Philip thought for a moment. "But then you would say that, wouldn't you?"

John chuckled. "Yes, you're right." He uncrossed his legs and stood up. Holding out his hand, he said, "Thank you for your time, Philip. Can I call you Philip?"

Philip stood too and shook his hand. "Yes, of course." He walked around the desk. "How long will you be here, John?"

John Hayes stopped by the door and looked back. Once more, Philip was struck by the intensity of his gaze. For a moment he thought he had somehow offended him, but then John smiled, "Well, that all depends on Mr Xie."

Philip watched him leave, then scratched his head. What did John Hayes mean by that?

He turned and walked back to his desk and stood with his hands on his hips, staring at his coffee cup as if he would find the answer in the black liquid.

Giving up, he called out,

"Helen, can you make me another coffee, please? And this time only one sugar."

19

John finished lacing his running shoes and stood up. He took a deep breath of fresh morning air, shook out his arms and rolled his head around, loosening up his neck. It was cool, his breath visible as he exhaled, but the sky was clear, promising another fine day. He'd been lucky with the weather since he'd come, expecting rain, but so far the days had been clear and sunny.

He walked down the path to the front gate and slipped through, the gate clicking shut behind him. He was about to turn left and head down the lane to the main road when he hesitated. Across the lane was a stile in the hedgerow that bounded one of the fields of the Atwell Estate. John stared at it for a moment, then crossed the lane and climbed the stile, dropping into the field on the other side.

Since his meeting with Philip Symonds the previous day, he had been wondering how to resolve the situation peacefully for his parents. They too could file a case with the relevant authorities, but it was bound to be tied up for years in the courts, and besides, if it wasn't working for the Council, then why would it work for his parents? They were elderly, and definitely couldn't handle the stress, let alone the cost of a lengthy court case. John stood with his hands on his hips, staring across the field. There had to be another way.

John took another deep breath and then began his run. He headed out across the field until at the top of the slope he could see the rest of the Estate unfolding in front of him. At the other side of the field, he ignored the 'No Entry' sign and vaulted the stile into the next field, following the bridle-path which ran along the hedge to his right. A pheasant burst out of the hedgerow, the sudden unexpected movement setting his heart racing. John slowed and grinned, watching it fly low across the field while he sought to get his heart rate back to a normal level.

Continuing on, he followed the hedgerow, taking a route that would circumnavigate the central part of the Estate. He ran from memory, the route etched in his subconscious from many runs and walks when he had been growing up. He had spent hours roaming the Estate in his youth, sometimes hunting rabbits and hares with a catapult, but most of the time simply enjoying the peace and quiet of the countryside.

He had forgotten how much pleasure he got from being alone in nature. It had been years since he had been in such an environment, his career taking him to huge crowded cities like Bangalore, Hong Kong, Bangkok, and now, with his home in central Lisbon, the chances of being away from it all were just as rare. He found himself slipping into a flow state, running easily, as if no physical effort was needed, his mind emptying of thoughts, and a broad smile filled his face.

About twenty minutes later, on the western boundary, he neared a gate secured by a heavy duty chain and padlock.

It was part of the public access, so John didn't hesitate, jogging to the hinge end of the gate, placing his hands on the top rail and vaulting over. It would take more than a padlock to stop him.

As he landed on the other side, he heard a shout and he paused, turning to his left to see a man running toward him, a dog snarling and pulling against the leash in his hand. John contemplated ignoring him and continuing on his run, but the dog would catch him in no time. So he waited, keeping his expression neutral, and stood with his hands on his hips, slowing his breathing as the man and his dog approached.

John recognised the breed, a Belgian Malinois, favoured by security forces worldwide. It looked fit and angry, continuously snapping and barking as they got closer, strings of saliva dangling from its large white teeth.

The buzz from his run quickly faded away.

"You are trespassing," the security guard called out before he had even reached John.

Here we go.

John didn't respond, instead waiting until the man stood in front of him, the dog just out of biting reach. It growled, and the man tugged on the leash, pulling it back a little further. He was dressed in what John now recognised as the uniform of the Atwell Estate security—black combat pants over high-top boots and the ubiquitous waxed green Barbour coat. He looked well built, his hair short, his face weathered from a life spent outdoors.

"I said you are trespassing." He spoke with an accent, European of some sort, but not one that John immediately recognised.

"I heard you the first time," John replied, supporting it

with a smile. "But I'm afraid you are mistaken. I am on a public bridle-path."

The guard frowned and shook his head. "No. This is private property. We have been told to keep everyone out."

John kept smiling, even though his amygdala was telling him to stop talking and get the hell out of there. But there was no way he could protect himself from the dog, so he had to keep the situation calm. "Told by whom?"

"The owner of the property."

"Ahh, Mr Xie," John said it as if he knew the man.

The guard blinked in surprise, but recovered quickly. "Yes. You need to leave now."

The dog strained at the leash, but it didn't affect the guard who stood with his legs apart, the end of the leash wrapped around a hand the size of a dinner plate.

"Where are you from? Eastern Europe?"

"None of your business," the guard growled.

"Czech Republic?"

"Ha," the guard snorted. "I'm from Albania."

John widened his smile. "I've never been there. You're a long way from home."

There was uncertainty in the guard's expression, then the deep creases in his forehead lightened out, and he tugged on the dog's leash while muttering a command. The dog growled once, then sat back on its haunches, ears cocked, and its head tilted to one side as it continued staring at John. At least its mouth was closed.

"What brings you to England?" John continued.

The guard shrugged and glanced over his shoulder as if to see if anyone was watching him. "Work," he grunted. "No work in my country."

"Well," John nodded in the general direction of the rest

of the Estate. "You've picked a beautiful part of England. It's lovely around here."

The guard grunted, as if he wasn't sure whether to agree.

John held out his hand, and the dog growled. "My name is John." He nodded over his shoulder. "I live nearby."

The guard hesitated, then, keeping the dog in place with a jerk of his left hand, leaned forward, reaching out with his right. "Admir."

"Welcome to my country, Admir."

Admir's mouth twitched, almost a smile that quickly disappeared. "Mr John, you must leave the property. Mr Xie will be very angry if he finds you here."

John sighed. "Admir, I know you have a job to do, but according to English law, this path I'm on is a public path. I am allowed to be here." He turned and pointed at the gate he'd just vaulted. "Do you see that yellow arrow on the gatepost? That's a public footpath marking."

He turned back to look at Admir, who was frowning again.

"I don't know English law. I just do what my boss tells me."

John nodded and smiled at the same time. "I understand, my friend, but I think even your boss, Mr Xie, doesn't understand the law." He winked at Admir. "Maybe he thinks he's still in China."

Admir couldn't help himself, and the left side of his mouth twitched again. "But I can't let you stay here. I have my orders."

"Yeah... I understand." John turned and looked up the pathway. "See that stone wall there at the end of the field?"

"Yes."

"Well, that's the outer boundary of the Estate. On the

other side is a road." He turned back to Admir and smiled again. "I'll continue along the road."

"Good... thank you."

John nodded at the dog. "What's his name?"

"Brutus."

"Hey, Brutus."

Brutus's ears twitched at the mention of his name.

"Are you a good dog, or are you going to bite me?"

"I won't let him bite you."

John grinned. "That's good to hear, Admir. You have a good day."

John turned and began to run away, up the path toward the stone wall. He raised one hand and shouted over his shoulder, "See you tomorrow."

20

Once on the road, John followed it for another kilometre south, then took a left and ran along the wall that formed the southern boundary toward the front gate.

The gate was closed, and he glanced toward the gatehouse as he passed. He had met two guards now, and he was sure there were more patrolling the grounds, but he doubted he would be as lucky with the others as he had been with Admir.

He was still unsure of what to do next to help his parents, but as he reached the lane that led to their cottage, an idea popped into his head.

He could fix the road. He would have to pay for it himself rather than wait for Xie to fix it, but at least it would be done.

With renewed enthusiasm, he picked up his pace and ran the last couple of hundred metres hard, his eyes on the broken road surface, dodging the cracks, and leaping over the larger potholes. He slowed once he reached the cottage and continued past at a jog for several metres before turning back. At the gate, he leaned on the gatepost while he regained his breath and studied the front lawn. He'd mow the lawn today as well.

Moving his attention to the house, he frowned. There was something not quite right. He stared at the windows for a moment longer, trying to work out what it was.

There were no lights on in the house.

Willow Cottage was an old house with small windows. The rooms were dark and until the sun was fully up, lights were needed. John turned his wrist and glanced at his watch, then shrugged. It was just after seven. Perhaps his parents had slept in?

He pushed through the gate and walked up the path to the door. Bending down, he shifted the flower pot, removed the spare key and, after slipping off his running shoes, let himself in.

"Good morning, son."

"Oh." John stopped in the doorway and looked over at his father sitting in the armchair by the window. Unusually, he was in his dressing gown and pyjamas. He hadn't even shaved, which was unheard of. "I didn't think you were up yet."

"Why? It's after seven."

John smiled and closed the door behind him. "I didn't see any lights on."

"Yes. That's because we don't have any power."

"What?" John stopped in his tracks. "There was power when I got up this morning." Once again, he looked at his watch. "Over an hour ago."

"Well, it's not there now. I can't even boil the kettle," his father grumbled.

"It's okay, maybe a fuse has blown. I'll check for you. Where's Mum?"

The Neighbor

"She's still in bed." His father looked away, his face sad. "She needs a hot shower to get started these days."

"Yeah." John sighed. "Don't worry, I'll sort it out. I'll check the fuse box. The power will be back on in no time."

David nodded. "You know where it is?"

"I used to live here, remember?" John said over his shoulder as he walked down the short hallway toward the back door. The fuse box was on the wall of the mudroom at the back entrance, and he flipped open the catch and swung the door open. Running his eyes down the rows of fuses, he checked each one individually, but they all seemed in order. John's frown deepened. Perhaps it wouldn't be as easy to fix as he thought.

He unlocked the back door, stepped out in his socks and looked up at the rear wall where the power cable entered the house. He then traced the cable across the garden to the power pole that stood in the neighbouring field. It was all still connected. He couldn't see any breaks. The power cable continued on from the nearest pole across the field until it joined the principal supply that ran along the main road. That was out of view, but if the problem was there, it was something only the power company could deal with. He'd have to give them a call.

Stepping back inside, he walked through the cottage to the front room.

"Dad, I'll need the number for the power company. The fuses are okay, so it must be a bigger problem. Maybe the power is out everywhere?"

His father muttered something under his breath. The only word John could catch was 'tea.'

"I'll boil some water on the stove for tea, don't worry. And I'll sort some hot water out for Mum. She'll have to have a bath this morning. Now, where can I find the number?"

"It's on the fridge."

John went upstairs to his room, retrieved his phone, and jogged back down the stairs, and entered the kitchen. Stuck to the fridge with a magnet was a sheet of paper with a handwritten list of phone numbers. He ran his finger down the list until he found the number for the power company and dialled. While it rang out, he wedged the phone between his ear and shoulder and filled a large pot with water, setting it to boil on the stove. Fortunately, the cottage still used an oil powered AGA stove for cooking.

Ten minutes later, he walked out into the front room with a teapot and cups. "Here you go, Dad. All sorted. The power company said it must be a local issue, so they'll send someone out straight away to check. Here's your tea, and water is boiling for Mum's bath."

His father nodded and looked a little more cheerful.

"Cheer up, Dad. It will all be fixed by midday. Pour yourself some tea, and then I'll take some up for Mum."

21

"Hello?"

"Mr Hayes?"

John pressed the phone closer to his ear and stepped toward the window, hoping for a better signal. "Speaking."

"This is Ethan from Southwest Power. We've identified the problem. Apparently, a power pole has fallen down. The technicians are repairing it now, but it will take most of the day before the power can be reconnected."

John frowned. "Fallen down? Where?"

"Near to your home, Mr Hayes. But rest assured, we will have the supply restored as soon as possible."

"Okay, thank you. I appreciate it." John ended the call and stared out the window, deep lines creasing his forehead. He had a nagging suspicion, but didn't want to accept it without proof.

"Mum, Dad, I'm just popping out for a few minutes."

He didn't wait for a reply and stepped out the front door, walking around the side of the house to the rear garden. John vaulted the rear wall and followed the power line across the field and up the slope. Cresting the slope, he saw a yellow vehicle parked on the edge of the road on the other side of the field. Beside it, two men stood looking at a power pole which leaned away from them at a thirty-degree angle. John walked over, carefully skirting the power lines lying on the ground, and raised a hand in greeting.

"Hi guys, I made the complaint about the power. John Hayes."

"Good morning, Mr Hayes," a stocky middle-aged man in overalls replied. "We'll have it fixed by evening." He gestured toward the pole. "We're just waiting on a crane to pull this upright."

John leaned over the wall and studied the power pole. "How did it fall over?"

The man glanced at his colleague, a younger man puffing on a cigarette, then replied, "It didn't fall."

John nodded slowly. "Somehow I didn't think so. We've had no wind." He glanced around. "No sign of a car accident, either."

"Nope." The man shrugged. "It was pushed."

"What makes you say that?"

"Well," said the man, warming to the subject. "There's yellow paint and scrape marks on the pole, and..." he gestured at several large tyre tracks John hadn't noticed, "there's these."

John placed his hands on the top of the stone wall and climbed over, landing easily in the uncut grass on the edge of the road. He studied the tyre tracks. They were large, much larger than a car's and there were signs of wheel spin where the vehicle had pushed up against the power pole. He then stepped over to the power pole and examined the scratches and deep indentations in the wood. As the man had said, there were traces of yellow paint and the indentations suggested something large and strong had pushed against the pole. Something like an excavator bucket. Looking back, he asked, "JCB?"

The older man nodded. "Or something similar. It's difficult to knock these over."

The young man spoke up for the first time. "Could be a farm tractor with a bucket on the front."

The older man shrugged. "Yup. Could be."

"Why would anyone do this? It looks deliberate."

The younger man cleared his throat and spat noisily into the grass. "Probably drunk."

John stared at him for a moment, then shook his head. "No. The power was on this morning when I went for a run." He nodded at the downed pole. "This happened between six and seven this morning."

The young man shrugged like he didn't care. "Could still be a drunk."

John didn't think so.

Neither did the older man, who rolled his eyes at John. "He's basing his opinion on his own habits. No, it was pushed over." He pointed at the tyre tracks. "That's why there is wheel spin there. Someone pushed it over on purpose." He narrowed his eyes and peered at John. "The question is, why?"

John had a pretty good idea, but no proof. Ignoring the man's question, he reached out a hand. "Thank you for coming out so quickly." He jerked his head in the direction he had come from. "It's my parents' house over the hill there. They are struggling with no power."

The older man took John's hand in a strong, calloused grip. "We'll have the power back on as soon as we can."

John smiled. "I appreciate it. If you need anything, please come up to the house."

The older man nodded a thanks.

John glanced at the younger man, who was lighting up another cigarette. "Thank you."

He got a grunt in reply and John turned, climbed back over the wall and walked back to the house, deep in thought.

22

"Hey, beautiful."

"John, is everything okay?"

John grinned and adjusted his grip on his phone. "Why? I have to have a reason to call you?"

He heard Adriana chuckle before she spoke.

"No, not at all. It's just that we spoke already this morning. I wasn't expecting another call today. Do you have power again?"

"Not yet, but it will be reconnected soon. A power pole had fallen down."

"Oh," Adriana paused. "I thought you said the weather was good?"

"Yes," John exhaled loudly and rubbed his head with his free hand. "It appears to have been knocked over... by a vehicle of some sort."

"Oh."

John turned and looked over his shoulder. His Mum dozed in the armchair and there was no sign of his father. "One sec." He moved over to the front door and let himself out, closing the door quietly behind him.

"I ahhh... need your help."

"Sure."

"Can you look into a man called Xie Longwei for me? Find out anything you can? He runs a multinational construction firm. I don't know the name, but I can find out."

"John, what's going on? Are you in trouble again?"

"No, no," John injected a lighter tone into his voice. "Not at all. It's nothing really."

"Tell me the truth, John. I know you're hiding something from me."

John sighed, "Yeah, okay." He thought about where he should start as he paced slowly across the front lawn. "He's my parent's neighbour, and he's hassling them."

He explained everything that had happened so far, while Adriana listened, occasionally interjecting with a question.

Once he had finished, she replied, "You seem to attract trouble."

"Like you, you mean?"

"Huh, very funny. So what will you do? Have you called the police?"

John made a face. To be honest, he had no idea what to do, but calling the police wasn't high on the list of options. "What can they do? There's been no crime committed."

"No, I guess not."

"I'll speak to him. I think that's the first step."

"Hmmm." Even over the phone, Adriana didn't sound convinced.

"But if you have time, see what you can find out. The more I know about him, the better. I'm sure he's involved in some dodgy stuff. He has armed guards roaming the Estate."

"Really?"

"Yes. I met one of them this morning."

"John, please be careful. Don't do anything dangerous. I wanted you to be with your parents, not get involved in property disputes with rich businessmen."

"What can I do, baby? It's my parents."

He heard Adriana sigh.

"Yes, I know. I just worry about you. There has to be a legal way."

"If I can find it, I will take it. Trust me. I don't want to create problems for Mum and Dad. They're getting old now. I want them to be safe and comfortable."

"I understand. I'll see what I can find out for you. Just be careful John."

"I'm always careful."

Adriana said nothing.

"I'd better go. Let me know what you find out. I love you."

"I love you too, John. Call me."

"I will."

John ended the call and stared blankly across the field. What was his next step? He slipped the phone back into his pocket and turned to look back at the house. A light flicked on in the living room and he nodded with satisfaction. At least the power was back.

He watched his father move across the living room and gently shake his mom awake. They spoke for a moment, and then he straightened up and glanced out the window. Seeing John looking back, he nodded, then turned away and headed for the kitchen.

John took a deep breath. Avoiding them for the past few years had been wrong, but there was no point in regretting the things he had or hadn't done. He had to move forward, and that meant ensuring the rest of their life was safe and secure.

23

Xie scooped grated ginger from the side plate and stirred it into his *congee*. Thin tendrils of steam spiralled upwards from the bowl of hot rice porridge, but he paid it no attention. His mind was on other things.

He'd slept badly, which wasn't unusual. The damp English weather didn't agree with him and neither did the drafty old house. They had conquered a large part of the world, but still couldn't build a warm house. The cold and damp seeped into his joints and it was not even winter. Hopefully, the renovations would be finished by the time the weather turned really cold, and the house would finally be liveable.

The thought of the renovations increased his irritation. As if he didn't have enough problems on his plate with his African projects, the stupid councillor was proving to be a thorn in his side. If it was Africa, or Myanmar, he'd use force, but here in England, where they still liked to believe in laws and regulations, he had to be a little more circumspect in the way things got done.

He sensed a presence behind him and he turned his head slowly to see Mingmei standing close by. He hadn't even heard her enter the room. She was like a ninja—his own personal middle-aged ninja—although in her shapeless grey suit and thick-rimmed glasses, she looked like one of those aunties who spent their days gossiping and playing *mahjong*. But her unassuming exterior hid a ruthless and highly efficient employee who had been with him for twenty years, and he trusted her implicitly. Whenever he needed something done, no matter the legalities, Mingmei always came up with a solution. Which is why he had turned to her when the solicitor had failed.

"Yes?"

"You have a call with President Tamba at ten o'clock."

Xie nodded slowly. "Is he coming round to our way of thinking yet?"

"Not yet, but this morning, with his breakfast, he will receive an envelope containing glossy and detailed photographs of his adventures last night with that young boy."

"Good."

"The boy is no longer..."

Xie stopped her with a wave of his hand. "Spare me the details. I only want results."

"You will have what you want after this morning's call."

"Good."

He gazed out the large windows across the broad swathe of grass that stretched toward a Greek-revival style folly on a distant hill, while he thought about the upcoming phone call. The previous government of the Democratic Republic of Nkuru had approved the Port he was building for them. But a new leader, President Tamba, had been elected, and construction had been shut down until he could negotiate a different deal. Although Xie was prepared to pay the new President generously, Xie had always believed in using the carrot and the stick approach. The photos were the stick because President Tamba was showing dangerous signs of developing a conscience.

He turned back to look at Mingmei. "Anything else?"

"The power is back on in the cottage."

"That didn't take long."

"No. Apparently their son is visiting, and he got it repaired."

"Son?" Xie frowned. "What do we know about him?"

"Nothing yet, but I'm working on it. He won't be a problem."

"I'm sure he won't. Anyway, get it done." Xie turned his attention back to his breakfast. He took a spoonful and raised it to his mouth, stopping when something outside caught his eye.

Midway between the folly and the end of the grassland, where it abutted the gravel parking area in front of the house, was a man. Xie narrowed his eyes. Despite his age, he prided himself on his superior eyesight. It definitely wasn't one of his security. He wasn't dressed like that. In fact, the man appeared to be in tracksuit pants and a t-shirt, and… was running toward the house.

He dropped his spoon into the bowl of *congee*, ignoring the hot liquid splashing onto his hand.

"Who is that, and how did he get in?" he growled.

24

To an outside observer, John looked relaxed as he jogged steadily toward the house. Internally, though, he was on high alert as his eyes roamed the house and the surrounding buildings.

When he had come up with the plan, it had seemed like such a good idea. But planning was one thing, doing was another, and now doubts were creeping in.

He had realised that phoning for an appointment would have been a waste of time. Xie's staff would have given him the runaround or passed him off to the lawyer, and John didn't believe in wasting time. So he decided to be more direct. He was taking a risk, but it was a calculated one. Even though Xie's security were armed, he didn't think they would shoot. It would create too many problems for Xie. The guns were a deterrent only... at least, that's what he hoped. The worst they would do, is set the dog or dogs on him.

John grimaced. Actually, that wouldn't be good either.

He pushed the negativity away and concentrated on the house.

Atwell Manor was just as he remembered it, with none of the changes Philip Symonds had hinted at, visible from the outside. The red brick of the Jacobean-era facade glowed warmly in the morning sunlight, several of the windows sending bright shards of reflected light across the manicured lawns. A black Range Rover and Mercedes were parked on the gravel area between the house and the lawns, and he could see an old Land Rover parked around by the stable block. But apart from that, there was no sign of life.

John was only a few hundred metres from the house when he heard barking, and he felt a stab of panic as a dog rounded the corner of the house and streaked toward him.

"Fuck," he cursed, and stopped in his tracks. Running would only make things worse, so despite all his instincts, he sat down on the ground, crossed his legs, and tried to look as non-threatening as possible.

"Shit, shit, shit," he muttered. What the hell was he doing? His heart hammered away in panic and he forced himself to take a deep breath. Hopefully, his seated position would confuse the dog, but, just in case, he clenched his right fist, ready to punch the dog in the head.

The dog closed rapidly, then slowed to a trot before stopping a few metres short of John. It bared its teeth in an angry snarl and a low growl rumbled from deep within its chest.

John hoped it was the same dog he'd seen the previous day.

"Brutus, come here, boy."

The dog cocked its head and John saw its ears twitch. It was.

"Good boy, Brutus."

John heard a shout and spotted two estate guards running toward him.

He ignored them, focusing his attention on the dog, continuing in soothing tones, "Good boy, Brutus, good boy."

He slowly raised a hand and reached out toward the dog, but Brutus growled.

"It's okay, boy, good boy. Come here, Brutus."

Another growl, but Brutus took a half step forward.

"Good boy. Look, I've got something for you." John reached into the pocket of his tracksuit pants and eased out a small packet he had prepared earlier. He unwrapped it and removed a rasher of bacon.

Brutus' nostrils twitched, and he took a tentative step closer.

"Good boy." John tossed the bacon toward Brutus, the meat landing halfway between them.

Brutus dipped his head cautiously and sniffed.

"Come on, Brutus, good boy."

John glanced nervously past the dog toward the men. They were close.

"Hurry up, Brutus," John said, fixing a smile on his face and keeping his tone encouraging. He didn't know whether dogs could understand a smile, but he figured it couldn't hurt.

Brutus stepped forward, sniffed the bacon, then picked it up in his teeth and wolfed it down.

"Good boy." John tossed another piece toward him, and this time Brutus didn't hesitate.

He moved closer, and the bacon disappeared down his throat.

John had one piece left, and he held it in his outstretched hand.

Brutus looked at him, then the bacon, then stepped forward, taking it from the palm of John's hand with a surprising gentleness.

The Neighbor

John grinned and slowly reached out, stroking the dog just behind the ears.

Brutus' tail gave a slight wag.

"Good boy, you won't hurt me, will you?"

Brutus licked his hand then sat on his haunches, his head tilted to one side, and licked his lips.

"Sorry boy, I don't have any more."

John turned his attention to the two guards. One was Admir, but the second one he hadn't seen before.

"Good morning, gentlemen."

The two men slowed to a walk, then stopped, their mouths hanging open, and exchanged a look of disbelief.

Admir was the first to speak. "What have you done to my dog?"

25

Xie clenched his fists, then swept the bowl of *congee* off the table with his right arm. It flew across the room, hit the floor and shattered, strewing rice soup and fragments of porcelain across the floor.

He closed his eyes, took a deep breath, regained some measure of control, then turned slowly and glared at Mingmei.

Mingmei, her face impassive, gave a slight nod, then tapped her phone, raised it to her ear and walked away from the table toward the window.

Xie turned his attention back to the scene outside. When the man had sat down as the guard dog raced toward him, he thought his eyes were playing tricks on him. Who in their right mind sits down in front of an angry attack dog?

Then, when the dog sat down, he couldn't believe it. What kind of clown show was his security? This is what happened when you had to use outside contractors. No-one did anything properly. It would never have happened if he had his normal Chinese security.

Xie struggled to get his temper under control as he watched a guard answer his phone while turning to face the house.

"He says his name is John Hayes, and he has come to see you."

Xie frowned and looked over at Mingmei. "Who?"

"John Hayes."

"Do I know him?"

"No. He says he's your neighbour."

Xie blinked, his brain still confused by what he'd just seen.

"The cottage. Their name is Hayes."

"But they're old. He looks young... ah, their son?"

"Yes."

"And?"

"I don't know."

"Then find out," Xie growled. "Deal with it. I'm not interested in seeing him."

"Yes." Mingmei nodded, muttered something into the phone, then turned toward the door.

Xie looked back out the window. One of the guards reached down and helped the seated man to his feet, and Xie shook his head. "Idiots," he muttered. "Mingmei."

Mingmei stopped by the door. "Yes?"

"Get rid of that dog."

26

Admir let go of John's arm as he stood and John nodded a thank you without showing recognition. In their two brief encounters, the guy had been decent and John didn't want to get him in trouble.

The other guy was less friendly.

"Move," he grunted.

John eyed him for a moment. He was broad shouldered, as if he was once fit, but now had a belly that strained at the buttons of his shirt. Two days' stubble peppered his chin, his nose was crooked, a small scar split one eyebrow, and he had a black dot tattooed between the first and second knuckles of each of his fingers.

John gave him a broad smile. "Where?"

The man shoved him toward the house as if that was enough of an answer.

John shrugged and began walking. "Beautiful morning, isn't it?"

"Shut up." He was English... a northern accent.

"No coffee this morning?"

The man gave him another push, and John stumbled

before regaining his footing. He threw a quick glance at Admir, who was following behind, Brutus now leashed at his side.

Admir gave a slight shake of his head, and John turned back and continued walking. He scanned the windows of the house, but the morning light reflecting off the windows prevented him from seeing inside. He assumed he was being watched, though.

They crossed the large gravel parking area in front of the house, and John headed toward the wide stone steps that led toward the front door.

"Hey!"

Broken Nose grabbed his elbow, jerking him sideways away from the entrance. "This way."

John shook his arm free and fixed Broken Nose with a stare. Broken Nose glared back, but John refused to look away. After a moment, Broken Nose broke eye contact, jerking his head to the side, and said, "The boss will see you in her office."

John frowned. Her? Interesting.

Broken Nose led him round the house toward the stables, and John examined the building as they approached. Here, Xie's alterations were obvious. Gone were the horses gazing out of half open stable doors. Instead, large aluminium framed windows punctuated the brick facade in a complete mismatch of style and proportion. John shook his head. No wonder Philip Symonds was upset.

Broken Nose led him toward a door and knocked. John didn't hear a reply, but Broken Nose must have because he opened the door, then stood back and sneered at John. "Inside."

John stepped forward and peered through the doorway.

Inside was a large sparsely furnished office. The walls were bare, and the only furniture was a long row of filing cabinets and two metal folding chairs in front of a large white formica desk. Behind the desk sat a woman. A middle-aged Chinese woman. John glanced at Broken Nose, then stepped inside, Broken Nose following behind him.

"Sit." Broken Nose instructed, pointing toward the two chairs.

So far, the lady had remained silent.

John walked over, smiled, and said, "Good morning." He held out his hand. "My name is John."

The woman stared at his hand for a moment, then reached out and took it. Her hand was soft and small and she let go of his hand quickly.

"Please sit down," she spoke softly, without an accent.

"Thank you." John sat, gave her another smile, and said, "I was hoping to meet Mr Xie."

"Mr Xie is a very busy man, and he doesn't see people without an appointment."

"And how do I make an appointment?"

"You speak to me."

"I'm sorry you have me at a disadvantage. Who are you?"

"Wang Mingmei. I am Mr Xie's assistant."

"A pleasure to meet you, Ms Wang. Can I have an appointment to see Mr Xie?"

"Why do you wish to see Mr Xie?"

"It's a personal matter."

"You will have to tell me more than that, Mr... Hayes... is that correct?"

"Yes, John Hayes." John sighed. "Look, it's about my parents. They own a property next to the Estate."

"Which property is that?"

She knew exactly which property he was talking about, but John humoured her. "Willow Cottage."

Mingmei nodded. "I see. I didn't know they had a son."

John smiled again. "Well, here I am."

"Indeed. So what exactly did you wish to discuss, Mr Hayes?"

"I want to make it clear to Mr Xie that the property is not for sale."

"I see," Mingmei repeated.

John waited, but she said nothing else, just looked at John, her face giving nothing away. Then she sat forward and brushed an imaginary speck of dust from the otherwise empty desktop.

"It must be difficult when you get to your parents' age to maintain an old house like that. Surely they will be more comfortable in a newer property? Perhaps one in a community more geared to people of their age? We are prepared to increase our offer to make it happen." She looked up at John, "perhaps a side agreement for you, to aid with any... expenses you may have? Helping your parents move out."

John stared back with the same lack of expression. She was really starting to annoy him, but he didn't want to show it. "I said the property is not for sale."

"Are you sure?"

"I'm sure."

"Don't you need to ask your parents? Everyone has their price, Mr Hayes."

"Well, this may surprise you, but my parents don't have a price. Willow Cottage is their home. They've spent many happy years there and have no desire to leave."

"I see."

John ground his teeth together. "I don't think you do. It's

their property, and they will not sell. No matter how much you offer."

"That's unfortunate."

John ignored the strange choice of words and continued, "I also want to point out that Mr Xie, as owner of the Atwell Estate, has a legal responsibility to maintain the byway that forms the access to my parent's cottage. It is in a very poor state of repair and is difficult for my parents to drive across."

"I wasn't aware of that, Mr Hayes. I will look into it."

"Thank you," although John doubted she would do anything at all. "So I'll assume that you'll pass on my message to Mr Xie?"

Mingmei nodded but said nothing.

John watched her for several moments and when it was clear she wouldn't add any more to the conversation, he stood up. "Good. I'll continue on my run then."

Mingmei glanced over his shoulder at Broken Nose. "My staff will escort you to the gate."

John turned to see Broken Nose nodding. With his left hand he opened his jacket, giving John a glimpse of a weapon in a shoulder holster.

The message was obvious. John turned back, gave Wang Mingmei a curt nod, then stood and headed for the door.

27

There was no sign of Admir and Brutus outside, but a battered old Land Rover 90 with a canvas roof stood idling in the parking lot.

John felt a push in his back, sending him off balance, and he stumbled. He regained his footing, turned around, and glared at Broken Nose.

"What?" Broken Nose sniggered.

"That's the last time you lay your hands on me."

Broken Nose scoffed and once more opened his jacket. "Or what?"

John refused to look at the holstered weapon, keeping his eyes fixed on Broken Nose. The man stared back, but his sneer slowly faded, and then he jerked his head toward the rear of the Land Rover. "Get in."

John thought about refusing, but then figured he'd fought enough battles for the morning and reluctantly climbed in the back.

Broken Nose climbed in after him, then without closing the tailgate, banged the flat of his hand twice on the steel bench seat.

The driver glanced back over his shoulder, nodded, then with a crunch of gears the Land Rover lurched into motion, and headed away from the stables and down the long driveway toward the front gate.

John sat glaring at Broken Nose, but the guard studiously avoided eye contact, preferring instead to look out the back of the Land Rover as it drove away from the house. He thought back over the meeting, wondering if there was anything he should have done differently, anything he should have said, but no matter which way he looked at it, there was nothing he would change. But he still hadn't met Xie and after the empty promise from his assistant, there was no guarantee his parents were going to be left alone. On the face of it, the whole thing had been a complete waste of time... and a waste of a good run.

Two minutes later, the Land Rover jerked to a stop, performed a three-point turn and then backed up to where another guard was holding the gate open.

Broken Nose looked at John and with a jerk of his head, indicated he should get out. John stared back for a moment, then pushed himself off the seat, landing easily on the driveway in one smooth movement.

Broken Nose climbed out with less ease and pointed toward the gate. "Off you go then."

John nodded, then turned and walked through the gate without acknowledging the guard. As the gate swung shut behind him, John heard a gunshot. Frowning, he turned and looked back into the Estate. Broken Nose was grinning and when John caught his eye, he threw back his head and howled like a wolf.

John stared back, puzzled, then the realisation hit him. "You dirty fucking bastards," he growled. Clenching his fists, he turned away and began the walk back to his parents' home.

With each step, the fire in his belly grew until it spread outward, filling his whole being with rage. He leaned forward into a jog, then upped his pace, his hands squeezed into tight fists, his jaw clenched. He pumped his arms, pushing himself faster and faster, until he was sprinting down the road. Opening his mouth, he roared in anguish, pushing himself onwards, faster and faster, allowing the rage to exit his body.

28

His energy ran out as he neared the Willow Cottage lane and he slowed to a more sensible pace, panting heavily.

He had parked the Porsche in a small lay-by on the main road, and there was now another car parked behind it, a light blue Kia. A man stood with his hands on his hips, gazing down at the Porsche. He looked vaguely familiar and when he turned at the sound of John's approach, John realised who it was.

Philip Symonds.

Breathing heavily, John slowed to a walk, then stopped and nodded a greeting.

"Good morning, Mr Hayes."

"John," John replied in between breaths.

"Yes... sorry, John. Been for a run?" Philip asked, then shook his head. "Sorry, stupid question. Of course you have."

John nodded, then, his breath almost under control, asked, "What brings you out here?"

Philip gestured toward the lane. "I thought I would come and see for myself."

John checked his watch. "You start early."

"Yeah, well, I live out this way, so I thought I'd take a look on the way into the office."

"Well, don't let me stop you." John jerked his head toward the lane. "Come and see what it's like."

"Yours?"

"Sorry?"

"The Porsche?"

"Yes, one of my few indulgences."

"She's beautiful. Seventies?"

John looked back at Philip, who hadn't moved from the car.

"1970."

Philip nodded slowly, his eyes roaming the car's lines with obvious admiration. "They don't make cars like this anymore. Instead, we get..." he gestured toward his Kia and trailed off.

John agreed, but didn't want to make Philip feel bad about his choice of transport, so he kept quiet. John was fortunate he could afford the car he had always wanted. If things had turned out differently... he shuddered... he too might have been driving a Kia.

Philip's shoulders rose and fell as he took a deep breath and sighed, then he turned to follow John up the lane.

Within twenty metres, it was obvious to Philip how bad the lane had become.

"I can see why you parked where you did. I didn't realise. The photos didn't..." he trailed off, shaking his head.

John stopped and stared into a crater, taking up two-thirds of the road. "Yeah." He sighed loudly. "You can imagine how difficult it is for my parents."

"I can."

John turned to look at Philip. "So, what can we do about it?"

Philip made a face and looked away. He was silent for a long time, and when he looked back, his expression was apologetic. "Well, as I said yesterday, I can issue a notice to the Atwell Estate. They'll have thirty days to rectify it."

"And if they don't?"

Philip's sigh was audible. "Legal proceedings."

"Legal proceedings," John repeated. "Against the same lawyer who tried to bribe you?"

"Yes."

"So, in reality, nothing will happen. Xie will ignore you, the road will get worse... if that's possible... and my parents will continue to suffer."

Philip looked away and stared at the bottom of a large pothole.

John watched him, then reached out and placed a hand on his shoulder. "Come up to the cottage. Last time we met, I promised you a good coffee, and I don't know about you, but I sure as hell need one this morning."

29

John carried the French press and two mugs outside, setting them on top of the stone wall separating the lane from the cottage lawn. Philip had stayed outside, ostensibly to continue checking the lane, but John suspected he was avoiding his father.

"I still can't believe the road surface has deteriorated so badly in such a short time." Philip said as John stood beside him.

"Yup," John agreed. "And it will only get worse once winter comes."

Philip shook his head and stood with his hands on his hips, staring down at the cracked and pitted surface. "I'll try to do something," he said eventually, his voice barely audible.

The stopwatch on John's wrist beeped, and he depressed the plunger on the French press. "Four minutes," he explained to Philip, then poured coffee into a mug and handed it over to Philip before filling his own. "Milk, sugar?"

Philip shook his head.

"Good, I didn't bring any." John grinned and inhaled the steam rising from his mug. "Coffee makes everything good."

Philip half smiled and took a sip. "Mmmm, this is actually good. Really good." He looked over at John. "When you said you would make me a good coffee, I thought it was an empty promise."

"I don't make empty promises."

Philip's smile faded, and he nodded. "No, somehow I don't think you do." He held up his mug. "Thank you."

John sipped his own coffee, then set the mug down and leaned on the top of the wall with both hands. "So... what do we do?"

Philip stepped back and leaned his butt against the wall, both hands cupped around his coffee mug, and John heard him sigh. "Well, I've told you, I will..."

John interrupted him. "No, I mean, what can we do that will actually work?"

Philip shrugged, but didn't look up.

John picked up his coffee mug and took another sip. He had known the answer before he asked the question.

He turned and glanced back at the house. Someone was moving around in the living room, probably his dad keeping an eye on them.

John had to do something. He owed it to his parents. At their age, they shouldn't be dealing with this shit. Their life should be comfortable, stress free.

Turning back, he cleared his throat. "I'll get the road repaired. I'll pay for it myself."

Philip nodded slowly. "I'll send you a contact. Someone who'll do it for a fair price."

"Thanks."

"Keep the receipts. We can try and claim it from Xie."

"Huh," John scoffed. "I don't think that will go anywhere."

"No," Philip agreed and shrugged. "But we have to try."

"Yeah." John made a face. "It's a waste of time, though." He took a large mouthful of coffee, seeking comfort in his regular morning drink. "I tried to meet him this morning."

Philip turned and frowned. "Who?"

"Xie."

"And?"

"I went for a run on the Estate and went up to the house. Thought I'd catch him at breakfast."

Philip's eyebrows arched in disbelief.

"Two security guards and a dog stopped me from getting too close."

"Oh."

"Yes. They took me to see a woman, Wang Mingmei."

"Xie's assistant."

"Yes. Although... I don't think assistant is the right word for what she does. I'm sure she's more than that."

"I've not met her. Just seen her name on correspondence."

"Hmmm, well, she had me shown into her office and told me she would look into the matter."

Philip smiled without mirth. "Don't hold your breath."

"I won't." John thought about telling Philip about the dog, but he didn't know for sure, so he kept it to himself. He felt himself growing angry again, his grip tightening on the coffee mug until he forced himself to relax.

"So, I'm no further forward."

"No." Philip looked down into his mug, then drained it and set it down on top of the wall. "Look, I wish I could do more, but..." he trailed off with a shrug.

"Do what you can, Philip. If I think of something, I'll let

you know." He nodded back over his shoulder toward the cottage. "I just want to save them from stress. They're too old for this."

Philip looked over the wall toward the cottage and nodded. "Yeah," he sighed. Glancing at his wristwatch, he said, "I've got to head to the office. Thanks for the coffee. It was excellent."

"My pleasure. Come and have another whenever you feel like it."

Philip smiled and offered his hand. "I might do that."

John shook hands and then watched him walk away down the lane toward the parked cars. He seemed like a decent guy, but John doubted there was anything he could do.

John needed to find a solution himself, but he had to be careful. There was a fine line between standing up against a bully and making things worse for his parents.

30

Philip was true to his word and within an hour, John received a call from a contractor who said he could repair the road. John sent him a couple of photos showing what was needed, they agreed on a price and the contractor agreed to be around first thing the next morning.

John decided to keep it a surprise and not tell his parents—his dad would stress if he knew too much in advance. For the same reason, he didn't tell them about his encounter with Xie's security earlier that morning. His parents didn't need to know details, they just needed the problem to go away.

John spent the rest of the day attending to the house. He mowed the lawn, weeded and turned over the flowerbeds at the front of the property, and did a quick trip to the supermarket in his parents' car.

His parents seemed to enjoy having him around. Carole sat out in the sun while he tended the flowerbeds and updated John on their life since the last time he'd seen them. His father pottered around, occasionally inserting himself into the conversation, but kept to himself most of the time.

It was late in the afternoon when John's phone buzzed and he smiled when he saw Adriana's name on the screen.

"Hey. I was just thinking of you."

"Good. You should think of me all the time."

John chuckled and mouthed the word 'Adriana' to his mum, who nodded, her eyes filled with amusement.

"How's your day been?" Adriana continued.

"Good. Just been doing some things around the house, cleaning up the garden."

"Your parents must be happy."

John glanced at his mum and smiled. "I think so. How about you?"

"Happy?"

"Well yeah, but I meant how was your day?"

"Busy, as usual, but I did some research on your..." John heard a shuffling of papers, "Xie Longwei."

"Oh, good, thank you." John moved away from his mother and walked toward the other side of the front lawn. "What did you find out?"

"Not a lot about his early life. Born in 1960 in Shanxi, China. Poor farming family. Left school early and worked on a building site, working his way up to foreman, before leaving and starting his own construction business. Houses, then apartment buildings, and now he runs the Golden Fortune Corporation, an international construction firm. Does a lot in Africa and Asia, but not so much elsewhere. Apparently extremely wealthy."

"Hmmm, sounds like a standard self-made man story."

"Yes, but he seems to have come out of nowhere. Everything I've told you is what he's said in interviews. I've not been able to find out anything from independent sources.

There's actually nothing on the web about him before ten years ago."

"Is that normal?"

"No," Adriana sighed. "Not for someone who is honest."

John thought about what she had said as he paced back and forth across the lawn. "You said he does a lot in Africa and Asia?"

"Yes."

"Do you have a list of the countries he's involved in?"

"I've sent everything to your email."

"Thanks. I'll take a look. See if there's a pattern."

"What will you do with the information?"

John sighed and massaged his forehead. "Honestly? Right now I don't know, but..." he looked back at his mother sitting in the deck chair. "There has to be something."

"You'll be careful, won't you, John?"

John smiled at the concern in her voice. "I'm always careful."

"That's what worries me. Your definition of careful is not the same as mine."

John chuckled and decided against telling her about his adventure that morning. "Well, I'm getting the access to the cottage repaired tomorrow, and I'm clearing up the garden. That's all, so don't worry."

"Hmmm." Adriana didn't sound convinced.

"Anyway, I'll have a look through what you've sent and if you find out anything else, let me know."

"I miss you."

John smiled again. "I miss you too. Hopefully, this will be resolved soon."

"I hope so."

John nodded. So did he.

"I'll call you tomorrow."

"Bye, John."

John ended the call and slipped the phone back into his pocket. The sun was low in the sky and the temperature had dropped noticeably. He turned and walked over to his mum. "Come on, let's get you inside before it gets too cold."

31

John was sitting on the front step, lacing up his running shoes, when he heard the rumble of engines. He finished knotting the lace and stood up, looking for the source of the noise. It was just after six in the morning, so it was unusual to hear anything other than the usual dawn chorus.

A white Mitsubishi Pajero with a yellow light bar on the roof crawled up the lane and pulled to a stop outside the front gate. John frowned until the driver raised a hand in greeting. John walked over as the man climbed out. He was a powerfully built middle-aged man in a high-vis vest. His face, tanned and lined by long periods outside, beamed with a broad smile.

"John?"

"Yes."

"William Sanderson. We spoke yesterday."

"Yes, William. I didn't expect you so early."

"Call me Will." Will reached over the front wall and grabbed John's hand, shaking it vigorously.

John tried not to wince as Will's large, calloused hand crushed his. "Thank you for coming out so quickly."

"No problem. Philip is a good friend of mine and he told me you needed help." Will let go of John's hand and jerked his head toward the lane. "You weren't joking when you said it needed work."

"Yeah," John sighed loudly as he flexed his hand behind his back. "Can you fix it?"

"Easy. But we'll need the day." He nodded toward the Ford Focus parked in the driveway. "If you need to go out, I'd take the car out now."

John shook his head. "Not today."

"Good. And the pretty little Porsche down on the main road?"

"Yeah, that's mine. Should I move it?"

"It's safer. My guys are good, but I'd prefer if it was parked elsewhere." Will grinned. "I'd hate to see it scratched."

"Me too. Give me a minute. I'll grab the keys."

"Will do. My boys are waiting down on the main road. I'll get them started."

John waited for Will to climb back into his Pajero, then, as he did a three-point turn, John headed back to the house to grab his car keys.

His father stood in the doorway in his dressing gown, a frown etched deeply into his forehead. "Who was that?" he growled.

"I'm getting the road fixed. That's the contractor."

"You what?"

"The road will be fixed by the end of the day, Dad. Nothing to worry about."

"Who's paying for it?"

"Me."

David was shaking his head. "No, no. I'm not allowing it."

John gritted his teeth and forced a smile. "Dad, I'm getting it done, and you can't stop me."

"That bastard is getting away with it."

John didn't need to ask who the bastard was. "I know, Dad, but you can't carry on with the road like it is. I'll get it fixed and we'll worry about Xie later."

David Hayes opened his mouth to protest, but John ignored him and squeezed past into the house. "I have to move the car."

He grabbed the Porsche keys from the side table, then jogged out the door and down the path before his dad could say anything.

His dad was right, of course, but being right wasn't getting the road fixed.

32

By midday, John's father had come to a grudging acceptance and was taking an active interest in what was going on. He stood watching by the front gate as the contractors filled the holes with a base of crushed stone and compacted it with a heavy roller. They were making rapid progress, and John had no doubt they would finish by the end of the day.

Carole had also joined in by supplying the workers with pots of tea and a batch of freshly baked scones.

After a break for lunch, the contractor began adding a layer of bitumen, and John was standing next to his father watching the hot black material transform the surface of the road when a movement in the opposite field caught his eye.

A battered green Land Rover, similar to the one John had ridden in the previous morning, rolled to a stop on the rise opposite the house and a figure climbed out. John couldn't make out who it was, but could see him raise a pair of binoculars to his eyes and, after scanning the road and the workers, speak into a handheld radio.

John frowned. He had hoped the work wouldn't be

discovered until it was finished. He glanced at his father to see if he had noticed, but David was too busy watching the machinery. John looked around for Will, who was standing on the edge of the road with his back to the field, and after another quick glance at his father to make sure his attention was elsewhere, John raised his hand.

Will looked over, and John jerked his head toward the Land Rover. Will stared back, puzzled, then turned slowly to look behind him. Spotting the Land Rover, he observed it for a moment, then jogged across the road to John, who had moved to the far end of the garden, away from his father.

"We've got company."

"Yeah. I was hoping they wouldn't notice until you were done." John had already explained the problems his parents were having with the neighbor and Will had been sympathetic.

"What do you think they'll do?"

John grimaced. "Hopefully nothing, but somehow I doubt it."

As he spoke, the guard climbed into the Land Rover and drove away over the rise.

Will put two fingers to his mouth and whistled loud enough to be heard over the machinery. His men turned to look at him and he beckoned one of them over.

"Paul, go down to the entrance of the lane and tell Trevor to park the truck across it. Don't let anyone in. And stay with him."

Paul looked from Will to John, then back again, and grinned. "Sure thing, boss."

John watched him turn and jog away from the house before turning back to Will with questioning eyebrows.

Before he could ask, Will winked. "Don't worry, Paul and Trevor are as hard as nails. No-one will get past them."

"Good. Thank you."

Will looked as if he was going to say more when his eyes flicked over John's shoulder and John felt someone behind him. He turned to see his father.

"Is everything okay?"

"Of course, Mr Hayes. We should be finished in a couple of hours, and then we will be out of your hair."

John's father nodded, glanced at John, then turned away without saying a word, and walked back toward the house.

John watched him go, and then turning back to Will, said, "Don't worry about him. He doesn't like change. He won't admit it, but he's happy the road is being fixed."

Will nodded thoughtfully. "My old man is the same. I think it's an age thing."

"Yeah," John sighed. "Let's hope it doesn't happen to us."

Will laughed and slapped John on the shoulder. "My missus will shoot me if that happens."

John attempted a smile, but his thoughts were already elsewhere.

As if reading his mind, Will gripped his shoulder with his shovel-like hand. "Don't worry about my boys. They'll handle anyone that comes along. You stay up here and relax. It's probably better you're not around anyway, so the boys can plead ignorance and say they're just following orders."

John thought about it and then nodded. "Yeah, you're right. But let me know if you need anything." He jerked his head toward the cottage. "I've got some stuff to do around the house. It'll keep my mind off things while you finish up."

"I'll let you know when we're done." With a nod, Will turned and went back to his work.

33

Xie ended the video call with a tap on his keyboard and sank back in his chair. Frowning deeply, he watched Mingmei, standing at the rear of the room, her back to him, a cellphone pressed to her ear.

Something was going on, and it was irritating him. She had been distracted during the call with his team in Burundi, taking many calls on her phone, and he needed her to be focused.

She ended her call and turned around to see him watching her. For the briefest moment, a look of surprise passed across her face before it returned to her normal emotionless expression.

He waited silently, not taking his eyes off her.

Getting the hint, she cleared her throat before answering. "The Hayes'. They've got someone to repair the road."

Beneath the desk, his hands clenched into fists. "Shut it down."

"I'm doing that."

"Now," he growled.

She nodded and left the room.

Xie closed his eyes and exhaled, opening his fists and wiggling his fingers to remove the tension. He then leaned forward, resting his elbows on the desk, and steepled his hands under his chin while he frowned at the numbers flickering across his computer screen.

Who would have thought the old man would have the balls or the money to fix the road himself? It didn't make sense. He could have done it a long time ago. Why the sudden change of heart?

It had to be his son. What was his name? John?

Xie had paid him little attention yesterday, dismissing him as a minor irritation, nothing Mingmei and his men couldn't handle.

But had he got it all wrong?

Xie drummed his fingers together. Maybe he should find out more?

He reached over to his desk phone, and without picking up the receiver, pressed a number on speed dial.

It wouldn't take long to find out everything he could about this guy, and once he did, he would quickly put an end to any hope he had of helping his parents.

34

John found a set of binoculars in his dad's shed, and he took them off the hook on the wall, looping the strap over his head. They were small and underpowered, but suitable enough for what John wanted.

Walking out of the shed, he closed the door behind him, glanced toward the house to make sure he wasn't observed, then walked around the back of the shed and jumped over the dry-stone wall into the field behind.

Keeping the binoculars steady with one hand, he jogged up the slope, slowing just before the top, where he could see down toward the entrance to the lane.

The Land Rover and a black Range Rover with heavily tinted windows were pulled up at the entrance to the lane, Will's dump truck preventing them from going any further.

John raised the binoculars, at the same time moving to his left so he could get a better view around the dump truck.

Two of Xie's security guards were, judging by their hand gestures, arguing with a man John assumed to be Trevor.

He stood at least a head taller than both the men and twice as wide, and with his legs spread and arms folded, it was obvious he wasn't moving. Paul stood behind him, leaning back against the truck, casually smoking a cigarette.

John was well out of earshot, so he watched carefully, observing their body language. One of the men—it looked like Broken Nose—stepped forward until he was just inches from Trevor. He craned his head back to look up at the big man's face, failing miserably in his attempt at intimidation. Paul flicked his cigarette butt onto the ground, ground it out with his boot, then moved next to Trevor. He too folded his arms and stared down both the security guards.

The second guard reached out and pulled Broken Nose away. He leaned forward and spoke in his ear before retreating to the Range Rover.

John followed him with the binoculars and watched the rear window slide down as the guard approached. He adjusted the focus of the binoculars, trying to get a glimpse inside. Was it Xie?

The guard leaned over, blocking John's view, and had a brief conversation with the occupant, before stepping back and the window glass slid closed again.

The guard called out to Broken Nose, then walked away toward the Land Rover. Broken Nose looked angrily over his shoulder, then back at Trevor. He said something, spat on the ground, then walked away.

The Land Rover turned and headed back to the Estate, but the Range Rover didn't move.

John kept his binoculars trained on it, wondering what would happen next.

After several moments it rolled forward, but instead of taking a u-turn it continued until it was parallel to John's position, then stopped.

John frowned, adjusting the focus on the binoculars as

the rear glass slid down. A figure inside leaned forward into view.

Xie's assistant. Mingmei.

She stared back at John for a moment, then leaned back out of sight as the Range Rover accelerated away, and the window slid closed.

John lowered the binoculars and looked back at the dump truck, where Paul was lighting another cigarette.

They had won this battle, but John had an uneasy feeling the war was not over.

35

In the late afternoon, Will pulled up in front of the cottage in his Pajero and tooted the horn.

John walked around from the back of the house and crossed the front lawn, ignoring his father, who stood on the front step.

"We're all done, John," Will called out, his eyes flicking past John. He smiled and spoke louder. "Your road is like new, Mr Hayes."

John turned and saw his father raise a hand, then walk back inside.

John stared after him, then turning back to Will, shrugged and shook his head at the same time.

Will chuckled and reached an arm out of his vehicle to shake John's hand. "I'll be off then."

John braced himself for the painful handshake and replied, "Let me know how much I owe you. I'll transfer it straight away."

Will winked. "It won't be much. I had some material left over from a council job, so I'll only charge for the labour."

"Oh, thank you. Are you sure?"

"Yeah, besides, I don't like how these guys are treating your parents."

"No." John glanced back toward the house, then stepped closer. "Hey, thanks for sorting them out earlier. I was watching from a distance. Your guys did a good job."

Will grinned. "I told you my boys can handle themselves. Those buggers weren't too happy."

"No... I saw. But I appreciate it, and..." John gestured at the road, "this too. It will make Mum and Dad's life so much easier."

Will's smile faded, and he gazed forward through the windshield, not saying anything for a while. When he turned back, his eyebrows were drawn together and his voice was low. "Look... hopefully it won't happen, but... if you ever need any help... anything... just call me. I don't like this kind of behaviour."

"Neither do I." John studied the man's face, then nodded. "Thank you. I appreciate the offer." He sighed and looked back toward the house. "As you say, hopefully I won't need to take you up on it." Even as he spoke the words, John noticed the lack of conviction behind them. A rich, powerful man like Xie, wouldn't give up so easily. He forced a smile and turned back to Will. "I'll keep in touch."

Will nodded, his grin returning, then did a three-point turn and drove away with another toot of the horn. John watched him go and leaned back against the wall. The pristine new road surface glistened in the late afternoon sun, smooth and black, completely unspoilt.

John took a deep breath of tar scented air and exhaled slowly. He hoped the road stayed that way.

36

"Dad?" John stood in the doorway and called out, "Come and see your new road." He turned and winked at his mum sitting in the living room.

"All done?" she asked.

"Like new."

"Thank you, John."

John's cheeks flushed, a warmth filling his body. It always felt good to do something for others, and when it was your parents, it was even better.

"Dad?" he called out again.

"I'm coming, I'm coming," his dad grumbled from the kitchen doorway, while drying his hands on a dishcloth. "What's the urgency?"

John shrugged. "No urgency. I just thought you would like to see it before the sun goes down."

David muttered something unintelligible, disappeared from sight for a moment, then reappeared without the dishcloth. John stepped back and waited for him to step outside, then looked back in. "Won't be long, Mum."

"I'm not going anywhere," she chuckled in reply.

The Neighbor

David was already halfway across the front garden and John jogged to catch up, then moved past to open the gate.

"Come, we'll walk down to the main road and pick my car up, too. At least now I can bring it in."

David Hayes grunted softly, his eyes on the newly laid road surface. He slowly turned his head, looking up and down the lane, then finally nodded his approval. "Thank you, son."

John smiled. The warmth continued to spread through his body.

They walked away from the cottage toward the road, both in silence. The sun was low in the sky, tingeing the edges of the clouds with orange, yellow, and sending long shadows across the landscape.

John inhaled deeply, the scent of freshly laid tarmac intermingling with the crisp country air. It was the smell of a job well done.

"How much did it cost you, son?" David broke the silence.

John looked over at his father. He walked with his hands clasped behind his back, and to John he seemed taller, his head held high, shoulders pulled back, as if he was ten years younger.

"I don't know."

David Hayes stopped in his tracks and he turned to look at his son. "You don't know?"

One side of John's mouth curled in a smile and he shook his head. "No."

"What do you mean, you don't know?" David's volume increased as he repeated the question.

John reached out and placed a reassuring hand on his father's arm. "It's okay. The contractor, Will, is giving me a good price. He's only charging for the labour. All the material is surplus from other jobs."

"Why would he do that?"

"Because he, too, doesn't like what Xie's people are doing to you."

His dad's eyebrows knit together in a deep frown, then slowly separated, the lines easing out. He nodded slowly, then began walking again.

John exhaled and fell in step beside him.

"You shouldn't have to pay for this, though. Your mum and I have some savings..."

"Dad, don't be silly. I'm happy to do it. I can afford it, don't worry."

David gave him a sideways look, then his gaze returned to the road in front of him. After a long silence, he said, "I didn't mean to sound ungrateful, John. I know your mum is thrilled, and that's the most important thing to me."

John grinned. "Does that mean you're not happy?"

Surprisingly, David didn't answer immediately, but then he stopped walking and turned to face John. "Son, I'm more than grateful for what you've done. Please don't get me wrong... It just sticks in my throat that you have to pay for something you shouldn't have to. That..." his mouth curled in a sneer as he nodded toward the Atwell Estate, "man has more than enough money to pay for this and it's his responsibility. It's just wrong."

John chewed his lip and studied his father's face. He was right, of course. "I know, Dad. But..." he shrugged, "how long should we fight with the guy? It wasn't helping you and Mum. At least now you can come in and out of your own home."

He took his father by the arm and started walking again. "He'll get what's coming to him, eventually."

He could sense his father giving him the side eye as they walked. "What do you mean?"

John shrugged. "Well, I've seen that eventually everyone receives the fruits of their actions."

"You've seen that?"

John nodded thoughtfully as they reached the end of the lane and stepped out onto the main road. "Yup. You do good or bad, the universe keeps a ledger. In the end, it has to make it balance."

He turned left and walked slowly toward where he had left the Porsche.

"Son... I know we haven't talked about it... but what actually happened in India?"

John pretended he didn't hear.

"I don't mean what happened to Charlotte. God rest her soul. It's just... you've changed."

This time, John responded. "Changed? How?"

"I don't know, son. I don't mean in a bad way... You're just not the same John that left home all those years ago."

"Well, I'm older, Dad."

"No. It's more than that. You seem stronger, more determined. Like nothing can affect you. You've... become a man."

John was about to chuckle when something caught his eye. He picked up his pace and hurried toward the Porsche. Stopping beside the car, he looked down at the tyres. Both front and rear tyres were flat and when he crouched down for a closer look, he could see large slashes in the tyre wall.

He heard his father step up beside him, but said nothing. All the goodwill he had felt earlier had gone. Instead, a fire was growing in the pit of his belly and he ground his teeth together, his hands balled into fists.

Saying nothing, he straightened up and walked around to the other side. Both those tyres had been slashed as well.

His father was saying something but he couldn't hear, the sound of rushing blood filling his ears. He took a deep breath and with an extreme force of will, fought to keep his rage under control. As he turned away from the car, his pride and joy, his eyes met his father's.

Genuine sorrow filled his father's face. "Do you think...?"

John couldn't answer and looked away. He stood, his hands on his hips, fingertips digging into his abdomen, and stared in the direction of the Estate.

"John?"

John took a deep breath and turned back to face his father. "It's okay, Dad. It can be fixed. About time I got new tyres, anyway."

37

"Is that to show the police?"

John had just taken several photos of the slashed tyres with his phone, then returned the phone to his pocket. He stared for a while at the car before answering. "No."

"No? But you must report it."

John pursed his lips, then turned away. "Come on, Dad. It's getting dark. I'll sort it out in the morning." He walked away, back toward the house, not waiting to see if his father was following.

He'd lied about the tyres. They had plenty of wear left in them.

"John, call the police." David had caught up and was a little out of breath, so John slowed his pace.

"What's the point? What can they do?"

"Well, they can..." his father trailed off.

"They can't prove who did it. We'd just be wasting our time... and theirs."

"But you know who did it, right?"

John nodded. "I have a pretty good idea."

He felt a hand on his arm, pulling him to a stop. He turned and looked at his father. The angle of the setting sun deepened the hollows of his cheeks and darkened the circles under his eyes, making him look older, thinner, but there was no mistaking the determined thrust of his jaw. "So, what are you going to do about it?"

John told him the truth. "I don't know, Dad."

The grip on his arm tightened. "But you're going to do something, aren't you?"

John didn't answer immediately. His anger told him he had to do something, but concern for his parents told him otherwise.

As if reading his thoughts, his father spoke again. "Don't you worry about your mum and I. We'll be okay." He paused and when he spoke again, he spoke with a force that surprised John. "But you can't let that bullying bastard get away with it."

John stared at his father for a long time, hundreds of thoughts swirling around in his brain. Eventually, he shook his head. "Just let it go, Dad. It's not worth it. They're just tyres."

Later that night, unable to sleep, John lay staring at the ceiling in his bedroom. But he couldn't see the ceiling. All he could see was the look of profound disappointment on his father's face.

38

John's father was avoiding him. At least as much as he could, given the small environment the three adults were living in. He kept out of John's way, and limited communication to mono-syllabic answers.

John would be lying if he said it wasn't affecting him, but he had to push it aside. He was flattered that his father assumed he could do something about Xie but it would not be as easy as he thought. Xie was an extremely wealthy man and hadn't got where he was without being ruthless and corrupt. He could crush John and his parents on a whim. In fact, John was a little surprised it hadn't happened already.

Common sense said to leave the matter alone. The access was fixed, the tyres could be replaced, and his parents were happy. John was out of pocket for a few expenses, but no big deal. It was a small price to pay for his parent's safety and comfort.

So John kept himself busy. It took him two days to source the correct tyres for his Porsche and have the vehicle picked up by a flatbed and taken away to get them fitted. The garden was looking neat and tidy; all the flowerbeds had been weeded and fertilised, and the edges of the lawn along the footpath trimmed. He'd made a start on the wooden window frames, stripping them down to bare wood and sanding them smooth. He'd get a coat of undercoat on them by the end of the week.

But on the third morning after the road repairs, things changed and John knew there would be no going back.

He was about to leave for a run when the phone in the pocket of his shorts vibrated with an incoming call. John glanced at his watch and frowned. Who was calling at six in the morning? He pushed himself to his feet, slipped the phone out of his pocket, and glanced at the screen as he walked away from the house. His frown deepened as he read the name on the screen. Adriana. Why was she calling so early?

"Is everything okay?"

"John, *graças a Deus!*"

"What's the matter? Are you okay?"

"Yes, I..." Adriana sounded a little breathless. "I don't know. I think..." John heard her swallow. "I think someone has been in the apartment."

John's grip tightened on his phone. "What do you mean?"

"It's... strange."

"Adriana, tell me what's happening," John growled impatiently.

"*Si*, sorry, ahh, I woke up this morning and there is one of those Chinese cats on the dining table."

John blinked in surprise, struggling to make sense of what she was saying. "Chinese cat?"

"Yes, you know the ones they put in the shops for good luck? The ones that wave their paw?"

John screwed his eyes shut and bit his lip, his grip on the phone so tight he was in danger of crushing it.

"John?"

He took a deep breath through his nostrils and exhaled through his mouth before answering. There had to be a logical explanation, although his gut already knew what it was. "Fernanda didn't put it there?" he asked, mentioning the name of the housekeeper who came in three times a week.

"She didn't come yesterday." Adriana paused. "John, it wasn't there last night when I had dinner."

Fuck! "Did you set the alarm before sleeping?"

"I... I... think so." Adriana hesitated and he could hear her footsteps across the tiled floor of the apartment. "I thought I did, but..."

"But what?"

"It's... off now. John, I always set it when you aren't home. Maybe... the battery has gone dead?"

John rubbed his face and pinched the bridge of his nose. "Adriana, I need you to listen to me very carefully." He spoke slowly and clearly, "Pack a bag and leave the apartment. Go and stay somewhere else until you hear back from me."

"John, what's going on? You're scaring me."

John took a deep breath. He had always been honest with Adriana, no matter what the consequences. Now was not the time to stop.

39

"Look, I thought things were sorted, now the road's been done. But..." he sighed. "I think I've made things worse."

"What do you mean?"

"I don't think Xie likes losing face."

"Losing face?"

John nodded to himself as his thoughts became clear. "Face. It's... it's a hard concept for us in the West to understand, but I came across it a lot when I was in Hong Kong[1]. Face is like honour, I suppose. In any dealings I had when I was there, I always had to ensure the other felt respected, even if I was getting the better end of the deal. Now, by going against Xie and doing the road myself, it's like... a slap in the face for him. He won't let it rest until he gets the upper hand."

"So you're saying he's had someone come to our apartment?" Adriana replied, her voice filled with doubt.

"I think so. It's a warning. No, not a warning, a threat. He's saying he can reach my loved ones anywhere."

"But how?"

John exhaled loudly and shook his head. "I don't know. But you don't get to his level of wealth doing what he does, without having dodgy connections."

"Do you really think he can do this?"

"Adriana, if it wasn't a Chinese cat, I wouldn't make the connection, but this is pretty obvious. Nothing's been stolen, right?"

"Not that I know of."

A thought struck John. "Hey, stay on the line, but don't say anything. Grab your keys and go out into the corridor. In fact, better still, go into the stairwell. Don't speak until you're there."

John concentrated on the sounds coming from her end of the phone. Footsteps, the jangling of keys, the sound of a door closing. He could hear her breathing, shallow and fast. His stomach roiled. He wished he was there to protect her. He heard another door and then her voice.

"I'm in the stairwell. You... you think they bugged the apartment?"

"We can't rule it out. Another reason for you to leave. Can you do that?"

"I can."

"Good."

"But what about the police? I should call them, right?"

John thought for a second. "There's little point. What can you tell them? That someone broke into your apartment and left a souvenir? They won't take you seriously."

"Yeah, you're right."

"Best thing to do is get out of there. Stay somewhere that can't be linked to you. Pay cash and try not to be followed."

"Followed? *Merda!*"

John grimaced. Adriana rarely swore. She was scared.

"Hey," John forced himself to smile so the tone of his

voice would change. "It's going to be okay. You can do it, I know you can. Remember what we did in Thailand?[2] In Syria?[3] That was you and me. This is nothing compared to that."

Adriana was silent for a long time and John removed the phone from his ear and checked the screen to make sure the call hadn't dropped. When she spoke again, he could hear a new determination in her voice.

"We need to stop this guy, John."

Despite his concern, John couldn't resist a smile. A real one this time. This was the woman he loved. "I plan to."

"Let me know what I can do, John."

"I will. But get yourself to a safe place first. That's the most important thing."

"Your parents? Will they be safe?"

The thought was lurking in the back of his mind. Would Xie harm them? Or was he just about intimidation? It was something he had to address, and sooner rather than later.

"I'll think of something."

"Do you think he'll actually do something to them?"

Even while he was thinking about how to reply, he registered she was no longer concerned about herself. The thought went some way to calming him down. "I don't think so... I think he's just trying to frighten us." John hoped what he'd said was true.

"Hmmm."

"Another thing. Get a burner phone. From now on, only call me from that."

"Maybe you should get one too."

John hadn't considered that. His phone had always been in his possession, but Adriana was right. "I will."

John's brain churned with a million permutations. "Hey

remember the Indian guy[4] who helped us before with IT? Don't say his name."

"Yes."

"Call him from the burner. Give him your number. I'll call him and get it from him."

John heard a long exhalation from Adriana's end of the call. "Are we being... paranoid?"

"Always better to be cautious, Adriana."

"Ok." Adriana went silent.

"I'll work this out, don't worry."

"Be careful, John. I love you."

"I will and I do too." John smiled. "Now sort things out there and call our Indian friend when you are safe."

40

John ended the call and stared blindly across the fields. He was angry, but also slightly nauseated. Someone had been in his house while Adriana was sleeping. Xie, and he had little doubt it was Xie who had sent the message, had gone too far.

Adriana could get herself out of harm's way, he was confident of that. She had proven herself before in times of crisis, but if these were the lengths Xie was prepared to go to, what would he do to John's parents? John wasn't worried about himself. Well, he was a little, but the thought of protecting his parents overruled everything else. The question was, what could he do about it?

He took a deep breath and looked at his watch and did a quick calculation. Dubai was three hours ahead of the UK. He needed to tell Ramesh to expect a call from Adriana, but he didn't want to do that from his own phone in case it too was compromised, and the shops didn't open for another two hours at least.

He looked down at his running shoes. He needed to fill

time, burn off the anger, and think, so he might as well go for a run. There was nothing else he could do at that moment and besides, he got his best ideas while running.

John checked the phone ringer was on—he didn't want to miss a call—slipped his phone back into his pocket and zipped it so it wouldn't fall out. Then he stepped through the front gate, clicking it shut behind him, and contemplated the stile in the hedgerow in front of him. After a moment he thought better of it, instead turning left down the lane toward the main road. There was no point in stirring things up even more by taking his usual route across Xie's property. The time for stirring things up would come later.

He forced himself to run slowly, allowing the blood to circulate around his body, warming up his muscles and joints. But by the end of the lane, his anger got the better of him, and he increased his pace, turning left away from the entrance to the Estate. He clenched his fists, pumping his arms and legs up and down, the image of a waving *Feng Shui* cat in his mind's eye. Before long, his muscles burned with lactic acid and his lungs gasped for air, but he kept going, pushing himself faster and faster. Eventually he stumbled, his muscles giving out, and he forced himself to slow down.

It took a while for him to regain his breath and settle into an easy pace, but the anger had dissipated and he allowed his mind to wander freely, ideas popping up and then being dismissed. Eventually, his mind emptied, and it was just the road, the sound of his feet hitting the road surface, and the steady inhalation and exhalation of his breath.

Despite everything that had happened, a feeling of calm gradually infused his body, and he began to feel confident.

Confident he would find a solution. He always did. A soft smile played on his lips and he ran on, further and further away from the cottage, the Estate, and the man whose greed wouldn't allow his parents to live in peace.

41

By the time John returned to the cottage, there was no trace of anger. Instead, he was energised, and he knew what he had to do next.

Saying nothing about Adriana to his parents, he showered and changed, skipped breakfast, and made an excuse about having to buy something in town. The Porsche was still not back, so he grabbed the keys to the Focus and drove into Winchester.

The shops were just opening by the time he parked, and he picked up two burner phones and a large coffee, and sat back in the car. He unboxed one of the phones, wrote the number on his hand with a pen he found in the cup holder, then scrolled through his own phone for the number he needed, entered it into the burner, and saved it in the phone book before dialling.

It rang twice before going to voice mail. John suppressed a curse, then left a message. "It's John. Call me back urgently on this number." He read out the number he'd written on his palm, then hung up. Setting the phone to charge using the car charger, he sat back in the seat and sipped on his coffee. Hopefully, Ramesh would call back immediately.

Just two minutes later, the phone buzzed with an incoming call.

The screen said *number withheld,* but it could only be one person.

"Ramesh."

There was silence on the other end for a couple of seconds, then a familiar voice. "John Hayes. Don't tell me you're in trouble again."

John grinned. "You could say that. Thanks for calling back so quickly."

"A UK dialling code. You get around. I thought you were in Australia."

"No. Not now." John took a deep breath. "Look, I need your help again."

"Anytime, John."

John nodded. The young Indian hacker had been a valuable resource for John several times in the past.

"First of all, Adriana will call you on a new number. I want you to give her this number."

"Done. What's going on?"

"I'll tell you."

John spent the next five minutes giving Ramesh a rundown of the events since he had come to England and when he finished, he heard a soft whistle from the other end of the phone.

"Life is never boring for you, is it, John?"

"No. Sometimes I wish it was, though."

"Huh. Okay. Count me in. Let me know what you need."

"Well..." What did John need? He wasn't sure. "I don't know right now, but I think I'll need your skills soon. In the meantime, can you dig into Xie and his company? See if there are any weaknesses we can use to our advantage?"

"It will be a pleasure."

John thought for a moment. "Do you think you can access the security cameras in our building in Lisbon?"

"If it's online, piece of cake."

"Okay. When Adriana calls, get whatever info you need to access the cameras. I want to find out who was in the apartment last night."

"Done."

"Thank you. Don't forget to keep an account."

"John, why are you talking about money? You should know me well enough by now that fixing these rascals is enough reward."

"Rascals?" John chuckled.

"Well, I don't like to use bad language. Anyway, whatever you need, John, I'm here."

"Thank you, Ramesh, I appreciate it."

John ended the call and smiled, thinking back over all the times Ramesh had come to his aid. They had been through a lot together in a relatively short time and their relationship had grown from mutual suspicion to a deep trust. Ramesh did a lot of shady stuff online, but with John, he'd always been a hundred percent trustworthy and enjoyed scoring victories against the evil that filled the world.

John picked up his other phone and scrolled through his contacts. He had another very important call to make.

He found the number, entered it into the burner, and dialled. Again, the call went unanswered and this time there was no voicemail. John frowned and ended the call. He thought for a moment, then typed a message and sent it to the same number. *This is John Hayes. Please call me back.*

He didn't have to wait long. The phone buzzed almost immediately and John answered. "Mr Yu, *lay ho,* hello. Thank you for calling me back."

"John Hayes. It's been a while. *Lay ho ma?*"

"*Ho, ho,*" John replied in Cantonese. "Good, good."

"I'm glad you haven't forgotten your Cantonese."

"The few words I know." John smiled at the still familiar voice of the Hong Kong billionaire and chairman of the multinational property developer, Pegasus Land.[1] It had been a while, but he would never forget the events that had led to their meeting. "You know I'll never forget Hong Kong. It will always be a part of me."

Ronald Yu chuckled with approval. "You know you will always be welcome here."

"That's kind of you, *ng goi sai lei.* Thank you very much." The pleasantries over, John hesitated, unsure of how to start the conversation. How do you ask one of Hong Kong's richest property tycoons for help?

Ronald helped him out. "I'm sure this is not a social call, John. What can I do for you?"

John got straight to the point. "What can you tell me about Xie Longwei?"

There was a lengthy silence, then Ronald replied, "Let me call you back." The line went dead.

John blinked with surprise. What happened there? Had he upset him? Said something wrong?

A moment later, his phone buzzed again. A Hong Kong number but one he didn't recognise.

"Hello?" he answered cautiously.

"Sorry, John. The other line wasn't secure. I hope yours is."

"It is."

"Good. Now tell me, why do you need to know about Xie Longwei?"

John told him.

42

"Hmmmm." Ronald Yu had remained silent while John explained the events of the past few days, and when he finished, this was his only response.

John waited for something more, listening carefully to the sounds on the other end of the line.

After a considerable time, Ronald spoke up, "John, you need to think very carefully about getting involved with this man. Knowing you, I'm sure you don't want to let things lie, but my advice is to walk away. Your parents should sell the house and move on."

John frowned deeply. This wasn't what he wanted to hear, but Ronald Yu hadn't finished.

"What is the expression in English? Biting off more than you can eat?"

"Chew. Biting off more than you can chew." John didn't like to be told what he could or couldn't do, even by a man he respected, and he could feel himself getting irritated. He took a breath and regained control. "Why do you say this?"

"Xie Longwei is a front for the Chinese Communist

Party's policy in the developing world. The Belt and Road. He has their full backing, both financially and... in other ways."

"In other ways?"

"*Guojia Anquan Bu*. The Ministry for National Security."

John's eyes roamed the street outside while he thought about what he'd just been told. "But here his security are all westerners."

"You won't see them."

"What do you mean?"

"Xie needs to appear to the West as a successful businessman with no connection to the CCP. Otherwise, he wouldn't get access to half the countries he does business in. The unsuspecting leaders of an African or South East Asian country think he's coming in to build the infrastructure they need. He'll create employment, boost the local economy, and even give them attractive funding terms to pay for it. But in reality, the labour gets flown in from China, the construction material is supplied by other Chinese owned companies, and the country won't have read the fine print on the loans. They end up heavily in debt, and beholden to China. That's how the CCP is slowly and steadily taking over the world."

"But that would take years."

Ronald chuckled. "It's a game of chess, not checkers. China always plays the long game, unlike the West. The West wants instant results. They assassinate a leader, bomb a country into submission... do whatever they want to gain control, but in the end, the country is destroyed, and the population turns against them. When a B52 rains bombs down on you, you know instantly what's happening. You have to give it to the Chinese. Their way is more subtle."

"The result is the same, though."

"Indeed. But by the time you realise, it's too late to do anything about it."

John took a deep breath. He'd suspected there was more to Xie all along, but hearing it from Ronald Yu made it more real. "So what do I do then?"

"I told you what you should do."

"Yes."

"But you aren't going to do that, are you?" Ronald chuckled again.

John rubbed his face in frustration. "No."

"Good. I wouldn't either if something like this was happening to my family."

John nodded silently, as if Ronald Yu could see him.

"John, I don't know how I can help you right now, but if there is anything you need, let me know." Ronald sighed. "I have to be careful. I'm in Hong Kong after all, but where possible, I will help."

"Thank you, Mr Yu. I appreciate it."

"You need to be very careful, John. The *Jiu Choi Maau*, the cat, was a warning. But the fact he can find your home and gain access shows you what you are up against."

"Yes." John felt a tightness in his chest.

"You'll find a way. Good luck."

The line went dead before John could respond. He tossed the burner phone onto the seat beside him. The positivity he felt after the run had vanished, replaced now by a nervous apprehension... maybe a trace of fear.

He was glad Ronald Yu had faith in him, because he was beginning to doubt himself.

43

John shook off the negativity. He had one more call to make. Dialling Philip Symond's number, he sipped his coffee while he waited for it to connect. A lady's voice answered, and John frowned, glancing at the phone screen to check he had dialled the correct number.

"I wanted to speak to Philip. Philip Symonds."

"I'm sorry, he's in a meeting right now. Can I take a message?"

"Yes. Please ask him to call John Hayes when he gets a chance."

"Oh, Mr Hayes."

John heard the lady's voice change, becoming warmer.

"This is Helen. How are you?"

Helen, Helen? John thought fast. Oh yes, Philips' secretary. "I'm well, Helen. How are you?"

"I'm very well, thank you. Will we be seeing you today?"

"No, not today."

"Oh." Helen sounded disappointed. "Umm, I'll ask Philip to call you as soon as he's free."

"I've changed my number." John read the number from

his palm and after a couple more pleasantries, ended the call.

He took another sip of coffee and grimaced. It had gone cold. Opening the door, he poured the remaining coffee onto the road, returned the empty cup to the cup holder, and started the engine. The coffee hadn't been that great, anyway. He'd make a better one at home.

Just over thirty minutes later, he pulled off the main road and entered the lane. The new road surface glistened in the morning sun and John allowed himself to feel a little better. If nothing else, at least his parents could drive in and out easily.

As he neared the cottage, he noticed a Land Rover sitting near the top of the field opposite the house. A figure leaned against the hood, a pair of binoculars held to his eyes. He was too far away for John to recognise, but it was obvious he was watching. John ground his teeth together, and his grip on the gear shift tightened. Why couldn't they leave his parents alone?

He pulled up just past the open gate, selected reverse, backed the Focus into the driveway, then switched the engine off and sat staring at the distant Land Rover.

What could he do? He couldn't stop the Estate staff from parking in their own field, and based on his experience a couple of days ago, would be accused of trespassing if he went over there. John took a deep breath. He had to ignore it. Climbing out of the car, he locked it, ignoring the watcher in the field, fixed a smile on his face, and walked into the house.

His mum sat in the front room, knitting something with a ball of pink wool.

"I hope that's not for me," he quipped.

"You don't like the colour?" she giggled. "No, don't worry. It's for Sylvia's new granddaughter."

"Sylvia?"

"A friend from the Bingo club. You don't know her."

John held up the shopping bag containing the burner phones. "I'll just put this in my room. Where's Dad?"

"In his shed."

John smiled, then left the room, jogging up the stairs to the bedroom. He placed the bag on his bed, removing the burner he had used and slipping it into his back pocket. Looking up, he glanced out the window that looked out over the rear garden and spotted another Land Rover sitting in the field behind the house. He stepped closer to the window. It was a 110 with the longer wheelbase, but again there was a figure outside, leaning against the front wing of the vehicle. John narrowed his eyes, trying to see if it was a guard he recognised, but the man was too far away. What the fuck were they doing?

At that moment, the burner in John's pocket vibrated, and he pulled it out, holding it to his ear without taking his eyes off the Land Rover.

"John? This is Philip."

"Oh, good morning. Thanks for calling back. I just wanted an update. Have you been able to make any progress with the Atwell Estate?"

"Well..." Philip hesitated, "it's..."

John switched his attention to the call. "What's the matter?"

There was silence and then, "They've removed me from the case."

"What?"

"Yes. I've just come out of a meeting with the Head of

Planning. I've been told to stop everything I'm doing and to hand over all the files to him."

John had held little hope for the legal route, so the news wasn't much of a surprise, but it did little for his mood.

"And he will do nothing about it, of course."

Philip didn't reply.

John exhaled loudly, his eyes moving back to the vehicle in the field. "I guess it's up to me then."

"John... um..." Philip cleared his throat. "I... um..."

"Don't worry about it." John ended the call.

44

John sat on the edge of the bed, closed his eyes, and took a couple of deep breaths. In through the nose and out through the mouth.

It didn't help.

Opening his eyes, he stared at the wall in front of him. *Eat the elephant, one bite at a time.* That's all he could do.

He stood up, took one more look at the vehicle in the back field, then went downstairs.

"Mum, I want to treat you and Dad to a holiday."

Carole looked up from her knitting and raised her eyebrows. "A holiday? Why?"

"Well." John leaned against the doorframe. His father would never agree straight away, but if he could convince his mum, she would talk him into it. "I was thinking, it's probably been a long time since you two went away together."

She nodded, smiling at her knitting. "Your father doesn't like to go anywhere."

John listened to the click-clack of the knitting needles. He had to find a reason to get them out of the house. Keep them somewhere safe for a while. "I'm planning to repaint the inside of the house."

The click-clack stopped and Carole gazed around the room, her eyes roaming the furniture, the pictures on the walls. Finally, she replied, "You don't need to do that."

"Mum, look at this door frame." John stepped out of the doorway and ran his hand up and down the frame. "It's chipped, discoloured." He nodded toward the wall. "The wallpaper is peeling off. It's high time the place had a freshen up."

"John, that's very kind of you, but there's no need. And besides, you will never convince your father."

John made a dismissive gesture with his hand. "Don't worry about him." He grinned. "You're the boss, aren't you?"

She giggled. "Definitely don't let your father hear you." She looked around the room again. "It would be nice, though. Maybe a brighter colour."

"Yes, let more light into the room. A fresh coat of paint will make everything look new again."

"Hmmm."

"Good. That's settled. I'll make some bookings for you both right away. Perhaps Cornwall or Devon. Somewhere by the coast."

"John, really, you're doing too much," she protested, but her eyes said otherwise.

"It's no problem. Anyway, the hard work is up to you."

"What's that?"

"Getting Dad out of his shed."

45

John maintained a wary eye on the watchers for the rest of the morning, but avoided mentioning them to his parents. He kept his mum busy discussing options for their holiday, and deciding on wall colours for the cottage, and his dad didn't emerge from the shed until just before lunchtime. If he had noticed the Land Rover in the field, he didn't mention it to John, and shortly afterwards, the Land Rovers drove away, no doubt going off for their own lunch.

John had prepared a simple lunch of salad, ham, and cheese, and waited until his father was halfway through the meal before bringing up the holiday.

As expected, David Hayes grumbled at first, but by the end of the meal and after a lot of arm twisting by his wife, grudgingly agreed.

John knew his father would enjoy himself once he was away, but avoided telling him about redecorating the house. That would have been a bridge too far, so he and his mum decided to keep it a secret.

But John waited until they had done the dishes, and

were sitting in the living room drinking tea, before telling them when they were leaving.

"So, once you've finished your tea, I recommend you start packing. Because you're leaving tomorrow morning."

"Tomorrow?" Even his mum was surprised.

"Yes, I've booked you into a lovely bed-and-breakfast down in Torquay for five days, starting from tomorrow."

"What will we do for five days?" David grumbled.

John shrugged and grinned. "Hell, I don't know, Dad, maybe enjoy yourself?"

"Oh ignore him, John. He'll be happy once he's there," Carole reassured him. "But is five days enough time?"

"Enough time?" David snorted, not understanding her meaning.

John did, though his answer meant something else. "I hope so, Mum. I hope so."

46

The Land Rovers didn't return, and by the end of the afternoon, John was wondering if he had overreacted. Perhaps it wasn't intimidation? What if it had just been a regular patrol?

But then Adriana called on the burner and he remembered the waving cat in their apartment.

"One second," John walked out into the garden so his parents couldn't hear. "Are you safe?"

"Yes. I think so. I'm in Cascais."

"Cascais?"

"Yes, Fernando in marketing has a house here, and he's lent it to me for a while."

"Good." John nodded thoughtfully. "What about work?"

"I told them I'm working on a story and need to be away for a few days."

"You weren't followed?"

"I don't think so. I was careful."

John felt a sense of relief and allowed himself to smile. "There are a lot worse places to hide out."

Adriana chuckled. "Yes. I have a view of the sea too, from one of the bedrooms."

"Even better." John glanced back at the house. "I'm sending my parents away for a few days, too."

"Do you really think something would happen to them?"

John grimaced. "I hope not. But better safe than sorry." He paused and took a breath. "Remember, I told you about Ronald Yu? In Hong Kong?"

"The real estate, how do you say… tycoon? The one who gave you the shares?"[1]

"Yes." John nodded, and turned to face the house, leaning back against the wall. "I spoke to him today. He confirmed what I suspected. Xie is heavily connected to the Chinese Government and the Communist Party."

"Oh."

"And apparently, he has the support of the Chinese Security Service. That must be how they found our apartment and got inside."

There was a protracted silence, filled only with the sound of Adriana breathing. Adriana didn't scare easily and John imagined he could see her now, perhaps in the upstairs bedroom looking out at the sea, while she thought about what he had said.

"Ramesh hacked into the security company and got access to the cameras for the building," she replied eventually.

"And?" John suspected he already knew the answer.

"There's no footage between three and four am this morning. Either the cameras were off or the footage was erased. I'm surprised the guard saw nothing."

"Luis?" John scoffed. "He was probably asleep. He's always asleep when I go for a run. Never even notices me leaving the building."

"Hmmm."

"And if Ramesh can access the cameras, who's to say they couldn't do the same and erase the footage remotely?"

"John..." Adriana hesitated. "Maybe it's better for your...?"

"Parents to sell the cottage and move elsewhere?" John finished the sentence for her. "You're the second person to tell me that today."

"Isn't it good advice?"

John could feel himself getting annoyed, and he made a conscious effort not to react.

Adriana continued, "After all, it's not just you. You know I would never tell you to back down if it was just you, but it's your parents. Why put them at risk? If the price is right, let them sell, and move somewhere else where they won't get hassled."

John's head told him she was right, but still... "My parents love this house, Adriana. It's their home. They brought me up here. There are so many memories. Why should they be uprooted at their age?"

"I understand that, but—"

John interrupted, "I may have agreed with you a couple of days ago, but coming into our apartment and threatening you has made it more personal." A hint of anger slipped into his voice. "I will not let him get away with it."

"John, that doesn't matter. We can change the locks, upgrade the alarm. You don't have to worry about me, and if your parents sell, he won't pay them or us any more attention."

John was shaking his head. "No. I disagree. People like this always think they can get away with it. He's a bully and I can't stand bullies."

"John, you can't fix the world. There are millions more

like him. Will you spend your whole life being some... crusading vigilante?"

John couldn't help himself. He felt his jaw tighten, but still he fought to keep control and not snap at her. It wasn't her fault. She was worried, and her advice was sensible. Years ago, he might have listened, but Charlotte's death had changed him. Her killers had been rich and powerful too, used to getting away with things. But he had dealt with them. Him. John Hayes. Not anyone else. He would not stand for that sort of behaviour. Not anymore.

He took a deep breath, held it for a moment, then exhaled slowly. "I'll think about it. I'm glad you're safe, anyway." He rubbed his temples, then pushed himself off the wall. "My parents need help packing. I'll call you tomorrow."

"John, baby, please be careful."

"Always."

"And please think about what I said."

John nodded, "I will."

"Promise me?"

John hesitated, screwed up his face, then replied, "Yes."

"Good."

Just from the sound of that one word, John could tell she wasn't convinced, but he would keep his promise. He would think about it.

For a second or two.

47

There was a toot of the horn from the little Ford Focus as it pulled out of the driveway into the lane, and John smiled and waved at the same time.

His parents were leaving an hour later than planned, last-minute packing, a slow breakfast, and some anxiety on his father's part, delaying their departure.

But they were happy, Carole beaming from the passenger seat, and even David giving John a smile and a squeeze of his upper arm before getting into the car.

John waited until they were down near the end of the lane before turning away and pulling the gate closed behind him. He stood looking at his beloved Porsche, which had returned the previous evening, and wondered what he should do next.

He had five days to sort Xie out, but did not know where to start.

Another coffee might help.

He walked across the front lawn, into the house, and entered the kitchen.

Grabbing the French press from the sideboard where it was draining after breakfast, he turned it the right way up and, with a spoon, measured out the coffee powder. He then picked up the kettle, flipped open the top, and crossed to the sink to fill it from the tap. Twisting the tap... nothing happened. John frowned. He turned it the other way, then back again. A slight trickle of water dribbled out, then stopped. Strange.

He put the kettle down and walked into the laundry area and turned on the tap there. Again, just a trickle of water before it stopped completely.

John stared at the tap. He could feel himself getting angry. Taking a deep breath, he opened the back door and stepped out into the rear garden. He tried the garden tap. No luck. He took another deep breath and clenched and unclenched his fists. It was probably nothing.

There was one more thing to try.

Walking around to the front of the house, he crossed the lawn toward the front boundary, then knelt down on the ground beside the hatch covering the mains stop tap. Dusting off the dirt, he lifted the hatch and peered inside. Beetles and woodlice scurried away from the sudden influx of light, and John waited until they had cleared before reaching in and twisting the tap. It was fully open. He twisted it the other way and back again, turning his head and leaning close so he could hear the flow of water.

Except there wasn't any.

"Fuck!"

It had to be him. It was too much of a coincidence. Sitting back on his heels, John balled his hands into fists on his lap. What the hell was wrong with the guy?

John leaned forward, banged the hatch shut, then

pushed himself to his feet, and brushed the dirt from the knees of his jeans and then his hands. Looking up, he saw a Land Rover crawl slowly across the opposite field.

It was all John could do to stop himself leaping over the wall and chasing after it.

48

John didn't feel like hanging around in a house without water, and besides, he needed to burn off his anger.

What if he hadn't been here? What would his parents have done? It was a good job he'd sent them away.

He took his phones, laptop, and the keys and climbed into the Porsche. He needed coffee and time to think.

At the end of the lane he turned right and drove slowly, waiting for the engine temperatures to rise, but as he neared the main entrance to the Estate, he slowed, then pulled up in front of the gates. He looked up at the cameras on each side of the large wrought-iron gates, then down at the gatekeeper's cottage. On the end of the wall, just under the eaves at the far corner of the cottage, was an alarm box with the initials of the security firm. He picked up his phone, zoomed in and took a photo of the alarm box, then tossed the phone on the seat beside him.

John slipped the car into first gear and was about to pull away when a guard came out of the cottage and stood smirking at him.

"Fuckwit," John cursed under his breath, blipped the throttle pedal, then dumped the clutch and pulled away, the tyres squealing in protest. By the time he was done, no-one would be smirking.

With one hand, he dialled Ramesh, placed the call on speaker, and waited for it to connect.

It rang twice before Ramesh answered. "I need more time."

"What do you mean?"

"I'm trying to get into his system, but this guy has got some major internet security. I mean, whoever is doing it for him is next level."

John heard rapid typing on a keyboard, and Ramesh muttering to himself.

"But can you do it?"

"Huh," Ramesh scoffed. "Of course I can... it's..." more typing and muttering, "... going to take some time."

"Ok. Keep me posted. Can you do something else for me? I'll send you a photo of an alarm box and the address of the property. It's Xie's place. See if you can hack the security system for me?"

"Easy." More frantic typing. "I came up blank with your apartment, by the way. All the footage was erased."

"Yeah, Adriana told me."

More typing, muttering, then "Shit, I've got to go."

The call went dead.

John glanced down at the phone in his lap and frowned. Had Ramesh just cursed?

Spotting a lay-by ahead, John slowed and pulled over. Picking up the phone, he shared the photo and the location with Ramesh and then added a message. *Be careful. This guy has the backing of the Chinese Govt.*

That was all John could do. Ramesh would have to look after himself.

John stared through the windshield and considered his options.

It didn't take long.

He was about to drive off when his phone buzzed with an incoming message and John glanced down at the screen.

Ramesh's reply. *India 1 China 0.* Followed by a winking emoji.

John's face softened.

Perhaps things would work out okay after all.

But he had one more call to make.

49

"John?"

"Can you speak?"

"One second."

John heard footsteps, then a door closing.

"Now I can."

"Can you get me plans for the Atwell Estate?"

Philip Symonds replied with a hesitant, drawn out yes.

"I mean building plans, water and power connections, etc. Anything you can get your hands on."

Philip was silent for several moments.

John filled in the gap in conversation. "If it's difficult, don't worry. I don't want to get you into trouble."

"No, I can do it. I was just planning how... in my head, now the files have been taken off me. But I can do it."

"Great. Thank you. How quickly?"

"Give me a couple of hours."

"Even better. Ummm..." John thought for a moment. "Probably better I don't come to your office again. Lunch? My treat."

"Done. Ahhh... Wykeham Arms at one?"

"See you there."

John stood across the street and gazed at the once familiar brick facade of the pub he had frequented with Charlotte when she was alive. There was a strange feeling in the pit of his stomach... nerves, sorrow... he wasn't sure. The last time he had been there was with her, and the memory played across his mind's eye. For just the second time in a long time, he saw her clearly, her teeth flashing as she smiled, the blue of her irises, the crinkle in the corners of her eyes. He closed his eyes and exhaled slowly, but it didn't help. There was a tremor in his fingers... as if he'd overdone the caffeine.

Perhaps he should have suggested somewhere else?

He glanced at his watch. He was early. Taking a breath, he looked up the street to his left and then to his right. He could walk around for another ten minutes. Maybe pop into the nearby cathedral? He chewed his lip for a moment longer, then made up his mind. No. He would go inside and deal with whatever demons he had to deal with. Charlotte was gone. Nothing would bring her back, and he had to get on with his life.

Crossing the street, he pushed open the door and paused while he waited for his eyes to adjust to the dim light inside. It instantly felt familiar. The low buzz of conversation, the smell of beer mingling with the aroma of food from the kitchen.

The pub was already busy. Several elderly men sat on stools at one end of the bar and half the tables were occupied. A pretty waitress bustled past with a plate of food in each hand and she smiled a greeting to John. John smiled back, although the feeling in his stomach had risen to his chest. Definitely nerves. He nodded at the barman, then looked around for somewhere to sit. His eyes fell on a table beside the window, next to the fireplace to the left of the bar.

Charlotte's table.

They had spent many a weekend lunch in that spot, holding hands across the table, joking, making plans for the future. His heartbeat began to increase, and he frowned. *Come on John, pull yourself together.*

Walking over, he dropped his keys and phones on the table, pulled out a chair, and sat down facing the entrance. Closing his eyes, he took another deep breath.

"I miss you, Charlotte."

"I'm sorry?"

The waitress was standing beside him, holding a menu.

John quickly regained his composure and gave her a broad smile. "Sorry, I was just thinking out loud."

"Isn't that the first sign of madness? Talking to yourself?"

John chuckled, "Ha. Then I'm well on the way already."

The waitress returned his smile, her eyes holding his, placed the menu on the table, then her fingertips on his arm, and winked. "Somehow I doubt that. I'll be back in a minute to take your order. You'll be having lunch, right?"

"Ummm," John realised the nerves had been hiding his hunger. "Yes, I will. Just waiting for a friend."

The smile on the waitress's face slipped a little, but she nodded and walked away from the table.

The door opened, and John saw Philip silhouetted against the outside sunlight. He held something long under his arm and hesitated in the doorway, peering around the dimly lit interior.

John raised his hand, and Philip closed the door behind him and walked over. He handed John a plastic tube, the type architects and designers carried plans in. "Here you go."

Philip shrugged off his tweed jacket and draped it over the back of his chair before sitting down.

John looked at the tube in his hands and raised an eyebrow.

"Everything you asked for you." Philip glanced around the pub, his eyes roaming the faces of the diners and the men sitting at the bar. "Floor plans, drainage, electricity, rights-of-way, maps of the land, you name it."

John stood the tube on the floor between his chair and the wall, leaning it against the wall so it wouldn't fall over. "Thank you. Any trouble?"

Philip exhaled loudly and shook his head as he leaned back in his chair. "None at all. It's all in the public domain anyway, if you know where to look. I just didn't want to draw attention to my interest."

John nodded slowly, his eyes on the man in front of him. He looked on edge, as if something was bothering him.

Philip chewed his lip and looked down at the empty table, then over toward the bar. "I need a drink." He looked back at John quizzically. "You're not having anything?"

John shook his head. He hadn't felt like a drink. It almost felt like a betrayal of Charlotte, but he couldn't explain that to Philip. Instead, he said, "I just got here myself."

Philip made to get up, but John raised a hand to stop him. "I'll get it. It's the least I can do." He nodded toward the menu. "Have a look at that while I get the drinks."

"Thanks. Pint of Guinness, please."

John stood and walked over to the bar. The barman was busy pulling a pint, and he acknowledged John with a nod. "Be with you in a minute, mate."

John nodded back and watched the young man as he

went about his work. His accent was antipodean, Australian or Kiwi, but John had to hear him speak more, to be certain which one. He leaned sideways against the bar and turned his attention to the group of men at the other end. They were all in late middle age, with the ruddy noses and thread-veined cheeks of heavy drinkers. Large bellies hanging over their belts reinforced his conclusion. They weren't talking either, just staring at their drinks on the bar.

John frowned. *That could have been me if I'd stayed here.*

He had been through a lot since he had left the town he'd grown up in. There were many things he wished had never happened, but he had to admit, despite all he'd been through, the world had opened up for him. A world full of danger, risk, loss and sorrow, but also one filled with wonder, beauty, kindness... and love.

Any regrets?

He pursed his lips and frowned.

Maybe some.

John nodded slowly, his eyes still on the men at the end of the bar.

Would he change anything?

The answer was clear, and he smiled as the barman walked over.

"A pint of Guinness, please." He scanned the bar, the beer taps, then the bottles of spirits displayed behind the bar. He would have a drink, after all. "A Botanist and tonic, lots of ice."

"Large or small? If you ask me, you can't taste a small, but it is lunchtime," the barman said with a wink.

John chuckled, his mood lightening for the first time since he'd entered the pub. "Large, and one for yourself."

"Sweet! Cheers."

John watched the young man grab a pint glass, tilt it, and open the Guinness tap. "Kiwi?"

"At last! Everyone here thinks I'm an Aussie."

"Perish the thought."

"Ha," the barman was highly amused. "Too right, mate." He turned the Guinness tap off when the glass was two-thirds full, allowing the liquid, cloudy with bubbles, to settle. "I can tell you're a man of discernment." He grinned and winked at the same time. "So would you like a highball or a copa?"

"What do you think?"

"I'd go with copa."

John nodded with a smile. He turned back to look at Philip, who held the menu in his hand but was staring out the window, his forehead creased with deep lines.

"Here you go. See if that puts some lead in your pencil."

John turned back and examined the drink on the bar-top. "Grapefruit garnish." John gave a nod of approval.

The barman winked. "Only the best, mate."

John picked the drink up, held it to his lips, and before taking a sip, he made a silent toast. *For you, Charlotte, wherever you are.*

The drink was as good as if John had made it himself. "Very good."

"Thanks. And here's your Guinness."

"Thanks. Can you run a tab? I'll pay for it with the food."

"No worries."

John picked up the drinks and then glanced at the three men at the end of the bar. "Get those guys a round too. They look like they need cheering up."

"Ha! A free drink will do that, for sure."

50

"Here you go." John set the Guinness in front of Philip, took another sip of his own drink, then sat down.

Philip stared at him, ignoring the drink. "What are you going to do?"

John reached for his glass and took another sip, giving himself time to formulate a reply. Putting the glass back down, he shrugged. "Honestly, I have no idea."

"Then why the plans?"

John pursed his lips and turned to look out the window. An elderly lady stood on the footpath opposite while her dog, a miniature poodle, squatted and did its business in the middle of the footpath. The poodle finished, turned around, sniffed at what it had deposited, then looked up at its owner for approval. She said something, then tugged at the leash and walked away, making no attempt to clean it up.

John turned back to Philip. "I guess... I'm hoping a solution will present itself. The more information I can gather... maybe something will come up."

Philip continued staring at him for several long

moments, the forefinger of his right hand tapping a silent rhythm on the table. Then he nodded and reached for his glass. He took a long pull, drawing off a quarter of the drink before setting it down. With the back of his hand, he wiped the creamy froth from his upper lip. "Okay." He picked up the menu. "I know what I'm having. What about you?"

John shrugged again. "I haven't looked to be honest."

"Have you gentlemen decided yet?" As if by magic, the waitress had appeared by John's side. She looked at Philip, then John, and her original smile returned.

"I'll have the ploughman's," Philip replied.

John looked up at the waitress and returned her smile. "What do you recommend?"

"You look like a roast beef kind of guy."

John handed her the menu. "Done."

She flashed another smile, ignored Philip completely, and walked away.

Philip watched her leave, then looked back at John, the trace of a smile on his lips. "She's pretty. I think she likes you."

John changed the subject. "I have a question for you, Philip."

"Okay."

"Why have you agreed to help me?"

"I haven't."

"The plans?"

Philip reached for his drink and took another long pull. His glass was already half empty. He set the glass down, licked his lips, and then looked at John. "My boss came in today in a new car. A BMW X3."

John shook his head. "That didn't take long."

Philip sighed loudly. "I've spent my entire career making

sure rules and regulations are followed. Ensuring the beauty and architecture of this county is preserved." He made a gesture with his hand to encompass the interior of the pub. "So that places like this are retained." He took another sip of his drink before continuing, his tone increasingly bitter. "I've put up with a shitty salary, not taken a holiday for years, and I still have a mortgage to pay off. Meanwhile, that... bugger," he spat the word, "turns up in a brand new car."

"You could have done the same. Taken the money the lawyer was offering."

Philip looked at John as if he'd just insulted the Royal Family. "Would you have taken it?"

John shook his head.

"Exactly. If we don't stand up against this sort of thing, the whole world will go to hell in a handbasket."

John nodded, still content to listen.

"It just... makes me so angry that dishonesty always seems to be rewarded."

John nodded, sighed, reached for his drink, and took a sip. He didn't disagree.

Philip lapsed into silence, staring morosely into his drink, then picked up the glass and drained it.

John glanced toward the bar, caught the eye of the bartender, and nodded at Philip's empty glass. The barman replied with a thumbs up and grabbed a fresh glass. At the same time, one of the men at the end of the bar raised his pint of bitter, and nodded a thanks to John.

John acknowledged him with a nod then turned his attention back to Philip. But before he could say anything, their food arrived.

"Here you go, gentlemen. One ploughman's and a roast beef." The waitress set the plates down, then placed her fingertips on John's shoulder again. "If you need anything, please don't hesitate to ask. My name is Charlie."

"Charlie?" Philip asked.

"Yes, short for Charlotte."

John's head whipped round, and he stared up at the young lady as the colour drained from his face. She didn't seem to notice, fixing him with a big smile before walking away from the table, her hips swaying a little more than was necessary. John watched her go, then turned back and looked down at his plate.

"Is everything okay?"

John smiled weakly before looking up. "Yes, yes,... umm the food looks good."

"Always good here." Philip was still watching him warily.

John picked up his cutlery and changed the subject. "So, what are you going to do about your boss?"

The question worked, because Philip turned his attention to the plate in front of him. He sliced a piece of ham, speared it with his fork, and stuffed it into his mouth. He chewed for a while, swallowed, then nodded a thanks at the barman who had appeared with a fresh pint of Guinness.

John's drink was still relatively untouched.

Philip took a sip, wiped his mouth, then replied, "I don't know. But I'll do something. It's not right."

John nodded as he chewed his food, but his mind was elsewhere. He looked up, his eyes finding the waitress attending to a table at the far end of the pub. What were the chances of her being called Charlotte? Did it mean something? Or was it just a coincidence? John wasn't superstitious, neither did he believe in signs... but it was weird... and distracting.

He turned his attention back to his food and realised Philip was waiting for an answer. "I'm sorry?"

"What happened? You aren't listening and I saw your face when she said her name."

John took a breath, ran his tongue over his teeth, then reached for his glass. He took a large sip while deciding whether to fob him off with a lame excuse or to tell him more. Setting the glass down, he leaned back in his chair and crossed his arms.

"My wife was called Charlotte."

51

"Was?"

John nodded, and he turned to gaze at the street outside the window. "She's dead now," he said softly.

"Oh... I'm sorry."

John turned back to face Philip, but his eyes were distant. "She was raped and murdered while we were in India."

"Oh, my god. That's awful."

John nodded, his mind wandering back to the worst time of his life. A time when he thought life was no longer worth living.

"Did... they catch the people who did it?"

John pulled his attention back to the present, and he fixed Philip with a hard stare. "No..." he paused for emphasis. "But I did."

"What? You mean...? No..."

John nodded.

Philip's jaw flapped up and down, then his eyes faltered, and he turned to stare out the window.

John watched him closely and saw Philip's Adam's apple move up and down as he swallowed.

"I... I see," was all he could say in the end.

John turned his attention back to the meal, and the two men ate in silence. Eventually, John placed his cutlery down and wiped his lips with a napkin.

Philip was staring at his empty plate, a knife and fork still in his hands. Realising John had finished, he looked up. "Does that mean you will—"

John cut him off. "Philip, I still don't know what to do. All I can say is, I want my parents left alone, and I won't stop until they are."

He saw Philip gulp again.

Philip put his knife and fork down, then adjusted their position, so they were perfectly aligned in the centre of the plate. "I... ah... don't want to go to prison."

"Neither do I. Who said I'm going to do anything illegal?" John smiled, trying to put Philip's mind at ease. "Look, you've nothing to worry about. I asked you for some plans, you got them for me. That's the extent of your involvement."

Philip didn't look convinced.

"Philip, I told you before, I have no idea what I'll do. But this hassling of my parents has to stop. To be honest, I don't care if he's made alterations to his house without planning permission. Hell, I don't even care about him closing public access across his land. I mean, it's unfortunate, but to be honest, I don't even live here. Where I draw the line is when his actions affect my parents. And right now, that's what's happening. Do you know he's cut the water off to the house this morning?"

"Shit."

"Yes, shit. Now I can deal with this sort of thing, but my

parents? At their age?" John shook his head. "It's not right, and it's got to stop."

John picked up his glass, swirled the ice around in it and then drained it in one go.

"I understand."

"You do?"

"Yes. I..." Philip's chest rose as he took a deep breath. "I won't stand in your way, and... where possible, I will help you. But I won't do anything illegal."

John smiled at him. "Don't worry, Philip. You've done more than enough. It's down to me now."

Philip nodded slowly, then looked toward the bar. "Do you want another drink?"

John looked at his watch and shook his head. "No, thank you. I've got things to do, and I'm driving." John pushed his chair back and picked up the tube of plans. "But I'll order you another one and settle the bill." Switching the tube to his left hand, he held out his right. "Thank you, Philip. Look after yourself."

"You too, John. You too."

52

John strolled back through the Cathedral grounds to where he had parked his car. It was one of those pleasant spring days, with just a few clouds in the sky and warm enough for the college students to strip off and lie on the grass in groups, chatting and laughing without a care in the world. John paid them little attention, as he tapped a steady rhythm against his leg with the plastic tube, his mind whirring away. By the time he got back to his car, he felt he could see a way forward, a vague plan taking shape in his mind. It would take a lot of work, some help from others, and a considerable amount of luck. But it least he was taking action.

He unlocked the Porsche, tossed the plastic tube into the passenger footwall and then drained the takeaway coffee he had bought on the way before depositing the empty cup in a nearby rubbish bin.

Climbing into the car, he started the engine, then pulled out onto the road. He followed the one-way system west, then turned right onto Jewry Street and drove north until he joined the Stockbridge Road, which took him northwest out of the city.

He had been driving for less than ten minutes when he passed a police car sitting at a junction to his left. Glancing in his rearview mirror, he noticed it pulling out and following a couple of car lengths behind. He paid it little attention, his mind otherwise occupied, until the flash of blue lights in his mirror caught his eye. The police car was now right behind him, and he slowed a little to let it pass, but within moments, it was clear the lights were meant for him. With a frown, John indicated left and pulled to the side of the road, then reached automatically for the registration papers in the glove compartment. He was pretty sure he hadn't broken the speed limit, so guessed they had noticed the car's Portuguese plates and pulled him over for a document check.

He switched off the engine, the registration and insurance in his lap, and kept his eyes on the rear-view mirror to see what the cops would do next.

The passenger door opened and a young man, a high-vis jacket over his uniform, climbed out, and pulled on his uniform cap. He bent down, said something to the driver, then closed the door and walked towards the Porsche. John watched him approach, observing his body language, trying to get a read on the situation. The cop walked with the arrogance of a uniform, but looked like he was barely out of school. What was that saying about policemen getting younger?

John wound down the window and when the young man reached his door, turned and greeted him with a smile. "Good afternoon, officer."

"Can you please step out of the vehicle, sir?" It was a question, but the tone suggested otherwise.

John kept the smile on his face, opened his door, and climbed out. "Is there a problem, officer?"

Ignoring him, the cop leaned down and peered inside the car, then studied John's face. He stepped closer and sniffed. "Have you been drinking, sir?"

"Ah... not really." The smile left John's face, and he frowned. "I had a gin and tonic with lunch. That's all."

The cop nodded slowly, but stuck out his lower lip to show he didn't believe a word John was saying.

"We've been led to believe you've been drinking and were spotted driving erratically."

John's frown deepened. "What? That's rubbish. You yourself just followed me. Was I driving erratically?"

"Well... no..." The cop turned to look back at his vehicle as the driver's door opened and his colleague climbed out. He waited for him to come closer, then raised an eyebrow as if to ask him a question.

The driver, an older man with a handlebar moustache, ignored the eyebrow, and instead addressed John. "Is this your car, sir?"

"Yes, it is." John held out the registration papers. "You can check these."

Moustache took the papers and scanned them briefly before looking up. "License?"

John removed his license from his wallet and handed it over.

"Mr Hayes. You're English."

"Yes."

"But the car is registered in Lisbon?"

"That's right. I live there. You can see that from my driving license, too."

Moustache handed the license and registration back to

John, crossed his arms and stared at John for several moments. John stared back.

"You don't sound drunk."

"I'm not."

"He said he had a gin and tonic with lunch," the young cop interjected.

A look of mild irritation briefly crossed Moustache's face. Ignoring his colleague, he asked, "What brings you to Winchester, Mr Hayes?"

"My parents live near here, out by the Atwell Estate."

Moustache nodded thoughtfully, then broke eye contact with John and turned his attention to the Porsche. "She's beautiful. 69?"

"70."

Moustache nodded, his expression softening and he stepped away toward the rear of the car, squatted down and admired the three-quarter view before standing up again. "Those were the days. Real cars. Not like now. Boring crossovers that all look the same." He smiled at John for the first time, and John felt some of the tension leave his body.

"Enjoy your time here in Winchester, Mr Hayes. You're free to go."

"But aren't we going to breathalyse him?" Young cop protested.

Moustache frowned. "He's not drunk. It was probably a prank call." He smiled at John. "Someone jealous of the car." He finished with a shrug. "It happens."

"Do you know who called you?" John asked, glancing from one to the other, but addressing the older man who was obviously in charge.

Moustache shook his head. "We don't get to know. It goes through to the control room and we're told to act on it."

"Hmmm, not good for you guys, then. Wasting valuable police time."

Moustache smiled again. "It comes with the job, Mr Hayes. But at least I got to see this little beauty. Drive carefully."

"I will," John replied, but Moustache was already heading back to the patrol car, leaving the young cop standing alone on the footpath.

John smiled, gave him a wink, then climbed back into his car.

He waited until both men were back in their vehicle before turning on the engine and pulling out into the traffic. He kept one eye on the mirror until the police car took a left and disappeared, then thought about what had just happened.

Was it really just a random person? John didn't trust in coincidences and if it wasn't a coincidence, then who complained? The staff in the pub? John dismissed that quickly. The only person he'd met today who knew what he was driving was Philip, and there was no chance he would have called the police.

Then who? And how? Was someone following him?

He hadn't noticed anyone, but then he hadn't really been looking. He glanced over at his phone lying next to the burners on the passenger seat. Were they tracking his phone? If Xi had Chinese State Security on his side, they must have the ability. But would he get them involved in what was essentially a property dispute? Surely he wouldn't go to such lengths? But then they'd been in his apartment in Lisbon.

John slowed as a car pulled out from a junction in front of him, and as he did so, noticed a man mowing his lawn stare at the car as he drove past.

John shook his head. He needed to drive something a little less conspicuous.

53

John walked into the cottage, went straight to the kitchen, and turned on the tap. It coughed and spluttered, but no water came out. "Shit."

The water company said it could take a day to find out what the problem was and restore the supply, but he had hoped it wouldn't take that long. He leant with both hands on the edge of the kitchen bench-top and stared into the empty sink. The lack of water made his decision easier.

He climbed the stairs, packed an overnight bag, then plugged his regular phone into the socket behind the bedside table, turned it to silent and wedged it between the bedside table and the wall where it was out of sight.

"Have fun tracking that," he muttered under his breath, then took one last look around the room before grabbing his bag and heading back downstairs.

Hesitating at the bottom of the stairs, he glanced around the empty living room. The house felt different without his parents, almost... soulless. There was no warmth, none of the little background noises he had grown accustomed to in the short time he had been there. The radio, the sound of his mother's knitting needles clacking against each other, his father grumbling to himself in the kitchen. All he could hear now was the ticking of the old wooden clock on the wall above the fireplace.

Doubt crept in. What if he was wrong about everything? What if he was going to make things worse? He crossed over to the front window and looked out across the lawn toward the open gate. He could see his Porsche sitting on brand new tyres on the freshly tarred road.

No. He wasn't imagining it. Those things happened.

John scanned the field opposite the house to make sure he wasn't being observed, then stepped outside and locked the door behind him. He placed his overnight bag on the passenger seat of the Porsche, then turned a full 360 degrees, again looking for any sign he was being watched.

If someone was watching, they were well hidden.

Instead of turning right, past the Atwell Estate entrance and toward the city, John took a left, driving slowly with his eyes on the rear-view mirror, waiting to see if he'd been followed. The road behind him remained empty.

He rounded a curve and immediately the flashing of yellow warning lights on the top of a van parked on the edge of the road made him slow down. As he got closer, he recognised the name of the water company, and he pulled in behind the van and parked. Climbing out, he walked around to the front of the van and saw two men standing waist deep in a ditch, their overalls covered in mud while a third in a high-vis vest watched him approach with suspicion.

John smiled to put him at ease and introduced himself. "Hi, I live in Willow Cottage." He gestured back in the direction of the house. "I reported the problem with the water."

The man in the high-vis vest relaxed. "Well, we've found

the problem." He nodded at his two colleagues in the ditch. "But I'm sorry, it's going to take a while to fix."

John heard a curse from the ditch and stepped closer to see inside. The two men stood in muddy water that reached halfway up their rubber boots. Visible just above the water was a pipe... with a section missing in the middle.

John frowned and looked back at High-Vis. "How did that happen?"

High-Vis shook his head. "Honestly, I wish I could tell you."

"Not just a leak, then?"

"No. Some bugger has cut a piece out," he exhaled loudly. "Probably them bloody *pikeys* from the camp on the Down," he continued, using the pejorative term for the Gypsy community. "They'll steal anything that's not nailed down and sell it for scrap."

John knew it wasn't the Gypsies, but humoured him. "Why would they steal such a small section of pipe? It seems like a lot of work for a small piece of metal."

High-Vis shrugged. "Beats me."

"Hmmm. Strange." John looked back into the ditch. "Anyway, thanks for coming out. How long do you think it will take?"

"Couple of hours."

John nodded, then smiled at High-Vis. "I'll leave you to it then."

54

It was almost an hour before John entered Winchester from the opposite side of the city. He had spent the time driving slowly back and forth across the Hampshire countryside, occasionally stopping in a lay-by, but always with an eye on the rear-view mirror. By the time he entered the city, he was satisfied no-one was following.

Once in the city, he left the Porsche in a storage facility he had found online and then caught a taxi to a car rental company. He toured the lot before going inside, looking for something bland and unnoticeable. Parked in the corner against the fence, he found the perfect vehicle. A white Ford Transit van, the favoured transport of trades and delivery men countrywide. There were so many of them around that the vehicle was as good as invisible.

John paid for the week, then drove straight to a sporting goods store and picked up some waterproof clothing in dark colours, a sturdy pair of boots, and a head torch. Next stop was a 'big-box' hardware store on the edge of town where he bought bolt-cutters, a small tool kit, duct tape and a bunch of plastic cable-ties.

He stowed them all in the rear of the van, then drove to a motel just off the M3 motorway and checked himself in.

The first thing he did once he was in his room was call his parents.

"Hello?" His father's gruff voice was instantly recognisable.

"Dad, it's John."

"What number is this?"

"I got a local phone, so you don't have to phone my Portugal number. Use this from now on."

"Hmmm, ok."

John's explanation for the burner seemed to satisfy him.

"Now what's this your mother is saying about you decorating the house? I want nothing of the sort," he growled.

John winced. He hadn't even thought about decorating today. There were so many more important things to do. He could hear muffled arguing on the phone while he thought about how to respond, but before he could reply, his mum came on the line.

"Just ignore him, John, dear. You know he doesn't like change. You go ahead and do it. I'm excited to see it all refreshed by the time we get back."

John rubbed his face with his right hand. She sounded so excited about the renovation and he didn't have the heart to let her down. He shouldn't have promised, but it was the only thing he could think of to get them out of the house. But then, if he didn't sort Xie out, they probably wouldn't have a home to come back to. He puffed his cheeks and exhaled his frustration before tuning back into the conversation.

"... and the owner is so nice. She gave us a ground floor room so I don't have to use the stairs, and it has doors that open straight out onto the garden. You should see her garden, John, it's beautiful. Like mine used to be. Thank you so much for doing this. You are a good boy."

"Not a boy anymore, Mum."

"You'll always be a boy to me, John."

John smiled. "Well, this boy is happy you like the place. Now you and Dad, enjoy yourselves. Go for some nice romantic walks together."

His mother giggled. "Your father doesn't remember how to be romantic anymore."

John heard him say something in the background, but couldn't make it out. His mother's response was a 'shush' before she spoke to John again.

"There are some lamb chops in the freezer, John. Make sure you feed yourself properly."

John chuckled, "Don't worry about me, Mum. I'll call you sometime tomorrow."

"Okay, my love. Bye."

John ended the call and stared blankly at the wall. His mum sounded really happy, and despite his father's habitual grumbling, he was sure he was, too. Which made it even more important that he sort Xie out so they could come back home and live a stress-free, comfortable life.

"Huh, no pressure then," he said to the wall, then looked down at the phone in his hand and dialled Ramesh.

55

"Find anything?"

"Not yet, John... but I will."

"Okay. Was it difficult?"

"For the average hacker, yeah, but..."

"You're not the average hacker," John finished his sentence for him. "That's why I need you."

"The problem, John, is that most of his correspondence is in Chinese, and even when I run it through a translation program, the translation makes little sense."

"No. I had that problem when I was in Hong Kong. It translates each character literally, not as a native speaker would, then adds them together to make a word. It's so confusing."

"Exactly."

"Ok, don't worry about that. Just look at the English stuff. Financial transactions, anything like that. Anything you think worth looking into, send it through to Adriana. She'll dig deeper."

"Okay. But what are you looking for, exactly?"

"I don't know, Ramesh. But a guy like this has to have some skeletons in his closet. There has to be proof of dodgy deals somewhere."

"Understood. Oh, I've also got access to the security cameras on the property. I'll send you a link and you can watch the feeds on your laptop."

"You beauty. Now, I've seen this in the movies, but don't know if it can actually be done. Can you record the footage and then play it back to them in a loop, so they are not seeing what's actually happening? Do you understand what I mean?"

"Of course I do. And I can. How long do you need and when?"

John paced slowly from one side of the room and back again while he thought about it. "Maybe an hour? Yes... record an hour tonight and keep it ready. I'll let you know when I need it."

"Done. What are you planning? No, don't tell me. It's better I don't know."

"Yes," John agreed, although he didn't know either. "Okay, I'll get back to you soon."

John tossed the phone on the bed, picked up the plastic tube of plans, then walked over to the table set against the wall of the motel room. He unscrewed the top and shook the roll of papers out and spread them on the tabletop.

He nodded with satisfaction. Philip had done well. There were building plans, various maps of the Estate, and the last two plans made him chuckle. One showed the location of the water pipes, and the other showed the electrical supply.

He stepped back and sat on the edge of the bed, the plan that had been gestating in his subconscious finally coming into form.

"Well, Mr Xie, we know you can dish it out, but let's see how you take it."

56

After a dinner of takeout, and a fruitless attempt at sleep, John pulled on some dark clothing and drove the van out towards his parents' house.

He parked on the edge of the road, well short of the turning, and sat for a while with the engine turned off while his eyes adjusted to the darkness. When he was satisfied he could see enough without the head torch, he locked the van, then climbed a gate and set off across the fields towards Willow Cottage.

As he neared the cottage, he crouched in the field and waited, listening to the night. He could hear nothing at first, but slowly, as his ears tuned in, the night came alive. The chirping of insects, the rustle in the hedgerow as a rodent moved around, and away in the distance, the alarm call of a rabbit. It brought back memories from when John was a kid, sneaking out of the house and roaming the fields of the Estate, when he couldn't sleep.

But most importantly, the only sounds he could hear were the sounds that should be there. He turned his head slowly, eyes scanning the fields around the house, making sure there was nothing that didn't belong, then slowly got to his feet and crossed the final distance to the cottage. He let himself in the back door, easing the door closed, and again waited. The house was silent apart from the ticking of the clock.

Satisfied, he walked into the kitchen and turned on the tap. After a few coughs and splutters, a stream of muddy water poured out. The water company had done their job.

He let himself out of the house, locking the door behind him and crossed over to the shed. Once inside, he turned on his head torch and searched for the tools he needed. He picked up an axe and tested the blade. It was dull and rusted in places. Pulling open the drawers in the workbench, he found a whetstone and slipped it into his pocket. He then grabbed a wood saw, a hacksaw, a pickaxe, and a shovel, and stacked them on the floor beside the door. He scanned the shed, making sure there was nothing else he needed, and his eyes fell on a hessian sack in the corner. Walking over, he unrolled the top and looked inside. It was filled with potting mix, so he picked it up, walked over to the door, and after turning off his head torch, stepped outside and dumped the contents on the lawn. He then returned to the shed and stowed the tools in the sack before hoisting it over his shoulder and pulling the shed door closed behind him.

He had what he needed. Now it was time to put his plan into action.

57

Back in the van, John unrolled the plans and ran his eye over them once more. Once he had memorised where he needed to be, he started up the van and did a u-turn. He took the long way round the extreme boundary of the Estate, avoiding the entrance gate and its security cameras, and once he was near the chosen spot, he pulled into a lay-by and switched the engine off.

It was just after one in the morning. Reaching over for the flask he had prepared earlier, he unscrewed the cap and took a large swig of strong black coffee. It would take a couple of hours, and he wanted to make sure he was alert.

Again he unrolled the plans, this time taking his phone and zooming into the section of the Estate where he was parked, and took a couple of photos. Once done, he got out of the van, removed the sack of tools from the rear, then walked along the hedgerow until he found a gap he could climb through, and forced his way into the field.

John walked for about half a kilometre and then dropped the sack at his feet. He closed one eye so he wouldn't lose the night vision in both eyes, checked the photos he had taken on his phone, then looked around for the landmarks he had found on the plan. The field sloped upwards away from the road towards a copse of trees and a stream ran from the copse, bisecting the field before entering a culvert which ran under the hedgerow and beneath the road. By John's estimate, he needed to be another ten metres to the east of the stream. Putting the phone back in his pocket, he jumped the stream and then paced out what he estimated to be ten metres before setting the sack down again.

John stood waiting and listening, making sure there was no-one around, then removed the pickaxe from the sack, took a deep breath, and raised it above his head, swinging it down until it dug deep into the soil. Again and again he repeated the motion until he had loosened an area of soil about half a metre square. He then swapped the pick for the shovel and began moving the loosened soil to one side.

Despite the cool night air, he was soon soaked in sweat, so he stripped down to his t-shirt and continued digging. After several minutes, he had made a hole about half a metre deep, but there was still no sign of the water pipe he had seen on the plans. He stopped to rest and take a breath, wiping the sweat from his brow, then flexing his fingers. His hands had become soft with a lack of physical work, and the skin on the palms was already blistering.

The mains pipe to Willow Cottage had appeared to be around half a metre underground, so he was either digging in the wrong place or this pipe was buried even lower. John sighed. There was no easy way to find out. He had to keep digging.

With one eye closed, he checked the photo on the phone again, then double checked against the landmarks. Still sure he was in the right place, he took a deep breath, picked up the pick again, and began swinging.

It took forty-five minutes and three more holes before the shovel made a metallic clang. John bent down and, using his fingers, loosened the soil to make sure what he had heard was the buried water pipe and not just a stone. His fingertips brushed against the smooth curved surface of the pipe and he grinned. "Bingo."

Standing up, he stretched out his limbs and twisted from side to side to loosen up his spine. Turning his wrist, he checked the luminous dial of his G-shock. Just after two am. He still had plenty of time.

John refilled the holes he had dug earlier, smoothening the earth on top as best as he could, then went back to the hole containing the pipe, estimated the direction of the pipeline, then paced ten metres further into the field. After marking the soil with his boot, he went back for the pick and shovel. He began digging again at the new spot, this time exposing the buried pipe in half the time. He repeated the process again until there were three holes exposing the pipeline, each ten metres apart.

John rested for five minutes, then removed the hacksaw from the sack and, after clearing the soil from around the pipe in the first hole, began to saw. It took several minutes to cut through the pipe; the process made more difficult by water spurting out through the cut. By the time he had sawn through it, water filled the hole, and John was soaked, cold, and covered in mud.

John climbed out of the hole, and then, using the pick-axe, levered the two severed ends of the pipe away from each other until the water was flowing out unrestricted. John rinsed his hands off, then went to the next hole.

He repeated the process in the other two holes, the work

made much easier now most of the water was emptying into the first.

John rinsed off the tools and arranged them next to the sack, then picking up the shovel, filled in the holes, again smoothening the soil down as best as he could. When he finished, he stopped and listened, then satisfied he was still alone, turned on his head torch and ran his eyes over the ground. It wasn't perfect, and if one knew where to look, they would see the disturbed soil and the mud from the leaking pipes, but John figured it would take time for a casual observer to work it out. Even when the water company figured it out, it would be a while before they discovered the pipe was damaged in three places.

John stowed the tools back in the sack, then double checked he had left nothing behind. Swinging the sack over his shoulder and with the shovel in his spare hand, he made his way back toward the road.

"Let's see how you like that, Mr Xie."

58

John had more sabotage planned, but it was now almost three am and he was cold, wet, and exhausted from the digging. He called it a night and, after stowing the tools in the van's rear, drove back to the motel with the heater in the van cranked up to full.

He stripped off at the door to his room, leaving the wet muddy clothing in a pile on the floor, and stepped into a hot shower.

As he leaned against the wall, the hot water cascading over his head and down his back, he thought back over what he'd just done. It was unlikely the residents of the Estate would notice the lack of water until the morning, and then it would probably take them most of the day to find the leak. John hoped that damaging the pipe in three places would prevent the supply being restored too quickly, but didn't want to count on it. At the most, he guessed they would be two days without water.

Tomorrow night, he would move on to phase two. He'd been on the back foot since he arrived. Hopefully, that was about to change.

Warmed and relaxed by the hot shower, he felt a drowsiness taking hold. Turning off the water, he towelled himself dry and lay down on the bed, staring up at the ceiling. Again, he thought over what he'd done. Had he left anything behind? Would they know it was him? What would their response be? But before he could think of any answers, his eyelids closed, and he fell into a dreamless sleep.

An annoying buzzing sound dragged him from the depths of sleep and when he gained enough consciousness, he realised it was his phone. Rubbing his eyes, he sat up and reached for the phone on the table. He felt like he'd only been asleep for a few minutes, but the sunlight streaming through the gap in the curtains told him otherwise. He answered the phone without looking to see who it was, sleep still clouding his eyes.

"John, are you awake?"

"I am now," John rubbed his face. "What is it, Ramesh?"

"Have you been watching the security footage?"

John sat upright, now fully awake. "No. Why?"

"Something is happening. There's a lot of activity on the Estate."

"What do you mean?"

"Security guards running around, what looks like arguing... stuff like that. I think something has happened."

John chuckled and glanced at his watch. Seven thirty. He'd slept for only four hours. "I cut off their water supply last night."

"You cut off their water supply...?"

"Yup."

Ramesh laughed. "That explains it, I suppose. How did you do that?"

"I cut the pipe."

"Ha. Great."

"Listen, I plan to do more tonight. I'm going to cut off their power. Did you make a recording of the security footage?"

"Yes. One hour like you asked."

"Good. I don't think I'll need it yet, but can you stay awake for me tonight and monitor the cameras? Around two am?"

"No problem, John. I don't sleep much, anyway."

"Thank you. I'm assuming there's a battery backup for the cameras, so I'll need an extra set of eyes. Once they find out the pipe was cut, they'll be on extra alert."

"You can count on me."

"I appreciate it. I'll message you when I'm going in."

"Be careful, John."

"I'm always careful."

59

After the call, John couldn't relax, so he got dressed and went out for coffee and breakfast while he waited for the stores to open. He needed a fresh change of dark clothing to replace the ones he had worn the night before and muddied beyond repair.

John avoided his preferred coffee shop in case it was being watched and instead drove to a motorway truck-stop and parked in the furthest spot from the restaurant. He sat for a while watching the other vehicles coming and going and then, satisfied no-one was following him, climbed out, crossed the forecourt and entered the restaurant.

Restaurant was probably too kind a word, but it was warm and the smell of bacon filled the air. Truck drivers and tradesmen occupied the chipped formica tables, some in pairs but most alone. An open kitchen at the rear bustled with activity and steam, and a couple of tired looking waitresses in the latter part of middle-age attended to the customers.

John found an empty table in the corner where he could watch the door and sat down. The table was stained and in need of a good wipe. Pulling a paper napkin from the dispenser, he wiped the table's surface, then examined the menu in the plastic stand in the middle of the table.

Before he could choose something, a waitress appeared beside him. "What can I get ya, luv?"

John gave her a big smile and asked, "What do you recommend?"

She sighed as if she'd heard the question one time too many. "The bacon sandwiches are good."

"Done." John looked at her name tag. "And Sally, is the coffee any good?"

Sally snorted. "It does the job."

"Great. I'll have a black coffee too. Thank you."

She nodded and turned away, tiredness and boredom making her immune to John's attempt at charm.

John watched her walk away and thanked his stars he didn't have to struggle to make a living. He had been blessed and cursed in equal measure in his life, but at the moment, all things considered, the scales were tipped in his favour.

He leaned back in his chair and stared out the window, paying little attention to the activity outside; the trucks refuelling, the stream of traffic on the motorway beyond. Instead, he played out various scenarios in his head.

The best scenario was that it would take a couple of days for the leak to be found. But assuming the best scenario would not keep John safe. He had to assume that sometime today, the water company would find it and tell Xie the pipe had been vandalised.

John put himself in Xie's shoes. How would he respond? Would he know it was John? He might not think so at first, perhaps assuming John wouldn't have the guts to fight back. But when John hit the power tonight, it would be pretty obvious. In any case, if John was Xie, he would step up security. Which would make what John planned that night even more difficult.

After studying the plans and a satellite view of the Estate, John had found an area where the main power line ran through a small patch of forest. All he needed to do was cut down a tree and have it fall on the power line. In theory, it sounded easy, but he couldn't use a chainsaw in case someone heard the noise. Even an axe would be noisy. Which meant he was limited to using a handsaw and that would take time. The longer he was on the Estate, the more chance he had of being caught.

Sally, the waitress, reappeared with his bacon sandwich and coffee, and placed them on the table without a word. John attempted another smile, but she was already walking away and he reached for the chipped, stained mug and took a sip. He made a face and set it down again. The only thing going for it was it was hot. The bacon sandwich, though, was excellent. Juicy and dripping with melted butter and brown sauce. John took another bite and as he chewed, his eyes strayed to the activity around the petrol pumps outside. A van had just pulled in and something written on the side of it caught his attention.

It stirred up a memory in his subconscious. A public service announcement he used to hear on the MTR, Hong Kong's Mass Transit Rail system all those years ago. Something he had never paid attention to, but his subconscious had stored away.

John grinned as an idea formed in his mind.

60

Once the stores opened, John made a few purchases and then went back to the motel room to rest. In between naps, he filled time by watching the security camera feed via the link Ramesh had sent him.

He was amused to see a water tanker arrive through the front entrance late in the morning, but it wasn't until mid-afternoon that he saw a van from the water company arrive. It spent an hour parked outside Atwell Manor before driving off, presumably to check elsewhere on the Estate.

Judging by the time frame, John guessed they wouldn't have the water supply restored again until the next day, but once the sun had set, John jumped in the van and took a drive along the roads bordering the property. The security cameras only covered the main gate and the buildings, and John had no idea if the leak had been discovered.

Along the western boundary, John spotted slow moving lights in the field and as he passed, recognised the shape of one of the Land Rovers. He noted the time, but didn't slow, keeping his face angled away from the field, although he doubted anyone would recognise him. It was dark, and the van was anonymous enough that no-one would think twice about it.

John continued south, then turned southeast until he neared the field where he had cut the pipes. Flashing yellow warning lights lit up the night sky and John slowed to pass the two water company vans parked on the edge of the road. He looked to his left into the field where several flood lights on stands lit up four men standing around a hole in the ground. John grinned, and once past the vans, accelerated away.

They had only found one leak.

John continued on, then turned onto the main road that passed the front entrance to the Estate. His mood was lifted considerably by what he had just seen. Even if they repaired the leak they had found, he doubted they would continue working through the night, so it would be at least another day without water for Xie and his men.

When he cut the power later, they would have even more to worry about. John's grin widened as he drove along the boundary wall toward the front entrance.

Headlights lit up the road ahead and he braked hard, his heart leaping into his throat, as one of the Land Rovers pulled out in front of him. He angled his face away from the entrance as he drove past and followed the slow moving Land Rover up the road.

The road was wide enough to pass, but John wanted to see where the vehicle was going, so he followed behind until it braked and, without indicating, turned left into the lane that led to his parent's house. John continued on, using the gears to slow down so his brake lights wouldn't show in the darkness.

His mind raced as he coasted to a stop. *What were they*

doing? Were they going to the house? The lane continued past the cottage, meeting another narrow lane about half a kilometre further on which crossed the Estate. *Maybe they were just heading in that direction?*

John thought for several moments, his eyes on his mirrors. *Should he get out and see?* But if he was wrong, and if they came back this way, they would see the van parked on the edge of the road, possibly blowing his cover. John hesitated, indecision getting the better of him, before finally making up his mind. He took a deep breath, slipped the car back into gear, and drove on. There was nothing he could do right now except stick with his plan.

61

John spent a restless few hours back in the motel room, but eventually gave up trying to sleep, and spent his time watching the security feed and noting the times of the patrols.

He had counted two Land Rovers, but only one left the main house on the hour, sometimes heading down the main driveway toward the front entrance, other times heading out across the fields. Apart from the time, there was no pattern, their choice of patrol seemingly random.

The cameras only covered the buildings and the front gate, so he lost sight of the patrol after that. But they would return about forty-five minutes later, which gave John a window of fifteen minutes when no-one would be watching. There was no way a single Land Rover could effectively patrol three hundred acres, so he felt he could easily avoid them. But knowing he had a fifteen minute clear window was useful.

At two fifteen a.m., after a final look at the plans, John jumped into the van and drove out toward the Estate. He had planned his arrival for the fifteen minutes between patrols but kept alert just in case the patrol pattern had changed. Fortunately, the roads were empty, and the fields remained dark.

He passed the field where he had cut the pipes, the outer beam of his headlights picking up the reflective strips on the barriers lining the hole in the field. As he had thought, it looked like they hadn't finished the repairs.

About three hundred metres further along, he took a right and then slowed to a crawl until he spotted the power pole he had singled out earlier. It stood on the edge of the road, its wires leading across the fields into the Estate and toward Atwell Manor. John pulled to a stop just past the pole and, leaving the engine running, turned off the lights. He wound down the window and waited, but apart from the low idle of the van's engine, the night was silent.

Making sure the interior light was switched off, he opened the door and stepped out, leaving the door open, and walked around to the rear of the van. Opening the door, he reached in and felt for the strings of the bunch of helium-filled foil party balloons he had bought that morning. Pulling them out, he walked along the road toward the power pole, then stepped off the road onto the verge until he was underneath the power lines on the Estate side of the pole.

Looking up at the balloons, he made sure they were aligned with the power lines and said a silent thank you for the calm, windless night. Taking one last look around, he then released his hold on the strings and jumped back as the balloons rose into the air. Once his feet touched the road, he turned and sprinted toward the van, putting space between him and the power lines. At the rear of the van, he turned to see the balloons entangled in the wires.

"Come on, dammit," he cursed. He had watched a few

videos online, and something should have happened by now.

Frowning deeply, he reached for the van's door handle, ready to grab the extra bunch of balloons he had bought, when there was a blinding flash of white light and sparks rained down onto the ground beneath the power line. Too late John screwed his eyes shut and turned, blinking away the spots of light that filled his eyes. Keeping one hand on the van, he felt his way around toward the front and, once at the driver's door, his vision almost clear, glanced back at the power pole. He couldn't make out much, his night vision compromised, but the sparking had stopped. Climbing into the van, he slipped it into reverse and pulled back past the power pole before turning on the headlights. The balloons had melted, leaving just a few scraps and several strings hanging from the power line.

John grinned. All the warnings he had heard during the festive season in Hong Kong about the danger of foil balloons in the underground rail system weren't wasted after all.

62

Back in the motel, John rushed over to the table and opened up the laptop. The security feed was still running, so there was obviously some sort of power backup for the cameras, but the house and other buildings were dark. By the stables, several guards huddled in the headlight beam of the Land Rover, no doubt wondering how to turn the power back on.

John grinned. His plan wouldn't have worked in India, where regular power outages meant everyone had a generator. But here in England, where the power supply was constant, he had caught them unprepared.

John kicked off his shoes, picked up the laptop, and sat on the bed, his back against the headboard, the laptop open on his lap. He watched for a while, until his eyelids drooped and he drifted off to sleep.

John shifted position and groaned at the stiffness in his neck. He was still sitting up in bed and, judging by the light outside, had slept in that position for several hours. He moved again and felt the still open laptop slide off his legs onto the bed.

Something had woken him up. John rubbed the sleep from his eyes, then realised what it was. He reached for the phone on the bedside table, its screen flashing with an incoming call from his mum.

Frowning, he checked the time on his watch as he answered. Seven a.m.

"Good morning, Mum."

"John, thank God!" She sounded breathless, panicked. "Are you okay?"

"Yes, I'm fine, wh... what... why?"

"John, the house is on fire. We thought you were inside..."

John's heart skipped a beat as his brain struggled to understand. "Fire?"

"Yes, the fire brigade just called us... where are you, John?"

John froze for several seconds, then he jumped off the bed. "I'll call you back." He stabbed at the screen, ending the call, cutting off his mother's reply in mid-sentence, and grabbed the keys to the van from the table. He thrust his feet into his shoes, not bothering to lace them up, and ran for the door.

Fire! Fuck, fuck, fuck!

He jumped in the van and reversed out of the parking space without looking. Someone honked in protest, but he ignored them, mashing his foot on the throttle pedal and accelerating out of the car park as fast as the van could go. He did the thirty-minute drive in twenty minutes, ignoring the repeated calls coming in from his parents on the phone. Instead, he concentrated on the road, stretching the underpowered van's performance, the engine and tyres complaining repeatedly as he pushed the van to its limit.

The smoke was visible well before he reached the house,

and his chest filled with an aching dread. Had he left something on in the house? Had there been a short circuit?

He swung into the lane, tyres screeching, then slammed on his brakes and skidded to a stop. Fire engines and several police cars blocked the lane. John didn't bother switching off the engine, leaping out and running up the road, swerving between the vehicles and leaping over the fire hoses criss-crossing the lane. A policeman in a fluorescent yellow high-vis jacket blocked his way, and John tried to push past. The cop threw his arms around him, holding him back, and shouted something that John couldn't hear.

All he could see, as heat singed his face, were the flames eating away at Willow Cottage.

63

John stared blankly at the clouds of smoke and steam rising from the charred remains. The soot-blackened brick and stone walls were still standing, however, black stumps were all that were left of the roof and its rafters.

Someone was speaking, but he paid no attention.

How had this happened? What would his parents do? What would they say?

He heard his name and felt a hand on his shoulder. John looked at the hand, then at the person it belonged to. He looked familiar, but John's brain wasn't working.

The hand on John's shoulder squeezed and released, and that simple action helped John come back to the present.

He shook his head; the movement clearing his mind of fog. "Sorry, what did you say?"

"Will your parents be okay?" Sergeant Manners, the cop who had stopped him earlier, asked with what appeared to be genuine concern.

Would they be okay? John gulped. "They are away right now... in Devon."

"That's a relief. And you? Do you have somewhere to stay?"

John nodded.

"I'm sorry, Mr Hayes. I really am."

John didn't bother responding. There was nothing anyone could say that would help. He felt numb, hollow, his mind blank.

A fireman approached with what looked like a charred jerry can in his hand. John watched him call Manners over, and the two men huddled together in a discussion. At one point, both of them glanced in his direction then looked down at the jerry can, now lying at their feet.

John's brain was not really registering what was happening. He felt like he was watching a film with the sound turned off.

After a while, the fireman left and Manners came back over.

"Mr Hayes, did your parents have insurance?"

John shrugged. He was staring at the jerry can on the ground.

Manners asked something else, but John ignored the question, instead asking one of his own.

"Where did you find that?"

"The jerry can? In the house. Do you recognise it?"

John shook his head.

"Hmmm. What is it you said you do, Mr Hayes?"

"I didn't." John continued staring at the jerry can, his earlier despair turning to rage. He could feel it expanding, the heat spreading through his system.

"I'll need your phone number and an address where we can reach you."

"What?"

He heard Manners take a deep breath. "It looks like arson... an accelerant was used... so..." Manners cleared his throat, "we'll need you to stay around for a while..."

John clenched his fists as Manners continued.

"... until the investigation is finished."

The rage exploded and John rounded on the policeman, grabbing him by his jacket and thrusting him back against the side of the fire engine. His face just inches from the shocked policeman, he spat, "You think I did it? You think I burnt down my parent's home, destroyed all their belongings, all their memories?"

Manners protested, his eyes wide, darting from one of John's to the other, and he pushed back, struggling to get free. But the roar of rushing blood filled John's head. He couldn't see, he couldn't hear, he couldn't even register what he was saying as anger and frustration poured from his mouth in a stream of invective.

Powerful hands grabbed him by the arms, pulling him away, prising his fingers from the policeman's jacket. Once he let go, someone stronger and bigger than him wrapped their arms around him, holding him tight in a bear-like embrace. He struggled to free himself as the anger ebbed, slowly becoming aware of the firemen crowding around him. Sergeant Manners straightened his jacket, then picked his uniform cap up off the ground. His cheeks were flushed, hair dishevelled, and his chest rose and fell as he gasped for air.

John suddenly realised what he'd done, took a deep breath, and exhaled slowly.

"I'm okay, I'm okay," he repeated, and felt the grip on him loosen. He shrugged off the fireman's arms and shook the adrenaline from his limbs.

Manners flinched as John stepped forward, holding both hands up in a gesture of peace. "I'm sorry."

Manners nodded warily. "I wasn't accusing you, Mr Hayes."

John nodded and took another deep breath. His legs trembled as the adrenaline ebbed away, and he closed his fingers into fists to hide the shaking of his hands.

"But we need to investigate the cause of the fire, which is..." Manners nodded in the direction of the jerry can, "looking suspicious... and we need to speak to everyone who may have an interest."

John nodded and then his eyes flicked past Manners, and he felt the fire in his belly rekindle. He leaped forward and the powerful hands of the fireman caught hold of him at the last minute, pulling him back. Manners had retreated to safety, but John's attention was on the field behind him. Several hundred metres away at the top of the rise was a Land Rover. Standing beside it, a pair of binoculars held to his eyes, was one of the guards.

John roared and lunged forward against the hands holding him back.

"You fucking bastards, you motherfucking bastards, I'll fucking kill you all!"

64

There was a tap on the door, and Xie looked up as it cracked open.

He gestured for Mingmei to enter while continuing with his telephone conversation. "He'll sign. I guarantee it."

Xie listened to the voice on the other end, his eyes closed, his fingers tapping an irritated rhythm on the desk. As if the last two days hadn't been bad enough, now he had his weekly report to his superiors. He had always got them results, results that had increased their power and made him an extremely wealthy man. But they still insisted on micromanaging as if they didn't trust him.

He struggled to keep his cool. One wrong word, one thing said in the wrong tone, could mean the end of everything he had built. They demanded respect, undying loyalty, and obedience without question, and came down hard on anyone they suspected of straying from the fold.

He nodded and gulped at the subtle threat from the other end of the line, and once again reassured them. "It will be done. I've never let you down. You can always count on me."

He listened for several moments longer and then, when the call ended, exhaled loudly and banged the phone down on the receiver.

Mingmei had taken a seat in front of him and he fixed her with a hard stare while he replayed the call in his mind, checking he had been careful, and not said anything untoward. As satisfied as he could be, his eyes refocused on his assistant, and he raised a questioning eyebrow.

"The power is back on."

"I noticed that myself," he growled.

Mingmei didn't flinch, seemingly impervious to his mood.

"How did it happen?"

"Balloons."

Xie glared at her, waiting for her to elaborate.

"Some foil party balloons got tangled in the wires and shorted out the supply."

Xie's frown deepened. "Not an accident."

"No."

"That wasn't a question," he snapped.

Mingmei remained silent, her face a blank mask. Nothing ever seemed to bother her, but today, for some reason, it was irritating Xie.

"And the water?"

"Full supply will be restored today."

"Make sure nothing like this happens again."

The corner of her mouth twitched as if she was about to smile, but then thought better of it. "It won't. I've ordered a generator, we have a backup water supply and patrols have been increased."

"Do we know who did it yet?"

"Well..." Mingmei smoothed out a wrinkle in her skirt. "I think given what we have been doing to those people in Willow Cottage, it's too much of a coincidence that these same things have happened to us."

Xie narrowed his eyes. "Not the old man. He's weak... His son? The man who came onto the property the other day?"

"Yes, his son. The old couple are missing."

"Missing? What do you mean, missing? Since when?"

"Since yesterday, at least."

"Then find them. And sort the son out. Who is he? What do we know about him?"

Mingmei took a breath. "John Hayes. Lives in Portugal, Lisbon. Lives with a journalist for Publico, the newspaper. He doesn't work, but he seems to have plenty of money."

Xie leaned back in his chair and steepled his fingers under his chin. "He doesn't work? Then what does he do?"

Mingmei shrugged. "He worked for a bank in India, then his wife was killed."

"Killed?"

"Raped and murdered. The police never found out who did it."

Xie waited for her to continue.

"Then he moved to Hong Kong..."

Xie arched an eyebrow.

"... where he worked for a finance company before quitting and leaving the country. He's never worked since."

"He stole money from the company?"

Mingmei shook her head. "If he did, there's nothing in the press or any police report. He just left."

"Strange. What else do you know?"

"Nothing else. No criminal record, no employment record after Hong Kong, he's a nobody."

Xie sat forward and jabbed a finger at Mingmei. "He's

not a nobody. There's something you're not seeing. He doesn't work, but he has money. He has the balls to come onto my property, demanding a meeting. He cuts off our water and power. That's not the work of a nobody."

"I've taken steps to show him the extent of our reach."

"When?"

"Yesterday. I had a subtle threat placed in his home in Lisbon."

Xie slammed the heel of his fist down on the desk. "Well, it obviously didn't work!"

Mingmei opened her mouth to say something, but he cut her off.

"Find out who he really is and what he is doing here. Then get rid of him and his parents. I've had enough of that property. I've had enough of them. I've got the Nkuru project to sort out, and I don't want to waste my time on the neighbours."

He turned away, making a dismissive motion with his hand. He didn't like to lose his temper, but the water, the power, and his micromanaging superiors had gotten under his skin.

He stared at the charts on his computer screen, but couldn't focus. He heard the door open and without looking up, he called out. "Wait."

Swivelling around in his chair, he glared across the room at Mingmei standing in the doorway. "What's that smoke outside?"

She smiled. "A solution to your neighbour problem."

Xie was about to ask for clarification, but then thought better of it and waved her away. "Go."

He turned back to his computer and tried in vain to concentrate. Eventually, he pushed back his chair, leaned on the armrests and pushed himself to his feet, groaning at the pain in his left knee. He wished he'd never come to this wretched country. Cold and damp, and irritating neighbours. Walking over to the window, he ignored the thick column of smoke rising from the west of the Estate and instead gazed down on the broad expanse of grass that led away from the house toward the folly in the distance.

He remembered the man running down that patch of grass toward the house just a few days ago. Then watched him sit down on the ground as the guard dog raced toward him.

The ring of his desk phone pulled his attention away from the view and he turned away from the window. He had work to do. Let Mingmei deal with John Hayes.

He walked over to the phone and answered, trying to ignore the unease gnawing at his gut.

65

It took a while for John to calm down. The Land Rover had long gone, and when John had refused to explain his earlier outburst, Sergeant Manners had eventually given up on his questions.

John didn't have the heart to approach the house. Instead, he sat on the wall, miserable, wondering if there was anything he should have done differently. But try as he might, he could not make himself feel any better. It was because of him that his parents had lost everything.

John's phone buzzed again in his pocket and instead of ignoring it like he had countless times before, he took a deep breath and answered without looking at the screen. He knew who it was.

"What have you done?"

John winced and didn't reply. There was nothing he could say.

"Answer me, John. What have you done to the house?"

John rubbed his face with his spare hand and then slid off the wall onto the ground. "It's gone Dad..." his voice caught in his mouth. "Gone."

The Neighbor

"What do you mean, gone?"

A memory from John's childhood flashed before his eyes. Looking up at his father in fear, his lip trembling as the man berated him for something he'd done. John clenched his fingers and pounded his hip three times with the heel of his fist. He took a deep breath.

"The fire is out, but the house is destroyed, Dad. There's... there's nothing left."

"Wh... wh..." then his father fell silent.

John hesitated. The silence was almost worse. "I'm sorry, Dad. I..."

"Sorry? What did you do? Leave the stove on? Or was it your redecorating?"

John walked further away from the house, past the last remaining fire engine, putting space between him and the visible signs of his mistake.

"Speak up, boy! I want to know what happened."

"Nothing happened, Dad. I wasn't even here."

"You weren't there? What do you mean you weren't there? Then what were you doing? You're supposed to be looking after the house while we're away. Your mother has been in tears all morning. Everything we own was in that house, all our memories, our whole life. And you're saying it's gone?"

"Yes. I..."

His father interrupted, "What do I tell your mother? What are we supposed to do? Where do we live now?" David Hayes broke off in a fit of coughing.

"Dad, I'll sort it out. I'll get you a place to live while we rebuild..."

"Rebuild? At my age... have you taken leave of your senses? Haven't you done enough already? We never wanted the house to be renovated. We were happy until you came along and ruined everything. You should never have come back."

John gulped, and he looked down at the ground, his eyes welling with tears. Maybe his dad was right?

John closed his eyes and inhaled slowly and deeply.

No.

He wasn't a little boy anymore. He would fix it. His father would be proud of him.

He pulled back his shoulders, lifted his head, and opened his eyes. "It wasn't me, Dad. It was Xie."

But the phone had gone dead.

66

John stared at the phone. Would calling back make a difference?

No. He could argue his case all day long, but it wouldn't solve the problem.

Slipping the phone into his back pocket, he again stared down at the road surface. The pristine new tarmac, wet from the leaking fire hoses, sparkled in the sunlight.

John chewed his lower lip.

He had done that.

His Dad was wrong. He wasn't a failure. He didn't ruin things.

He had got the road repaired. A road that had been impossible for his parents to use. He had made things better.

John took another deep breath and looked back at the remains of the house. He squared his shoulders and lifted his chin. He would make things right again.

The sound of an approaching vehicle caught his attention, and he turned to see Will's white Pajero rolling up the lane toward him. Will climbed out and stared wide eyed at the smouldering ruins. John watched silently as Will shook his head, cursed under his breath, then walked over.

"I'm so sorry, John. I saw it on the morning news." He sighed and shook his head again.

John acknowledged him with a nod, but wasn't in the mood to say anything.

Will studied his face for several moments, then turned to face the house. A heavy silence hung between them until Will cursed again. Audibly this time. "Fuck." Then, as if he suddenly realised, "Your parents, they're not...?"

John exhaled loudly. "They're away. In Devon."

"Jesus. Thank Christ for that."

"Yup."

"Do these guys know what happened?" Will asked, gesturing at the nearest fireman. "Was it a short circuit?"

"It was the neighbour. Xie."

Will's head jerked back as if someone had slapped him. "What? What do you mean?"

"They found a jerry can in the wreckage. It's not mine."

"Jesus!" Will shook his head in disbelief. "But... what makes you think it was your neighbour? And... where were you when this happened?"

John hesitated. How much could he tell him? He thought back to how Will had dealt with Xie's men when repairing the road. He decided to trust him.

"It's a long story."

67

Will leaned back against the front wing of the Pajero, his arms crossed and his head tilted to one side. "So you shorted out their power supply with a bunch of party balloons?" He chuckled and shook his head at the same time. "Amazing." He opened his mouth, then hesitated as if he wasn't sure what to say, then shrugged. "Look, I know things haven't worked out the best, I mean..." he gestured toward the house. "But I think you did the right thing. That motherf..." he shook his head again. "He shouldn't be allowed to get away with it." Once more, he gestured toward the house. "Especially now."

"Yeah," was all John could say.

"John, I said it before and I'll say it again. If you need help, I'm here. I mean it more than ever this time."

"Thanks." John nodded. "Thank you. Yeah." He sighed. "I'll have to rebuild the place, so..."

"I don't mean re-building, John. I mean sorting out your neighbour."

John turned to look at Will.

"I'm serious."

John stared at him, trying to gauge his commitment, but Will held his gaze. "Are you sure? Even if it means... skirting the law?"

"I'm sure."

John continued probing. "Because there's no going back. He's gone too far and I'm going to make him regret it."

"I'm with you." Will grinned. "In fact, I think I'll enjoy it."

John studied him for a moment longer, then satisfied, nodded and finally looked away, turning his attention back to the house. He meant what he'd said. There was no going back. Even if he rebuilt the house, Xie would continue the harassment, and who knew what lengths he would go to next time?

John was going to make his life a misery. Xie would regret the day he'd set his sights on taking back Willow Cottage.

68

Soon afterwards, after agreeing to meet John later at his motel, Will left John alone with the remaining fire crew.

John stared at the smoking ruins, etching the sight into the deepest part of his memory. He wanted to make sure he would never forget the sight or the smell. If things got bad enough for him to doubt what he was doing, he wanted the image of his parents' destroyed home to be at the forefront of his mind.

Eventually he turned away and made his way back to the van, anger still simmering away inside him, but for the moment, just under control.

Back at the motel, he couldn't settle. His mind raced with a million ideas as adrenaline continued to pulse through his body. Pacing up and down the small room, he examined each idea but discarded them just as quickly.

For the briefest time, he considered giving Xie a taste of his own medicine, and setting fire to Atwell Estate, but quickly dismissed the idea. He didn't have the heart to destroy hundreds of years of history. The problem wasn't the house; it was Xie.

His phone buzzed in his pocket and he pulled it out and glanced at the screen. *Adriana*.

"Hey."

"John, is everything okay? I've called three times."

John sighed loudly. "Yeah, sorry... ahhh... my parent's house burnt down."

"What? Wh...?"

"This morning. Destroyed. There's nothing left, and it's my fault."

"Oh, John, I'm so sorry... but start from the beginning. What happened?"

John took a breath. Where did he start? "I got a call from my mum early this morning to say the house was on fire—"

"Are they okay?" Adriana interrupted.

"Yes, thank God. I had sent them away... on a holiday, at least that's what I told them. But I wanted to keep them safe."

"That's a relief. And you're okay?"

"Yeah."

"You weren't there? You said you got a call?"

"I'm staying in a motel."

"John, now I'm really confused."

"Okay, um... Xie was harassing my parents..."

"That much I know."

"Let me finish," John snapped, the frustration of the day getting the better of him. He closed his eyes and took a breath. "Sorry, I... it's been... a stressful few days."

"It's okay," Adriana replied, but John could hear the wariness in her voice.

"Xie cut the electricity to the cottage, then he cut the water, and even slashed the tyres on my car. I believe he's also had me followed. When you mentioned someone getting into our apartment, it was the last straw. So I sent my parents somewhere safe and got back at him."

"John..."

"I know, I know... but I couldn't sit by and do nothing."

"What did you do?"

"I cut off his water yesterday, and last night shorted out his power supply."

"Huh."

"But..." John rubbed his face. "I never imagined he would burn the house down. I just wanted to give him a taste of his own medicine. Now I've ruined everything..."

Adriana didn't respond and John listened to the silence on the other end while wondering for the millionth time whether he had done the right thing. Eventually he asked, "Why aren't you saying anything? Do you think I was wrong?"

"I'm thinking."

"Okay." John waited.

After a long moment Adriana followed up with, "No. I don't think you did the wrong thing. There's no way you could have foreseen he would go this far."

John exhaled slowly.

"But even if he hadn't burnt the cottage down, the fact he resorted to cutting off the power and water shows he is ruthless. Have you told the police?"

"No point. What do I tell them? I can't prove it."

"But you're sure he lit the fire?"

"Not him, his people. There was a jerry can in the wreckage. They must have used petrol to get it started."

"I'm so sorry, John," Adriana repeated. "What will you do now?"

"I'll have to get the house rebuilt. Find somewhere for my parents to live in the meantime..."

"I meant to Xie. You can't let him get away with it."

For the first time that day, John felt the beginnings of a smile. "Well..."

"If you rebuild, he'll continue the harassment. You have to put a stop to him."

John's smile grew. This was the Adriana he loved. "I'm going to. I just don't know how yet."

John's phone buzzed with another call and he held it away from his ear to look at the screen. His smile faded.

"I'll call you back. My parents are calling." He ended the call without waiting for an answer and, with his heart sinking into his stomach, answered the incoming call.

"Hello?"

"Your mother and I are coming straight back."

"There's no point, Dad."

"What do you mean, there's no point? You've burnt our house down and you expect us to stay on holiday?"

John ground his teeth together, closed his eyes, and counted to ten. His dad had every right to be angry, but John had to take charge of the conversation. He wasn't a kid. He was a grown man.

"Dad." John injected some force into his voice. "There is no point in coming back right now, because there is no house to come back to. There is nowhere for you and Mum to stay. Give me a couple of days to sort things out, and then you can come back."

"Sort things out? Haven't you done enough?"

John heard his mother's voice in the background and then further muffled conversation, as if the mouthpiece had been covered. After a moment, he heard his mother's voice.

"John, are you okay? Are you safe?"

The Neighbor

John swallowed the lump that appeared in his throat and nodded, then realising she couldn't see him, he cleared his throat and replied, "Yes, Mum, I'm okay. I'm sorry."

He swallowed again.

"As long as you're okay. Don't mind your father. He's very upset."

"I know. I'm really sorry, I really am."

He heard his mother sniff. "It's happened now. We have to move on."

John felt his eyes mist up, and he bit his lip. What could he say to make things right? "I'll fix it, Mum. I'll sort out the insurance, we'll get the house rebuilt, and in the meantime I'll find somewhere nice for you to stay."

"I know you will, dear."

"Just give me a few days, please. Tell Dad not to come back right now. I need some time."

"I understand. I'm relieved you're okay. We can replace everything else."

"Yeah," John sighed.

"How did it happen? Do you know?"

John took a deep breath. He briefly considered lying, but decided there had been enough dishonesty. "It looks like arson."

He heard a sharp intake of breath from the other end of the phone. "Arson? But why? Who would do that?"

"They, the fire department, they don't know, Mum. But they found a petrol can on the property, so everything points to a deliberate fire."

John's mother remained silent for a while. John could hear her breathing and his father muttering in the background.

"John?"

"Yes, Mum?"

"You don't think it was…?"

"I don't know, Mum. Let's leave it to the police to investigate."

"Hmmm. He wouldn't do that, would he? That man?"

She didn't have to say his name for John to know who she meant. "I don't know, Mum, I don't know, but I aim to find out."

69

With renewed vigor, John moved over to the table and opened up the laptop, switching to the security feed. He watched for a while, hoping for inspiration, but when that didn't work, he opened up the plans and spread them across the table.

That didn't work either, and he sat down and leaned back in his chair, rubbing his head with frustration. "Fuck it," he growled to no-one in particular.

Reaching out for his phone, he called Adriana back.

"Hey."

"Can you do a video call?"

"Yup," John replied, and tapped the screen to turn on the camera. Adriana smiled back at him, but her eyes were heavy with concern.

"You're looking tired, John."

John made a half-hearted attempt at a smile, but didn't disagree.

"How are your parents taking it?"

The smile slipped, and John looked away and stared out the window. "Dad's angry. Blaming me." John shrugged and looked back at the screen. "Mum said she's okay, but..." John sighed.

Adriana watched him, her lower lip held between her teeth.

John forced a smile. "Anyway, I'll sort it out somehow. How are you? Still in the safe house?"

"Yes. Ramesh has been sending me whatever he's finding on Xie's system, but it's very complicated. Lots of offshore accounts, shell companies... it's hard to make sense of it all. It's going to take time to find anything we can pin on him."

"That's a pity. I need to sort him out now." John took a deep breath and exhaled slowly through pursed lips. "I'm just not sure how." He lapsed into silence for a while, searching for comfort in the face of the woman he loved. "The thing is, I can do the same thing to him, but will it stop him? I don't think he will ever admit defeat. It would mean an enormous loss of face. This could go on forever."

"So, I know I said he mustn't get away with it, but... is it worth it?"

John frowned. Was it worth it? Was he just letting his ego get the better of him? Then he remembered his mum's voice on the phone. The sadness in her voice, despite the comforting words. And more than that, his father... accusing him of making a mistake, blaming the fire on him. He could picture the expression on his father's face. An expression he remembered from his childhood.

"No, Adriana, I have to do something. He can't get away with it. You won't understand, but it goes deeper than just the house. It's something I have to do for myself."

Adriana nodded slowly. "Okay, John. I'll support you in whatever you do, you know that."

John smiled, but his eyes were sad. "Thank you." He stared at the screen for a while. He wished Adriana was there with him right then, so he could hold her, run his fingers through her hair, kiss her soft lips. But there was no point in putting her at risk too, just because he needed comforting. He took a breath and sat up straight. The sooner he sorted this out, the sooner things could get back to normal.

70

John ended the call and sat staring at the laptop screen. Figures moved around in black and white on the various security feeds, but John's mind was blank.

Then he remembered something.

He checked the time and did a quick mental calculation. Dubai was four hours ahead. Should be okay.

He picked up the burner phone and scrolled through the messages, then tapped on a number.

It took a while to connect, but once it did, it was answered within three rings. The voice on the other end was deep, confident, and with the hint of an antipodean twang.

John sat forward and leaned his elbows on the table, the phone pressed to his ear. "Is this Jacob Watson[1]?"

"Yes. How can I help you?"

"My name is John Hayes. Ronald Yu sent me your number."

"Mr Hayes. I know who you are. Mr Yu told me to expect your call."

"Okay... good. Ahhh..." John composed the words in his head, "He ah... told me you might have some information regarding a Xie Longwei, the Chairman of Golden Fortune Corporation."

"The infamous Xie Longwei." Jacob chuckled. "I know him well, unfortunately."

"You do?"

"Yes. He's a competitor on some of our projects in Africa. He's... how do I say this... someone whose business tactics are often unsavoury."

"I'm not surprised. I need some dirt. Something I can use sooner rather than later. Is there anything you can tell me?"

There was a loud exhalation on the other end of the line, then all John could hear was the background noise of a busy office, phones ringing, muted conversations, then a door closing, and the background noise stopped.

"How much do you know about what we do, Mr Hayes?"

"John, please. I know about Pegasus Land, the real estate business in Hong Kong."

"Yes, of course. Okay... well... we are now much more than that. Since the pro-democracy protests in Hong Kong, and the crackdown by the Mainland Chinese Government, Mr Yu has been expanding operations elsewhere... diversifying, if you will."

"Okay."

"So I head up the overseas operations from here in Dubai and we have been involved in several large projects throughout the Middle East and sub-Saharan Africa."

"And so is Xie."

"Yes. Exactly. We've been working on a port project in the Democratic Republic of Nkuru. The project was about to be approved when Xie came into the picture. Our proposal stands to benefit the country significantly, and the new leader, President Tamba, sees that. He's keen to do things that benefit his people, and we were very close to finalising things when negotiations stalled. It looks like he's going with Xie despite his deal being much worse."

"Bribery?"

"Well, it could be, that's not unheard of... but I don't think so. I've spent a lot of time in the company of President Tamba. He's a good man and genuinely wants to improve the welfare of his people. He's always been completely open and gracious in all the dealings I've had with him. No, I think Xie has something on him. Something he doesn't want to come out in the open." Jacob paused. "I think he's blackmailing him."

"With what?"

John heard Jacob exhale loudly. "Well... I don't know for sure, but there are rumours he has a liking for young men."

"Hmmm. Okay."

"Now, as I said, I don't know if any of this is true, but the rumours are persistent, and Xie has used things like this in the past. It would certainly explain why Tamba has gone cold on our deal."

"Yes," John's mind raced as he thought about how this could be of use to him. Unfortunately, nothing jumped to mind.

"So..." he said, thinking out loud. "Does Xie have anything we can use against him? Any habits, addictions... girls... boys?"

"No, he lives like a monk. His only interest is money. If he has anything else, I've not heard of it. He keeps his private life extremely well protected. That's not to say there aren't any skeletons in his closet, though. I would think most of his projects in Africa have had some sort of undue influence applied to the negotiations."

"Hmmm." John frowned. He needed a scandal, something that would destroy Xie's reputation. Something that would make him persona non grata with the UK government, and he needed it to happen sooner rather than later. "Do you think President Tamba would talk to me?"

"No. He won't even talk to me anymore. And besides, if the rumours are true, Tamba will not want that information out there in public."

"No."

There was a long silence, then Jacob asked, "What are you thinking of doing?"

John sighed. "I don't know. I just want him kicked out of England."

"Okay. Look, I can't get you an audience with Tamba, but... how about his son?"

"His son?"

"Yes. His son is at Sandhurst."

"The military academy?"

"Yes. He's there as an officer cadet before rejoining the Nkuru Army."

"Why would he speak to me?"

"I can't promise he will, but like his father, he wants what's best for his country. I met him once. He's a decent young man."

John nodded to himself. He didn't know where this would take him, but he had to follow whatever leads he could. "Send me through his details. I'll try him."

"Done. And John..."

"Yes?"

"Good luck. Mr Yu speaks highly of you. If there is anything else I can do, let me know. Xie has been a thorn in my side for some time now, and I won't be disappointed if something happens to him."

"Well, I can't promise anything, but we'll see. Thank you, Jacob."

71

The phone buzzed with a message immediately after John ended the call. A phone number and a name. *Joseph Tamba.*

John stared at the phone for several moments, then composed a message and sent it to Joseph. It was a long shot, and he didn't know where it would lead, but he had nothing to lose.

It was an hour later when his phone rang. The voice on the other end was deep, confident, and spoke the clipped, well enunciated English of a public school education.

"Mr Hayes. How did you get my number?"

"A mutual friend in Dubai shared it with me."

"Who?"

"Jacob Watson, Pegasus Land."

Joseph was silent for a moment then, "I remember him. Hardly a friend, more of a business acquaintance of my father."

"Yes," Joseph still sounded wary and John needed to get him onside. "Your father and I have a mutual enemy."

"You said that in your message. But you didn't say who."

"Xie Longwei."

There was a lengthy silence before the next question. "And what is it you want from me?"

"I don't know, to be honest. All I know is that we would both benefit if he wasn't around to bother either of us anymore."

"And why is that?"

John took a deep breath. "My parents live next to Atwell Estate, Xie's property. Xie has been harassing my parents in an attempt to take over their property. I also know that your father is having some difficulties with Xie in Nkuru."

"Why do you think this has anything to do with me? I'm not involved in my father's work."

"No, I know... maybe I'm just clutching at straws, but look... today Xie took it too far when he burnt my parent's house to the ground. The home they have lived in for the past thirty years, all their possessions, destroyed."

"I'm very sorry to hear that Mr Hayes, but maybe it's better you have this conversation with the police?"

"That would be a waste of time," John replied a little too quickly. He took another deep breath, then exhaled slowly, struggling to keep his irritation in check. "Xie is rich and powerful. He has expensive lawyers. He'll probably bribe the police."

"In England?"

"No country is immune from corruption."

Joseph didn't reply.

John continued, "He should not be allowed to get away with it."

"It still sounds like a matter for the police, Mr Hayes."

"Huh," John snorted. "Just like the blackmailing of your father is a police matter," he retorted, finally losing his temper.

There was a heavy silence, before Joseph replied. "I'm afraid I have nothing more to say to you."

The phone went dead.

"Damn it." John cursed and threw the phone down onto the bed. "Fuck, fuck, fuck, fuck it!"

He took a deep breath, closed his eyes, and attempted to compose himself. He exhaled slowly and then inhaled again. Halfway through the next exhale, he opened his eyes.

There was someone at the door.

72

John moved quietly across the room toward the window. The outline of two figures was just visible through the net curtains.

Carefully he moved to the side of the window furthest from the front door and with one finger moved the net curtain aside so he could see out. Only then did he relax.

"I thought you might be hungry," Will grinned and held up a plastic bag of takeaway food, as John opened the door. John nodded a thank you, but his eyes immediately went past Will to the man standing behind him.

"Philip. I wasn't expecting you," John greeted him cautiously.

"You weren't answering your phone."

John frowned, puzzled at first. Then when realisation hit he smiled. "I'm using a different number at the moment," he explained, stepping to one side to allow both the men entry into the motel room. John took a moment to glance around the motel forecourt before closing the door behind them.

"I heard the news about Willow Cottage, and when I

couldn't get hold of you, I tried Will to see if he had any news," Philip continued. "I'm so sorry, John."

John shrugged and gestured toward the chair by the desk. "Take a seat. There's only one chair, I'm afraid."

Will walked over and placed the bag of takeout on the table, then leaned with both hands on the back of the chair and stared at the laptop screen showing the black and white camera feeds from the Atwell Estate.

"Will said it was arson?"

John nodded at Philip, who was still standing by the door. "Yup."

Philip stared down at the carpet, his head shaking slowly from side to side. There was a heavy sigh and only then did he move and sit down on the edge of the bed as if his legs had given out on him. "I can't believe it. How could he do that?"

John said nothing and glanced over at Will. He had turned away from the laptop and was grinning at John. With a jerk of his head toward the laptop, he asked, "How did you manage that?"

"I have some useful friends."

"Indeed. Have you eaten?"

John shook his head.

"Good, let's get stuck in then. I'm starving." Will turned back to the table and opened up the bag, removing several foil food containers and removing their tops. The pungent smell of spice filled the room. "I hope Indian is okay, because that's all I've got." He set out three paper plates and some plastic cutlery. "Come on, help yourself. I'm not serving."

John's stomach rumbled as his nose sent signals to his brain. He realised he had eaten nothing since the previous evening. Will had already started, so John grabbed a plate and helped himself to chicken curry and rice. He turned around to sit on the bed and noticed Philip hadn't moved. "Philip? You don't like Indian?"

Philip shook his head. "I'm not in the mood."

Will winked at John and continued eating as John sat down on the other end of the bed. The curry was over-spiced and oily, but he was so hungry he didn't care, and it was several minutes before he looked up from his empty plate.

Philip still sat in the same position, staring blankly into space while Will was over by the table, helping himself to seconds.

"What are you going to do?" Philip finally broke the silence.

John caught Will's eye, and he shook his head. "I've not told him anything."

John nodded and stood up, heading to the table for more food. "I'm going to do the same thing to him," he replied to Philip while spooning rice onto his plate.

He heard a sharp intake of breath.

"Burn down Atwell Manor? No, you can't!" Philip had risen to his feet, and he was shaking his head vigorously. "No, no!"

"No, I won't do that. I can't do that to such a beautiful building," John reassured him. "But I will make Xie's life difficult."

"How?"

John shrugged and turned his attention back to the curry. "I don't know yet." His plate full, he turned around and looked at Philip. "And it's probably best you don't know, either."

Philip's eyes darted from John to Will and back again, his

mouth opening and closing, and finally he sat down again without saying a thing.

John moved past him, sat back down, and concentrated on eating. He was halfway through his second helping when Philip spoke again.

"I don't know what you have planned, but I know something that might help you."

73

John stuffed his empty plate into the plastic takeout bag, wiped his mouth with a paper napkin and then turned to face Philip, who had taken the roll of plans and spread them out on the bed.

Will remained by the wall, still spooning food into his mouth.

Philip ran his fingers over the plan on top of the pile before discarding it and moving onto the one underneath. He did this once more, muttering to himself until his fingers stopped and he stabbed at the paper with his index finger. "Here."

John moved closer and frowned. He wasn't sure what Philip was showing him.

"Look."

"What?" John asked.

Philip straightened up, smiling for the first time since he had arrived. "Back in the 1700s, the Lord at the time was involved in smuggling. Mainly gin from Holland, but also tobacco and French brandy. He had a series of tunnels built, providing secret access to and from the Manor house."

Philip turned back to the plan and pointed again at a spot on the paper. "See this? In this area of woodland. This is one entrance."

John leaned forward and stared at the map of the Estate. "Are you sure?" He hadn't noticed the notations on the plan before, and even if he had, he wouldn't have known what they meant.

Philip grinned, his eyes flashing with excitement. "Of course I'm sure. I've not done my job for all these years without learning a thing or two."

"Is that the only one?"

"No, there's more. One sec..." Philip pulled the map closer and traced the markings with his finger. After a moment he said, "here's another one."

John looked back over his shoulder. "Throw me that pen, Will."

Will stopped eating to toss the pen across the room, and John caught it in midair.

"Make sure you save some food for Philip."

Will grunted and licked his lips.

John rolled his eyes, then turned and drew a ring around the area Philip had shown him. "Where was the first one?"

Philip pointed, and John drew another circle.

"Here's another one." Philip stabbed excitedly at another part of the map.

John circled it, then stood back and studied the circles he had drawn. "It looks like there's one at each point of the compass, so there should be another one..."

"Here," Philip beat him to it.

John drew another circle, then examined the map. Each tunnel entrance came out in an area of woodland, providing useful cover and shielding them from discovery.

"Do you think Xie knows?"

"I doubt it." Philip shook his head. "This plan is old. From our archives. He won't have a copy. In fact, the last Lord probably didn't know about it either."

"Will they still be operative?"

Philip sighed. "That I don't know. They won't have been used for decades, if not centuries."

"And do you know where in the house they come out?"

Philip reached for the plans and shuffled through them until he found a plan for the main house. He studied it for a moment, then pointed at the basement plan. "I would say somewhere here."

"But you don't know for sure?"

"No," the excitement faded from Philip's voice. "I don't."

John straightened up and gripped Philip's shoulder, giving it a squeeze. "Don't worry about that. This is very useful information, Philip."

"Do you think you can use it?"

John glanced over at Will, who had finally finished eating and was dabbing his lips with a paper napkin.

"There's only one way to find out."

74

"What do you think?" John asked Will as he closed the door.

Will waited for Philip to walk past the window outside, then nodded. "It's the right thing. He shouldn't be involved anymore than he is. Plausible deniability."

"Hmmm. What about you? Are you sure you still want to help?"

Will grinned. "Wouldn't miss it for the world."

"Good... thank you. It'll be easier if there are two of us." John moved back to the bed and looked down at the map of the Estate spread out on the bedcover. "I want to check out the tunnels. See if they're still accessible."

"When?" Will joined him beside the bed.

"Tonight." John looked up. "They've increased patrols since I cut off their water and power, so we'll need to be careful." He pursed his lips as he thought it over. "Although they might think now that they've frightened me off." He shook his head as he disagreed with the thought immediately. "No, I'll assume they're still on alert."

Will agreed. "Better safe than sorry."

John nodded thoughtfully, his eyes back on the map. "Tonight I'll just recce the tunnels. Once I know they can be used, I'll be better placed to decide a plan of attack." He turned and looked Will up and down. "Do you have any dark clothing? I don't think mine will fit you."

"In the Pajero. I've got a dark pair of overalls. A couple of head torches, too."

"I've got my own. We'll take some tools. I'm thinking a pry bar, bolt cutters, hacksaw..."

"Hammer and chisels. Screwdrivers. Oh, and some WD40," added Will.

John smiled. He was happy he had Will on his team. He checked his watch. "Ideally I'd wait until around two am, but I don't know how long it will take to recce all the tunnels, so let's head out at eleven?"

"Sounds good."

"We'll take my van. No point in your vehicle being spotted." He nodded toward the bed. "Grab some kip if you need it. I'm going to study Google Earth and get an idea of the lay of the land before going in."

"I don't need to rest. I'm going to pop out and grab some coffee and food to take with us."

John raised an eyebrow. "You're not still hungry, are you? You had Philip's share of dinner, too."

Will winked. "Nothing worth doing well should be done on an empty stomach."

75

Just after eleven, John pulled the van off the road and down a dirt track leading into a clump of trees. It provided suitable cover for the van and was just a short walk to the edge of the Atwell Estate.

Before getting out, he pulled out his phone, inserted an earbud into his right ear, and dialled Ramesh's number. "We're going in now. I'll keep the call open. Let me know if you see anything on the security cameras."

"Will do. It's clear right now. A patrol just came back, so you've got about fifteen minutes before they head out again. Good luck."

"Thanks. I'm sharing my location with you and going silent now." John checked the phone ringer was off, then slipped it into his pocket. He nodded at Will, then they both climbed out of the van, pushing the doors shut with a soft click.

From the rear of the van, they removed two backpacks laden with tools, and then each pulled on a head torch. Finally, John opened a tin of boot polish and, with two fingers, smeared the black paste over his face before handing the tin to Will.

Will did the same, then closed the rear doors of the van and waited for John's lead.

John stood quietly, listening to the sounds of the night. Something small rustled in the undergrowth, and there was the faint sound of a distant car engine. Otherwise, the night was silent and once his eyes had adjusted to the darkness, he reached out, tapped Will on the shoulder, then set off down the track toward the main road. Crossing the road, he followed the line of the hedgerow until he spotted a gap, then ducked down and pushed his way through, dropping to his knee in the field on the other side. He waited for Will to join him, the big man cursing the branches of the hedge that scratched and poked as he pushed his way through. John waited and listened before again tapping Will on the arm and gesturing for him to follow.

They had three fields to cross until they reached the first tunnel, and wary of being caught out in the open, John followed the hedgerow, keeping as low as he could.

At the edge of the next field, he leaned closer to Will and whispered into his ear, "All okay?"

Will replied with a nod, his teeth flashing in the moonlight as he grinned.

The next boundary was a stone wall and John tested it with his hands, checking for loose stones before hoisting himself up and over. Will followed quickly after with the agility of a man half his size. John nodded his approval, his confidence in his large companion growing with every minute.

Almost ten minutes later, they reached the edge of a small copse set in a fold of land bisecting a large field. John dropped to a crouch, waiting for Will to join him, then pointed into the trees. Will nodded his understanding, and John rose to his feet and stepped into the darkness under the trees.

There was a sudden movement from within the trees, and John froze, his heart in his mouth. Will ran into the back of him, almost knocking him over. John struggled to maintain his balance while his eyes widened, trying desperately to make out what was in the darkness. There was a screech and a flapping of wings and John breathed out as a startled pheasant made its escape across the field they had just come from.

"Bugger me," Will muttered.

John took a deep breath, calming his nerves, then looked over his shoulder to make sure they were hidden from the field. He whispered into his phone, "Ramesh, all clear?"

"A patrol just left, but they are a long way from you."

"Okay. Keep me posted."

"Roger that."

John grinned, not so much with amusement as relief, then slowly moved deeper into the copse. About ten paces in, he reached up and switched on his head torch, setting it to night-vision mode. The red LEDs gave off a soft red glow, enough to see by, but hopefully not enough to be spotted by a patrol.

The undergrowth closed in around them as they ventured deeper inside the trees, and without the head torches, they wouldn't have been able to see much further than the end of their arms. Progress was slow at first, but as their brains adapted to the red signals their eyes were receiving, their confidence grew.

When John estimated they were far enough inside, he stopped and looked around. On the map, the land sloped down toward a small stream and, although John couldn't see it, he could hear the faint trickle of water. He made his way carefully down the slope, moving the beam from the head torch from left to right, looking for anything that might be the tunnel entrance.

He whispered to Will, "It has to be around here somewhere. Look for anything that looks like a hatch or a door."

Will nodded, his grin still visible in the red glow of the lamp, and he pointed at himself, then gestured upstream. John understood and gestured downstream, then gave Will a thumbs up.

It took almost ten minutes for John to search the bank right down to the edge of the copse, but he found nothing. As he reached the edge of the trees, he heard a vehicle approaching.

John dropped to the ground and switched off his head torch, then watched the play of headlights across the field as a Land Rover passed close by. Once it had gone, he whispered, "Ramesh, the patrol has just gone past."

"Roger. Any luck?"

"Not yet," John muttered, then switched his head torch back on and made his way back into the woods. Reaching the centre of the copse, there was no sign of Will, so John made his way further up the stream. He spotted a faint red glow ahead, and he gave a low hiss, warning Will of his approach. There was a hiss in reply, and rounding a thick clump of bush, he spotted Will kneeling on the ground beside a pile of moss-covered stones.

Will beckoned him over and pointed at something to the right of the stones.

John squatted down and directed his head torch beam over the stones. In amongst them, he noticed something that was too regular to be natural. Leaning closer, he reached out and traced his fingertips over an old iron ring about six inches in diameter. Gripping it between his fingers, he tugged, but it wouldn't move. He couldn't make out enough detail in the red light, so he removed a penlight from the side pocket of his cargo pants and switched it on. Shining the beam on the ring, he could see it was heavily rusted and seized to the metal hatch behind it. He played the beam over the hatch, which was set at a forty-five degree angle in the slope. Several rocks obscured the bottom left quarter and a thick tree root partially covered the top edge. He turned off the beam and sat back on his haunches. "Looks like you found it."

"Yeah," Will breathed excitedly, "but I can't open it. I've been trying for the last five minutes." He held up his left hand. "I even busted a nail."

John chuckled, then slid the backpack off his shoulders, unzipped it, and removed a pry bar. Standing up, he inserted the end between one of the large stones and began levering it free. It took several goes before it loosened and then, with Will's help, they pried it loose and dropped it to one side. They repeated it several times until the bottom of the hatch was clear of stones. John then turned on the penlight and shone it over the root covering the top of the hatch. "We'll have to cut this out."

"I don't think it will do any good," came Will's reply. "Look here." He pointed at the edge of the hatch. "See the hinges. They're seized solid. I don't think we'll be able to open it."

"What if we apply WD40?"

Will shook his head. "It won't work quickly enough to open it tonight. I reckon we'll need to cut it out with an oxy torch."

"Shit," John cursed under his breath. "Just when things were going so well."

He turned his wrist and checked his G-shock. "We have a choice. Continue trying to open this, or find the others."

"Let's find the others. They might be easier. If not, at least we know where this is."

"Agreed. Let's go."

76

Almost two hours later, John sat in the cover of a hedgerow while Will passed him a mug of hot coffee. John took a sip, the hot liquid providing some comfort in what had so far been a frustrating night. Despite searching up and down the field for the better part of an hour, they had found nothing that even remotely resembled the entrance to the southern tunnel.

It was now well into the early hours of the morning, and both men were frustrated and tired. Will no longer grinned when John spoke to him, but he didn't once complain. Even now, he sat quietly beside him, sipping on his coffee as they gazed out over the fields. The clouds had cleared from the night sky, opening up a vast inky blackness dotted with pinpricks of white light. Something chirped repeatedly in the hedgerow behind them and in the distance, the bark of a fox punctuated the silence.

"I used to roam these fields as a kid," John said in a soft voice, his breath heated by the coffee, expelling a puff of steam. "I even used to sneak out after I was supposed to be in bed. I loved it out here."

"Did you hunt?"

John shook his head. "Not really. Rabbits and hares with a slingshot. But I just enjoyed being out on my own, in the silence." He sighed. "I'd forgotten how much I enjoyed it. I've spent most of my adult life in big crowded cities."

"Would you come back here, I mean permanently?"

John took another sip of coffee while he thought about it. "To be honest, I don't like to think that far ahead. And besides, what is permanent? Look at my parents' house."

"Yeah."

John heard a rustle and looked over to see Will unwrapping a foil package.

"Here."

John took the sandwich and held it up to his nose. "Bacon."

"Better hot, I know."

John shrugged. "Beggars can't be choosers."

The two men munched in silence, washing down the food with the remains of the coffee. With a full stomach, John felt revived and motivated to continue. He wiped his fingers on his pant leg, then looked at his watch.

"We'd better get a move on if we want to find the other tunnels before daylight."

"Yup. Let's hope we have better luck."

John said nothing. He hoped so, too.

77

John stood cautiously, looked around for patrols, then gave a low hiss.

There was no response. He frowned and narrowed his eyes, trying to see Will in the darkness. There was no sign of him and, unlike earlier when they stopped for coffee, clouds had rolled back in, cutting out the light from the moon.

This time John tried a whistle but when there was no acknowledgement, he crouched down again and edged forward toward the hole he had found in a steeper section of hillside. He had missed it the first time round; hidden by an overgrowth of vegetation, the steepness of the slope preventing that part of the field from cultivation. But when John double-checked, he spotted the small opening and pulled the weeds and branches out of the way to expose a hole that led into the hillside. Crawling inside, he reached up and turned on his head torch. Red light lit up walls of moss-covered stone. John smiled for the first time that evening. He had found it.

"Ramesh, can you hear me?"

"Just. Your voice is not clear."

John edged back out toward the entrance of the tunnel. "Now?"

"Loud and clear."

"Good. Are you still tracking my location?"

"Yes."

"Okay, mark this location on the map. I've found one tunnel. Just going inside to check it out."

"Good luck."

"Thanks." John thought briefly about waiting for Will, but then eagerness to make progress got the better of him and he moved further inside before removing his penlight from his pocket and turning it on.

The tunnel wasn't high enough for him to stand upright and was just wider than his shoulders, so bent double, he moved slowly forward. A web plastered its strands across his face, and he wiped it away with his left hand, trying not to think about the spider. He flashed the beam of the penlight ahead of him, looking for more webs. Beetles and bugs of all shapes and sizes scuttled away from the light, and a pair of red eyes shone back at him from the far reaches of the light beam. An involuntary shiver ran down John's spine. "Come on, man, don't be a wimp," he muttered under his breath, and pushed on.

The floor sloped gently downwards and the temperature noticeably dropped the deeper inside he went. His breath was visible in the glow from his head torch and he felt a chill from the sweat cooling on his skin. He briefly contemplated pulling on another layer of clothing, but the tunnel was too confined for him to move easily and he didn't want to waste any more time.

Eventually, the tunnel took a bend to the left and as he

rounded the bend, the beam of the penlight bounced back off something he hadn't wanted to see.

"Shit," he cursed, and sank to his knees, giving his quads a rest as he examined the rockfall ahead of him. A mound of rocks and earth from the collapsed roof completely blocked the way forward. Edging closer on his knees, John held the penlight in his mouth and with both hands tried to pry the rocks loose. He succeeded with a couple of them, but removing them encouraged more soil to fall from the roof above. He moved back to safety and sat back on his heels. Taking the penlight from his mouth, he gave up all pretence of silence and swore loudly. "For fuck's sake. When is my luck going to change?" He shook his head. "Bugger it."

With difficulty he turned around, switched off the penlight and made his way back toward the entrance, making sure to turn off his head lamp before getting out into the open. He stood upright, took a deep breath of fresh air, and shook out the lactic acid from his burning thighs. A movement in his peripheral vision caught his attention, and he slowly eased down into a crouch, making his silhouette as small as possible.

"Psst, John?"

John relaxed and stood upright. "Psst," he replied, and waited for Will to make his way over.

"Any luck?" Will asked, then noticed the tunnel entrance behind him. "You found it!"

"Yeah," John sighed and looked back at the tunnel entrance. "But it's blocked. The tunnel collapsed about a hundred metres in."

"Shit. Can we clear it?"

"No. At least I doubt it. Looks like it's been like that for years, and I'm worried it will collapse even more."

"Damn it."

"Yup." John exhaled. "Look..." He turned to face Will. "If you want to call it quits, I understand. You've done more than enough."

"Are you quitting?"

"No."

"Then why would I quit? I said I'd help and I mean it."

John studied Will's face in the darkness, then reached out and gripped his shoulder. "Thank you."

"Don't mention it. Come on, lucky last."

John grinned. As much as he tried to do everything himself, the universe always sent someone to help him out in times of need.

He gave Will's shoulder a squeeze. "Let's go."

78

The two men were now comfortable moving in the darkness, and the patrols seemed to have become less frequent as the night wore on. There had been no signs of movement for some time, only a herd of cows regarding them curiously as they moved through them, and a startled Roe deer escaping across the field and leaping the hedgerow in a single bound.

The final tunnel entrance was in an area of woodland in the north of the Estate. Upon entering the woods, the two men separated, turned on their headlamps, and began to search.

John moved slowly, searching carefully, ensuring he didn't miss his last chance at finding a viable tunnel. Fatigue was getting the better of him and his mind started playing tricks, turning shrubs into doors, boulders into tunnel entrances. The weight of the tools in his backpack increased with every hour, and the straps chafed against his shoulders. Blinking the tiredness from his eyes, he continued on as an owl hooted from the branches high above.

He was almost near the end of the woods, feeling

increasingly despondent with every step, when he heard a low whistle. Whipping around, he scanned the darkness and spotted the faint red glow of Will's headlamp. The whistle came again, and he made his way toward him.

"I found it," Will called out, giving up on silence in his excitement. John stepped up his pace and his headlamp caught the big man waving his arms in excitement.

"Over here."

John pulled out his penlight, and when he reached Will, switched it on. Will pointed to his left, and the flashlight lit up a rotten wooden door about three feet in height and about two feet wide. The bottom had rotted away, and a large crack ran up the middle of it.

John breathed out in relief, but tried not to get too excited. The tunnel still had to be accessible. He checked his watch. They had about an hour before it got light, so they needed to move fast.

He slipped the backpack off his shoulders and removed the pry bar. Passing the penlight to Will, he stepped forward and wedged the end of the pry bar into the crack in the door. He counted to three, then wrenched the two sections of the door apart. There was a loud crack and a piece of wood ripped from the door and fell to the ground. John waited, hoping the sound hadn't been overheard, then adjusted the position of the pry bar and applied pressure again. This time, with a protesting screech, the left side of the door separated from the right and fell to the ground. John dropped the pry bar and reaching forward, grabbed the remaining section with both hands, pushing and pulling until it came loose, exposing the tunnel behind.

He looked back at Will. "Let's check it out."

"Uh uh." Will shook his head.

John frowned. "What do you mean?"

Will shrugged. "I'm not going in there."

"But..."

"I said I'd help you. I said nothing about going into the tunnel."

"I don't understand."

Will was no longer grinning. "I'm ah... not good in enclosed spaces."

"Oh." John couldn't hide his surprise. "Okay... then keep watch outside for me."

Will nodded, looking sheepish, and handed over the penlight.

John took it, winked, then turned, crouched down, and entered the tunnel. Just inside, he hesitated. Checking his watch, he then looked out at Will squatting in the entranceway. "If I'm not back in forty-five minutes, don't wait for me. Meet me at the van. There's no sense in both of us being caught out in daylight."

"Got it." Will gave a thumbs up and John turned and made his way into the tunnel.

According to the map, the tunnel entrance was about eight hundred metres from the main house, so he doubted he would have time to reach the end and get out before sunup, but he had to try.

Despite the poor state of the door, the tunnel itself was in relatively good condition. The stone walls were dry and so was the ground underfoot. It sloped gradually downwards and ran in a straight line for as far as the beam of the flashlight would carry.

John moved as quickly as he could, given the limited space, bashing his head on the stone roof occasionally and stopping to ease the lactic acid buildup in his thighs several times. Despite this, he felt he was making good progress until he checked his watch and discovered thirty minutes had passed with no end of the tunnel in sight.

John sat down on the floor of the tunnel and shook out his legs while he decided what to do next. The sensible thing was to head back. He could always return the following night when he'd have much more time. John chewed his lip and once more glanced at his watch, as if doing so would rewind the clock.

"Fuck it."

He pushed himself to his feet and headed deeper into the tunnel.

79

Will shifted from one foot to the other and glanced up at the sky between the tree branches. Was it his imagination or was it getting lighter? He checked his watch. It was fifty minutes since John had entered the tunnel. He should be back by now.

Bending down, Will stared into the tunnel. It was pitch black, with no sign of the light from John's flashlight or head torch.

"Come on, come on, where are you?" he muttered, then stood up and looked at his watch again. Should he stay or should he go? John had told him to go, but Will didn't feel comfortable leaving him behind.

He crouched down and peered back inside. What if he was trapped and needed help? Will grimaced, took a breath, and began to crawl in. Reaching up, he turned on his headlamp, and a red glow filled the tunnel, sending a rodent scampering away into the darkness. A shiver ran down Will's spine, and he stopped. There wasn't much he was afraid of in life, but he'd always had trouble with enclosed spaces. Even more so when they were dark and filled with rats. He took a deep breath to calm himself, but the air was stale and musty, and it only made him feel worse.

"Don't be a wuss," he said out loud and moved a little further inside. His breathing became more rapid, shorter breaths, and now he could feel the rapid beat of his heart, almost as if the organ was trying to climb into his throat.

"Shit," he cursed, and shook his head. He took another deep breath. "John," he called out as loud as he dared, and waited for a response, but there was nothing.

"John," he tried again, but when there was no answer, he quickly shuffled backwards into the open and sat on the ground sucking in lungfuls of fresh air. He'd wait for another ten minutes.

Fifteen minutes later, Will peered into the tunnel again. Throwing caution to the winds, he called out, "John, where are you?"

There was still no answer, and reluctantly he shouldered his backpack, picked up the pack John had left behind, and turned away from the tunnel.

At the edge of the woods, he paused and looked back, still hoping he would see John emerging from the tunnel. Leaving him behind went against all his instincts, but what if John had found another exit and was already waiting in the van?

With that thought, Will stepped out into the field and turned left, keeping close to the edge of the woodland. The sky was transitioning from black to grey, and Will could see clearly across the field to the other side. If a patrol came past now, it would be difficult to hide, so he broke into a jog, stopping only by a small stream to splash water on his face and attempt to clean off the boot polish. His hand came away smeared in black, and he took his sleeve and rubbed his face as much as he could. He would have trouble explaining a blackened face once he was off the Estate.

Hoping he had removed most of it, he set off again, eventually reaching the boundary of the Estate where it touched a road. Once on the road, he increased his pace; a rifleman's march, alternately jogging and walking, but it still took another forty minutes before he reached the hidden van.

John wasn't there.

"Shit," he exhaled loudly and dropped both backpacks on the ground, turning to look back the way he had come. The sun was not yet above the horizon, but it was effectively daylight. He glanced again at his watch. Over an hour had passed since he had left the tunnel. He kicked the van's front tyre. Where was John? Should he have stayed? Why did he let fear get the better of him?

"You're a wuss, Will Sanderson, a wuss."

80

Will paced up and down beside the van for another ten minutes, but with no sign of John, he tossed the backpacks into the rear of the van, then climbed in and turned it around so it was facing the road. If John arrived in a hurry, he wanted to be ready to make a quick getaway.

Bloodshot eyes looked back at him from the rear-view mirror and boot polish residue still filled the lines in his face. He turned and reached for his backpack behind the seat and removed a spare shirt. He wiped his face as clean as he could before tossing the ruined shirt into the load space behind him.

He caught sight of the last remaining foil-wrapped bacon sandwich in the bag, and his stomach growled in anticipation.

No, he'd keep it for John. He would be hungry when he got back.

Five minutes later, Will wiped his mouth with the back of his hand and washed down the last of the bacon sandwich with a mouthful of tepid coffee. He'd get John a fresh one on the way back to the motel.

Settling back into the seat, he checked his watch again. "Come on, John, where the hell are you?"

Will contemplated taking a drive around the roads bordering the Estate, but then if John came looking for the van and it wasn't there, it would create another problem. Will checked his phone. The battery was almost dead and there were no messages or missed calls. Should he call John? But what if he was hiding?

Will frowned with indecision, then typed out a text. *John, where are you? I'm in the van.* He pressed send, then wedged the phone between the dashboard and the windscreen where he could see it.

Rolling his shoulders back, he settled back into the seat and yawned. He'd been awake for twenty fours and, after the physical exertion and stress, his body wanted to shut down. He wound down the window to allow some fresh air in, hoping it would keep him alert, but ten minutes later, his eyes drooped shut. Blinking them open and giving his head a shake, Will adjusted his position and glanced around, but there was still no sign of his friend.

His eyelids drooped again, and he struggled in vain to keep them open. Finally, exhaustion got the better of him and his eyes closed as the comforting arms of sleep wrapped around him.

Bang!

Will jumped in his seat, instantly alert, as his nervous system pumped adrenaline through his body.

Standing in front of the van, both hands resting on the hood, was a sinister-looking figure in black. Will reached for the door handle, heart racing, his left hand curling into a fist... then the figure grinned, a row of white teeth standing out in stark contrast in the black face.

"John," Will exclaimed in relief. "For fuck's sake, I almost pissed myself." He climbed out of the van and grabbed John, wrapping his arms around him and pounding him on the back with the palm of his hand.

"Thank God. I was worried you had got caught." Will released his embrace and held him out at arm's length.

"Not worried enough to stop you sleeping, though." John grinned back.

"Yeah," Will replied. He let go of John and looked down at the ground. "Sorry about that. I... ah... tried to stay awake."

John reached out and grasped his arm. "No worries, my friend. I'm glad you waited. Let's get out of here."

"Yes, but tell me what happened. Is the tunnel any good?"

John's grin widened, and he thumped Will on the shoulder. "I got all the way to the house, Will, all the way."

81

The tunnel stretched further than the reach of his flashlight beam. It seemed endless, and in the darkness, John lost all track of time. His back ached and his quads burned and shook with fatigue. Thick strands of spider web stuck to his hair and wrapped across his face, and he wiped them away with his spare hand. Rounding a slight bend, he stopped as the tunnel split into three. He flashed the beam down each one. Which one should he take? Where did they lead to? The flashlight beam flickered and died.

"Shit."

He banged it on his thigh, hoping it was a loose connection. The light came on briefly, then died again. John reached up and switched the red light on his head torch to white, lighting up the tunnels briefly before that too faded, plunging John into total darkness.

"What the...?" he cursed. He'd replaced the battery that morning.

He tapped it with his fingers, but nothing happened.

The darkness was absolute, and he reached out for the tunnel wall to reassure himself.

An alarm blared, and he flinched, his heart rate immediately doubling. *What the...?* Turning his head from side to side, he tried to workout where the sound was coming from. Was it the three tunnels in front, or was it from behind him? The alarm got louder.

He must have triggered a sensor. He had to get out before they caught him. With difficulty, he turned, but his backpack snagged on the stone wall. He pulled it free and began to move toward the exit, his shoulders rubbing against the walls... *hang on... what... was he imagining it?* The walls of the tunnel were closer, pressing in on him. What the hell was going on? His shoulders wedged against the walls on each side and he pulled them free, turning side on, but there was no way he could move forward. His breath quickened, becoming shallow, and he attempted to slow it down, taking a deeper breath, but there wasn't enough oxygen. He pressed back against the wall, trying to make more space, but the walls continued moving closer and closer.

John sat up in bed, and it took several seconds for him to work out where he was. His heart was pounding, his chest heaving in panic, and the alarm was still blaring in his ears.

It took several moments to realise his phone was ringing. He exhaled with relief and reached for the phone on the bedside table.

Ramesh.

"John, did you see my message?"

John rubbed his face and swung his legs off the bed. "What message? What time is it?"

"It's one thirty in the afternoon your time. Were you

sleeping?" Ramesh didn't wait for an answer. "I just sent a photo. Take a look."

John rubbed the sleep from his eyes, then thumbed through the apps on the phone and opened Ramesh's message.

"Can you see it?"

John stared at the black-and-white screen grab from one of the Atwell Estate security cameras. At first, his brain couldn't work out what he was seeing... then his eyes widened in shock.

"Is that...?"

"My father." John's heart sank.

His father was being pulled out of the back of a Land Rover by a security guard, while another stood to one side, holding a weapon at the ready.

What the hell was his dad doing there?

"He turned up at the front entrance and drove in without stopping. They blocked his way with a Land Rover, pulled him out of the car, and took him away. That photo I sent is when they got him to the house. After that, I lost sight of him."

"Shit," was all John could say. He couldn't believe it. He had told his parents to stay down in Devon. What the hell was his dad doing at the Estate? And where was his mum?

"I'll call you back. Let me know if you see him again." John ended the call without waiting for a reply and dialled his parents' phone.

It was answered immediately.

"Mum, where are you?"

"John, thank goodness. I've been trying to reach you. You didn't answer your phone."

John held the phone away from his ear and checked the screen. Three missed calls.

"Mum, where are you?" he repeated.

"I'm at a motel here in Winchester. We came back this morning. Your father went out to get some food. He should be back soon."

"Argh," John groaned and screwed up his face

"What's the matter, John? You sound upset."

"Mum, I told you to stay there until I sorted things out. Why didn't you listen to me?"

"You know your father, John. He's very stubborn. He insisted on coming back... but why are you so upset? We can help you fix things up."

John closed his eyes, stuck his fist in his mouth, and screamed internally.

"John... John, are you there?"

He took a deep breath, forcing himself to calm down, then opened his eyes, fixed a fake smile on his face and replied, "Yes, Mum, I'm here. Which motel are you in? I'm coming to see you."

82

John pounded on the door of the adjoining motel room he had rented for Will.

"Will, wake up!"

The door opened, and Will stood in a t-shirt and boxers, rubbing the sleep from his eyes.

"What's up?"

"Get dressed and come to my room. My dad's been kidnapped."

John left him standing there with his mouth hanging open and rushed back to his room. He grabbed his phone and dialled Ramesh.

"John."

"Any sign of him since we spoke?"

"I saw him being moved to the stable block, but there are no cameras inside."

"Shit!" John thumped the tabletop. "Shit," he repeated. "Stupid old fool... dammit!" He closed his eyes and ran his fingers through his hair. He needed to calm down. "I'm putting you on speaker. I need to think." John placed the phone on the table and began pacing around the room.

There was a knock on the door, and he walked over to let Will in. He was dressed but still barefoot, and his hair needed a comb.

"Ramesh," John called out, as he caught Will's eye and nodded toward the phone on the table. "I've got Will with me now."

"Hi, Ramesh," Will added.

Ramesh returned the greeting and then asked, "So, what's the plan?"

"I don't know." John shook his head in frustration. Turning to Will he said, "Will, my father, instead of staying down in Devon, where he was safe, drove up here, and for some fucking reason," he spat the curse word for emphasis, "entered the Estate and has been captured by Xie's security."

"Fuck."

"Yeah. Fuck." John kicked the wall. "The stubborn old bugger. He always thinks he knows best."

Will said nothing.

"I have to get him out."

"Let's call the police."

John stopped pacing and stared at Will. "How do we explain to the police that we know he's there?" John gestured at the laptop. "I can't tell them we've hacked into the security system."

Will shrugged. "Anonymous tipoff."

John thought about it. "What do you think, Ramesh?"

"You know my thoughts about the police, but putting that to one side, think about this. Why didn't Xie's security call the police? They could have said someone was causing a nuisance at the entrance and asked the police to intervene. Instead, they grabbed your father and took him prisoner."

"Yeah." John nodded.

The Neighbor

"Maybe they're holding him while they wait for the police to arrive?" Will suggested.

John considered this, too. More than anything, he wanted to believe his father was safe. His mind raced as he tried to workout all the possible angles.

"The police will ask Dad why he went there..." John voiced his thoughts. "He'll accuse Xie of burning the house down. The police already suspect arson, so..." John trailed off as he tried to put himself in Xie's position. "He won't call the police."

"Why not?" Will had moved over toward the desk and was leaning against the wall with his arms crossed.

"He won't want the attention. He definitely won't want the finger of blame pointing in his direction."

"He can blame the fire on his security. Make one of them the fall guy," Will countered.

John frowned. That was possible. He could promise one of the guards a cash payout as long as he took the blame and kept his mouth shut.

"Too many loose ends," the disembodied voice of Ramesh broke the silence.

John walked closer to the phone. "What are you thinking, Ramesh?"

"Well... based on what I've been able to glean from his computer records, he doesn't like to leave things to chance. He always wants to make sure all his options are covered. He's ruthless, John, and doesn't think normal rules apply to him."

John suddenly felt very cold.

"I don't want to say this, John," Ramesh continued, "but I think your father is in real danger."

"Oh, come on," Will interjected, "don't you think you're getting carried away? This is just over a..." He raised a hand, palm out. "Sorry John, but just a house. Harassment I can understand, and yes, arson is going a bit far, but you're suggesting..." He shook his head. "I don't even want to say it."

John didn't want to hear it.

"John, we've been through a lot together over the years," Ramesh added. "We've seen what people can do. There are all sorts of rumours surrounding Xie's projects in Africa. People missing, mysterious deaths--"

"But that's Africa," Will interrupted. "This is England. Things like that don't happen here."

Ramesh said nothing to that, and neither did John.

"And what about all his security? Aren't they a loose end, too?" Will continued.

"Carrot and the stick."

Will turned and leaned over the phone. "What do you mean, Ramesh?"

"He'll give them a choice. Keep quiet and take a huge cash payment, the carrot, or not take the payment and lose their life. That's the stick. He'll probably threaten their families, too."

Will shook his head in disbelief, then looked up at John as if expecting him to disagree.

John nodded. "He's right, Will."

"But..." Will protested.

"The world is not all fluffy pillows and bunny rabbits, Will. That's why I asked if you were sure you wanted to get involved."

"Yes, but that's when you were just going to teach him a lesson. Cut off his power, make his life uncomfortable."

"Well... yeah." John shrugged. "But then he took my dad, so... Look..." John sighed. "You've been a great help, Will. Done more than I could have expected from anyone. I really appreciate it. But I won't think any less of you if you want to back out now."

Will stared back at him, the confusion evident in his eyes and deeply creased forehead.

"Umm, gentlemen, can I interrupt?"

John maintained eye contact with Will. "Yes, Ramesh."

"Speaking of loose ends, where's your mother?"

The confusion left Will's face, and his eyes widened, mirroring John's own expression.

"Shit." John cursed. In all the discussion, he'd forgotten about his mother alone in her motel room. "Okay, Will, are you in or out?"

83

John drove as fast as he could without breaking the speed limit. Will sat silently beside him, one hand gripping the grab handle above the door as John rounded a corner, the van's tyres screeching in protest. John glanced over at his companion. Will had said he was in, but looked like he was still struggling with the decision.

"Will, I want you to do something for me."

Will turned his head slowly, and John smiled reassuringly before turning his attention back to the road.

"Don't worry, it's not illegal, but no less important."

"Okay," came the cautious reply.

"I'm moving Mum into our motel. So far, they don't know where we are, and I don't want to risk leaving her at hers. So I want you to watch over her, keep her safe."

Will said nothing immediately. John swerved around a turning vehicle, then glanced over. "Can you do that for me?"

Will swallowed and nodded. "Yes, I can do that."

"Thank you, Will. It means a lot. And I know I can trust you to keep her safe."

"You can, John," Will replied, sounding more confident.

John glanced over again, and Will smiled for the first time since John had woken him.

John let go of the steering wheel with his left hand and gave Will a pat on the thigh. "I know you will."

He spotted the sign for The Yew Tree Motel ahead, indicated, then pulled into the forecourt a little faster than necessary, earning a stern look from a guest standing outside the reception.

"Which room?" Will asked, his eyes scanning the numbers on the doors.

"321."

"318, 319... there."

John screeched to a halt, jumped out, and hurried over to the room. Stopping outside, he took a breath, composed himself and then, as calmly as he could, knocked on the door.

"It's open."

John stepped inside. His mother sat in an armchair on the far side of the room. The TV was on with the sound muted, and she had an open book in her lap.

"John," her face lit up. "Your father is not back yet. I thought..."

She trailed off, frowning as she caught sight of Will's large frame filling the doorway.

"Mum, this is my friend Will." John gestured behind him as he walked over.

"A pleasure to meet you, Mrs Hayes. John's told me a lot about you."

Carole's eyes moved from Will to John and back again. Her face relaxed as her frown changed to a smile.

"Will, please come in. I'm happy John has made a friend here."

84

John noticed a security camera as they were leaving, and he made a call to Ramesh, giving him the location and the name of the security company on the alarm box on the wall above the reception. Hopefully, he could hack into the system and let John know if anyone paid his parents' motel room a visit.

It had taken thirty minutes of fast talking and heavy explaining before John could finally convince his mother to leave the motel.

Her initial joy at seeing John was quickly replaced by confusion and fear, then finally concern for her missing husband. But John's promises to get him back safely had done little to reassure her, and she was silent as she sat in the passenger seat of the van on the way back to John's motel.

John used the silence to decide his next move. Originally, he had planned to use the tunnel to get into the house unnoticed and to carry out various nuisance acts to make Xie's life uncomfortable. But now the priority was to rescue his father. Dealing with Xie would have to wait.

The tunnel had ended in a sturdy wooden door, and he hadn't been able to test it the previous night. He was hoping he could lever it open with a pry-bar, and also hoped the entrance wasn't bricked up on the other side. If it was, then he was screwed.

There were still far too many unknowns, but he didn't have the time to work everything out. The longer he left it, the more his father was at risk. He had to go in as soon as possible, and would have to improvise.

"John, you look worried?" Carole spoke for the first time since she had sat in the van.

John gave her a smile. "No, just tired. Nothing to worry about." He didn't enjoy lying to his mother, but there was no point in adding to her stress.

"Here we are," John slowed, the motel arriving just in time to forestall further conversation. "Nothing fancy, but you'll be comfortable, Mum."

John pulled up outside his room and turned the engine off. He turned in his seat and smiled at Carole. "And I mean it. There's nothing to worry about. Dad will be back here grumbling away before you know it." He placed a hand over hers and winked. "And you'll be wishing he'd stayed away longer."

85

"There." John leaned in and pointed at the laptop. He and Will stood on either side of Carole, who sat on the chair in front of the desk.

Ramesh had hacked into The Yew Tree Motel's security cameras, and they watched as a black Range Rover pulled up outside Carole and David's room. Two men climbed out, both in dark clothing, dark wrap-around sunglasses hiding their faces. One stood by the Range Rover watching the car park and the other rooms, while the other walked straight to the door of the room and knocked. He waited for a reply, then tried the door handle. John had left the room unlocked after removing his parent's belongings, and the man glanced over his shoulder, then reached inside his jacket with his right hand while opening the door with his left.

John heard the sharp intake of breath from his mum when the man disappeared inside. "I can't believe this."

John placed a hand on her shoulder. "Now you understand why I got you out of there."

"But... why can't we just go to the police?"

"Mum..." John hid his impatience behind a smile and

crouched down until his face was at the same level as his mother's. He kept one eye on the screen as he continued, "By the time we explain everything to the police and get them to believe us, it might be too late."

The man exited the motel room and approached his colleague. They had a brief conversation, then both walked over to the reception.

"We can tell them they've kidnapped your father. They have to believe us."

John swivelled the chair around so his mother was facing him. "What do we tell them? How do we know they've kidnapped him?"

Carole glanced at the laptop.

John shook his head. "No, we can't tell them about this. It's illegal for a start, and will invite too many other questions."

"But..." Carol's eyes darted around the room as she struggled to understand.

John placed his hands over both of hers. He understood her confusion. Most people believed the world was a safe place filled with sit-coms and game shows, and farmers' markets on the weekends. That citizens obeyed laws, trusted the government, and depended on the police to keep them safe. That there was an order to everything. But John knew very well things didn't actually work like that.

"What about the constant harassment, the road, the electricity failure? I know that was them, even though you didn't tell me."

John grinned. Despite her current confusion, his mum was sharp as a tack.

"No, I didn't tell you. I didn't want to worry you."

"The fire was them too, wasn't it?"

John glanced up at Will, who was listening quietly, then looked back at his mum and nodded.

She turned back to watch the screen. The two men had left the reception and were standing next to the Range Rover. Judging by their hand movements and the way they were looking around, they weren't happy.

"I thought these things only happened in the movies," Carole finally said softly, as the two men climbed into the Range Rover and it drove out of view.

John squeezed his mum's hands and sighed. "Unfortunately not, Mum."

He released her hands, stood, and stared blankly at the laptop. The calm demeanour he had shown his mother was just an act. Inside, he boiled with rage. First, they detained his father, and then two armed thugs had gone to pick up his mother. Even he was struggling to believe it.

Xie clearly felt he was above the law. John could understand him operating like this in a third world country, but to be so brazen here in England was hard to believe, even to John's cynical mind. He took a deep breath and refocused on the room. Carole was looking up at him, deep lines across her forehead, her eyes wide with worry. She looked like she was waiting for an answer.

"Sorry, what was that?"

"Wh... what will they do to him?"

John forced a smile and crouched down again. He took both her hands in his and looked into her eyes. "Don't you worry, Mum, I'll get him out of there."

"But..." again her eyes darted around, and John could feel a slight tremor in her hands. "How? You are..."

John gave her hands another squeeze. "Mum, look at me."

Carole's eyes refocused on John, and he held her gaze for

a moment before speaking. "I've not told you much about my life after India. I've not..." he struggled to find the best way to put it. "I've not wanted to worry you unnecessarily." He took a deep breath. "But I've had some experiences, done some things... that would shock you."

"Bad things?"

John pursed his lips and tilted his head from side to side as if he was weighing up the rights and wrongs of his actions. "It... depends on one's perspective."

Carole looked even more confused.

"Look, what I'm trying to say is that I'm not the son you think I am."

Carole looked shocked. "Are you a criminal?"

John had to chuckle. "No, Mum, not at all." He took another breath and broke eye contact, looking around as if he would find inspiration elsewhere. "I'll explain everything after this is over. What I'm trying to say is I'm stronger and more resourceful than you think I am." He jerked his head toward the laptop. "Than Dad thinks I am. I want you to trust me, and believe that I'll get Dad back, and that Xie will not bother you again."

Carole studied his face for several moments, then the lines on her forehead eased out, her expression changing. She gripped John's hands. "You've always been special to me, John." She smiled for the first time, although her eyes remained sad. "I trust you to do what's right."

John returned her smile, gave her hands one more squeeze of reassurance, and then stood up. He looked over at Will, who gave him a nod of approval.

Everyone seemed to have faith in him to solve the problem.

He just wished he knew how.

86

John rechecked his backpack for the last time, then zipped it up and closed the rear door of the van.

He turned around and smiled at his mum. In the dim light of the setting sun and next to Will's hulking frame, she looked tiny and vulnerable. She returned his smile, but her eyes failed to hide her true emotions. She was a mother sending her son off to battle, but also a wife waiting for her loved one to come home from the war.

"Mum, everything is going to be okay. Trust me."

Carole nodded and gulped at the same time, her eyes welling with tears.

"No-one knows you are here. I have someone monitoring the security cameras, and Will will keep watch all night. This is the safest place you can be."

"I'm not worried about my safety, John."

John grinned and placed his hands on his mother's shoulders. "Don't worry about mine, either." He winked and then pulled her closer and held her in a tight embrace, the grin fading from his face.

He kissed his mother on the top of her head, then released her and turned away before she could see the moisture in his eyes. He walked around to the front of the van, opened the door, and climbed in. As he started the engine, Will appeared beside the door and John lowered the window.

"I still think I should come with you."

John could have used Will as back up. The big man had proven himself, and apart from his irrational fear of enclosed spaces, John would have welcomed him in his corner. But he needed someone to watch over his mother and there was no-one else he knew or could trust.

"I need you here, Will. I can't leave her alone while this is happening. She needs company and protection."

"Yeah..." Will looked away for a moment, then when he looked back, his expression was troubled, "but you can't do this on your own."

John shrugged. "I've done worse." He reached for the seatbelt and clicked it in place. "The best thing you can do for me right now, Will, is keep my mother safe."

Will nodded slowly, then reached his hand through the window. John took it and tried not to flinch, but Will stopped just short of crushing John's hand. "Good luck, John. May God watch over you."

John gave a wry smile. "I don't know about God, but someone usually does."

The comment didn't seem to reassure Will, but he let go of John's hand and stepped away from the window.

John selected first gear, and just before releasing the hand brake, he turned once more to Will. "If I'm not back by sunrise, call the police."

Without waiting for a response, he released the clutch and pulled out of the parking space.

87

The sun had set about thirty minutes earlier and John sat listening to the early evening. The birds settling down for the night, insects squeaking and chirping, and the ticking of the van's engine as it cooled. He told himself he was waiting for his eyes to get used to the darkness, and to make sure he hadn't been followed, but he knew he was lying.

John's fingers tapped a nervous rhythm on the steering wheel. He was about to take on the private security force of a ruthless millionaire with no plan, no weapons, and no one to help him. There were so many things that could go wrong.

John thrust his chin forward and pulled his shoulders back. He had to stop the doom spiral of negativity before it overwhelmed him. This wasn't the first time he'd faced an arduous task, or been up against huge odds. He had always come out on top in the past, more often by luck rather than skill, but he had done it, and he could do it again.

He remembered Will's parting words. *May God be with you.* With so much evil in the world, the concept of God made little sense to John. But he would take help wherever he could get it, and if God, Allah, Shiva, Obi Wan, whatever you called him or her, was looking after him, he wouldn't turn it down.

He took a long slow breath, filling his lungs completely, then exhaled slowly, feeling the tension leaving his body. One thing was definite. Sitting in the van feeling sorry for himself wouldn't help anyone. He closed his eyes, took another deep breath, exhaled slowly again, then opened the door of the van and stepped out into the clearing.

He pushed the door until it closed with a soft click and then stood, extending his senses outwards. Satisfied he was still alone, he walked around the van and eased the rear door open. He removed the backpack and slipped it onto his shoulders, adjusting the straps until it was comfortable. The pry bar was strapped to one side and inside the pack was a collection of tools, each wrapped in cloth so they wouldn't make a noise as he moved around. He had also packed two flasks of strong coffee, a bottle of water, and some of Will's famous bacon sandwiches wrapped in foil.

He blackened his face once again with boot polish, then pulled on a head torch. In the side pockets of his black cargo pants were another flashlight, spare batteries, and a power bank for his phone. Finally, he inserted an earbud, pulled out his phone, and dialled Ramesh.

"Ready?"

"Ready."

"Good. I'll keep my location sharing on for as long as it works, but once I'm underground, I'll lose the signal."

"Got it. Nothing unusual on the cameras yet. All quiet at the motel, and nothing out of the ordinary at the house."

John nodded. "Okay. Any sign of my dad yet?"

"Not since they took him inside the stables."

John's frown deepened. He didn't know if that was a good sign or not, but there was only one way to find out. "And Xie is there?"

"I've not seen him leave."

"Okay, thanks Ramesh. I'm going silent now."

"Good luck."

John made sure the phone was set to silent and then slipped it into his pocket. He took a deep breath, eased the rear door of the van shut, turned around, and faced the Estate.

All or nothing.

88

"What do we do with him?"

"Let him go, Lorik. He's an old man," Admir muttered. "We should never have brought him here."

"It was Gerry's decision." Lorik replied under his breath, nodding toward the guard with the broken nose.

Admir didn't reply, his eyes on Gerry, who was leaning over David Hayes, his face just inches from the old man's. They couldn't hear what he was saying, but judging by his expression, it wasn't pleasant.

Admir had formed an instant dislike for the man from the first day he'd taken the job. He'd met men like him before, when he was in the Albanian Land Force. Bullies in uniform. But Admir needed the job, so he turned a blind eye to many things. Work was in short supply in Albania, and even if you found it, nothing paid as well as Xie. Even when his beloved dog was shot, he bit his tongue and continued on, reminding himself that his family needed him to stay.

The two men stiffened as the door opened, and the woman they called 'The Dragon' walked in and stopped just inside the doorway, flanked by the two Chinese bodyguards in suits. Admir had a nickname for them, too. Yin and Yang. They spoke only Chinese, didn't mix with the other men, sleeping and eating in the main house, and never seemed to take a break. For all he knew, there could even be four of them. The Chinese all looked the same to Admir.

He suddenly realised she was staring at him, and his breath caught in his throat. Could she read his mind? It was only when she turned her attention to the old man that he breathed out again.

The old man sat on a chair in the centre of the room, his arms and legs secured with duct tape. Gerry stood behind him, his shoulders rolled back, chest puffed out like a rooster, an arrogant twist to his mouth.

The Dragon's gaze moved from the old man and fixed on Gerry.

The sneer disappeared, and Admir saw him gulp.

"Well?" she spoke softly, not needing volume to assert her authority.

Gerry blinked rapidly, his eyes darting toward Admir and Lorik for support, then back at The Dragon. He cleared his throat. "He... he says he doesn't know where she is."

The Dragon's right eye twitched. After several uncomfortable moments, she returned her focus to David Hayes.

The old man stared back, his chin thrust out in defiance.

"Mr Hayes, things would have been much simpler if you and your wife had accepted our offer. Now..." The Dragon shrugged and made a gesture toward Gerry, but left the threat unsaid.

The old man's posture didn't change.

Admir admired the old man's courage, but it was futile. He should have sold the house when he had the chance.

What could an old man do against a rich and powerful man like Xie? Or a woman like The Dragon?

She frightened Admir, and it took a lot to scare him.

"I will never sell the house."

There was a slight quiver in the old man's voice, and Admir watched him clench his fists to hide the tremor in his hands.

"There is no house now. Only ashes."

"I will not sell it."

Admir noticed The Dragon's eye twitch again, and he himself flexed and unflexed his fingers. He had learnt her tells. The eye twitch wasn't good.

"It's only a matter of time before we find your wife." The Dragon looked up at Gerry, then over at Admir and Lorik. When she looked back at David Hayes, it was with a smile that sent a shiver down Admir's spine.

"When we do, it won't take my men here long to convince her that the benefits of selling far outweigh the alternative."

"We. Are. Not. Selling."

The eye twitched again; her smile vanished, and her face became a blank mask. Then, without a word, she turned on her heel and walked out of the room, followed closely by Yin and Yang.

Admir felt the tension in his body leave with her, and he exhaled slowly.

The defiant David Hayes had left too, leaving behind a frail old man slumped in a chair.

89

There it was again.

John stopped mid-stride, one foot half off the ground, and didn't move. Something was wrong. The hair on the back of his neck was standing up, and he knew from experience not to ignore it. Holding his breath, he waited, his ears straining for a sign, but there was nothing. Just the sound of his heart beating a little faster than normal, and the occasional muffled sound from the live call with Ramesh in his earbud.

Slowly and quietly, he sank to the ground and lay flat in the long grass between the edge of the ploughed field and the hedgerow.

Exhaling slowly, he continued waiting and listening. A cricket in the hedgerow, a distant car on the road, a dog somewhere on another farm. Something crawled along his lower leg, inside his cargo pants, something small with lots of legs. He resisted the urge to move and brush it away. After what seemed like an eternity, he was satisfied he was alone. The prickling sensation was still there on the back of his neck, but he couldn't hear anyone or anything around him.

"Ramesh," he murmured. "Can you hear me?"

"Yes," came the reply in his earbud.

"All okay?"

"All quiet. Nothing at the motel, and the security patrol has been back for five minutes."

"Okay." John lay still. What was troubling him? "Any sign of my father?"

"No. But I'm guessing he's still in the stables."

"Okay. Keep me posted." John took a deep breath and exhaled slowly. Perhaps he was just getting paranoid? He pushed himself slowly to his knees and looked around. There was enough ambient light from the moon for him to see across the field to his left as it rose gently away from the hedgerow before disappearing behind the rise. It was empty and nothing moved for as far as he could see. He slowly got to his feet, and then, keeping close to the hedgerow, continued onwards.

He was close to the woods where the tunnel came out and even though he could make it easily before the next patrol started their rounds, he preferred to err on the side of caution, moving slowly and keeping to whatever cover he could find.

Reaching the edge of the field, he turned left and moved along the boundary as it climbed slowly toward the east. He located the stile which provided access into the next field, and keeping as low as possible, climbed onto it, then rolled over the top bar before dropping into the field on the other side.

He felt the warning tingle on the back of his neck again and he froze in a crouch, slowly moving his head to survey his surroundings.

A large, dark shape moved in his peripheral vision and he shrank back against the wooden post of the stile.

His heart beat a rapid tattoo in his chest as the shape moved again.

Then it snorted.

A chuckle escaped John's lips. Now he knew what it was, he could make out the shape of a large animal. A cow, probably more frightened than John at the unexpected intruder in its territory.

John rose to his feet, adjusted the straps of his backpack, and moved on. Not far now.

90

John checked his watch. It had taken almost three quarters of an hour to get from the van to the tunnel entrance. Longer than he had wanted, but at least he hadn't been spotted.

"Ramesh, I'm going into the tunnel now," John whispered. "I'll lose the signal."

"All clear from my side, John. Good luck."

"Thanks, Ramesh. Wait for thirty minutes, then play the recorded security footage over their system."

"Will do."

John reached up and switched on his head torch, keeping the light on red, bent over, and entered the tunnel.

Having explored the tunnel the previous day, and knowing it was intact and where it led, made all the difference to John's confidence, and he moved quickly, stopping only to stretch his thighs and lower back. The tunnel builders had lacked John's height, and he had to maintain a half bent posture to avoid hitting his head on the bricks and stone that lined the tunnel roof.

The air was still musty, irritating his nostrils and making

his eyes water. He felt a sneeze building, and rubbed his nose with the back of his hand, but it made it worse. He stopped fighting it and sneezed; the sound echoing up and down the tunnel. He hoped no-one could hear him, but then he felt the tingle on the back of his neck again. He stood still, listening, but the tunnel remained silent.

Paranoia.

He shook his head, wiped his nose with the back of his hand, and continued on his way.

By the time he reached the end of the tunnel, his back ached and his thighs burned. He lowered himself to the ground and stretched his legs out in front of him, rocking them from side to side, until the muscles relaxed, then leaned forward to touch his toes and stretch out his back.

Slipping the backpack from his shoulders, he removed the flask of coffee, unscrewed the lid, blew on the top, and took a sip. It was still hot, and expecting a long night, he'd made it extra strong. He shifted his position so he could lean back against the tunnel wall while he allowed the restorative power of the coffee to take effect.

So far, everything had been easy. Now the real work began. Enter the house, find his father, and get him out without being caught.

The task seemed impossible, but John knew from experience to break it down and focus only on the step immediately in front of him.

John took one more mouthful of coffee, then returned the flask to the backpack and zipped it closed. Removing the pry bar from the side of the pack, he hefted it in his hands, then moved onto his knees and faced the exit door.

He had taken a photo the previous night and studied it back in the motel. The wooden door was in much better condition than the one at the entrance, with large iron hinges that stretched halfway across the door. There was no door-handle, but halfway down on the left side was a large keyhole. John did not know how to pick locks and, after studying the photo of the door, had concluded the only way through was by brute force. He just hoped no-one would hear him.

Shuffling closer, he put his ear to the keyhole and listened. The space beyond was silent and he could feel a cool damp breeze on his ear. That meant it wasn't bricked up. Turning his head, he put his eye to the keyhole and peered into the blackness beyond.

Nothing. It was pitch dark, giving no clue of what lay beyond.

It had to be an unused basement of the main house.

John moved back, then inserted the end of the pry bar between the door and the frame, just below the lock.

Taking a deep breath, he gripped the end of the bar with both hands and pushed. The bar flexed but didn't move.

"Shit." John muttered.

He tried again.

Nothing.

John wiggled the pry bar loose, then inserted the end above the lock, and tried again. This time he felt a slight movement... or thought he did. The door looked the same.

Moving to the side, he leaned back against the wall, raised his right leg and placed the sole of his boot against the bar, and pushed. The bar flexed, there was a protesting groan from the lock, but the door remained closed.

"Fuck it," John growled, then in frustration, pulled his foot back and kicked the end of the bar with the heel of his boot. The bar sprang loose and clattered onto the floor.

John grimaced. He had to be patient. Losing his temper

would only get him caught. *Had anyone heard that?* He moved forward and pressed his ear against the keyhole.

The door moved slightly.

John leaned back and studied the door frame. Had he imagined it?

He retrieved the pry bar from the floor, inserted it between the door and frame, and applied pressure. The door moved.

Not much, but it was something.

With renewed enthusiasm, John pushed and pulled the end of the pry bar, one way, then another. He could now see the edge of the door sitting proud of the frame, but it remained securely locked.

John moved the bar to below the lock again, wedged his back against the wall, and raising his boot, applied pressure with the heel against the bar. At first it didn't move, then there was the sound of metal against metal and he felt movement. He pushed again, and the lock protested, a metallic grinding noise, then the splintering of wood, and John lost his balance as the pry bar fell to the floor, the sound of metal on stone echoing through the tunnel.

John picked himself up and turned, the red glow from his head torch lighting up the half-open door and disappearing into the dark space beyond.

All frustration vanished, and John grinned. He was in.

He peered around the edge of the door into the large space beyond, the red light from his headlamp just enough for him to make out the details of the room. It must have been a storage cellar some time in the distant past, but now appeared to be unused. There were old crates piled along one wall and at the far end, a stone stairway led up to ground level.

John stowed the pry bar, slipped the backpack over his

shoulders, and tightened the straps. He pulled the door fully open, ducked his head, and stepped into the cellar.

He had taken three steps inside when a hand covered his mouth and an arm wrapped around his neck, cutting off his air supply and pulling him backwards.

91

Xie Longwei took a sip from the crystal snifter and allowed the warm amber liquid to coat his tastebuds. Closing his eyes, he tried to identify the flavours on his palate. Candied fruit... almonds... and maybe gingerbread? He sighed with something close to satisfaction.

His compatriots back in the motherland favoured Hennessy, the more expensive the better, but he felt he had a more discerning palate. Tonight's drink was a Chateaux Fontpinot XO from Cognac Frapin. He'd tasted it once while on a trip to France and enjoyed it so much he'd ordered a case. It wasn't cheap at a hundred and fifty euros a bottle, but what was money for if it couldn't be spent on the finer things in life?

Xie opened his eyes and stared at the flames dancing in the hearth. Despite the approach of summer, the old house remained cold and damp and it was only the excellent cognac, and a fire every evening that made the house tolerable.

Buying the Atwell Estate was a necessity and part of a

grand plan he had set in motion many years ago. So far, he had achieved everything he set his mind to, amassing wealth, influence, and power. There was just one thing left, and that was to legitimise his place in society. To the western world, he was a shady foreign businessman who made his fortune in the Third World. But an English manor house, especially one previously owned by a Lord, provided an air of respectability, and it was only a matter of time before they had to accept him as one of their own.

Unfortunately, there remained two lingering sources of irritation, but once they were resolved, everything would be perfect.

Xie turned his thoughts to Nkuru. African leaders were nearly all the same. Just one step out of the jungle—unsophisticated, perverted, and above all greedy. But unusually, in Tamba's case, greed wasn't a factor. Xie was convinced he had found the one lever that would make him sign—no full-blooded African leader wanted his people to know he preferred members of his own sex—but despite having his balls in a vice, Tamba continued to stall. Xie just couldn't understand why he hadn't signed the contract.

Xie frowned and took another sip of cognac. He held the liquid in his mouth, savouring the complex spirit before swallowing. He would have to increase the pressure, raise the threat level.

Which brought him to the other problem.

Atwell Estate was perfect, his own private kingdom, apart from one thing. Willow Cottage. It should never have been divided from the Estate all those years ago, and Xie was determined to get it back.

Xie shook his head. He really couldn't understand white people. He had made a generous offer, more than enough money for the stubborn old man to live what was left of his pathetic little life in luxury. But he had turned it down, and what did he have left? A pile of smoking ashes. He was an idiot.

A tap on the door disturbed his train of thought, and he turned to see Mingmei enter the room. He said nothing as she approached and stood beside the leather armchair on the other side of the fireplace.

Xie placed the glass of cognac on the armrest and arched an eyebrow.

"He doesn't know."

"He doesn't know," Xie repeated slowly, carefully enunciating each word, his eyes locked on hers. She didn't look away. "You need to find her."

"I know."

Xie studied her for a moment, then turned his attention to the fire. "Your first mistake was to bring him onto the Estate."

"That was Gerry..."

Xie stopped her with a raised hand. "I don't want to know the details. You have started us down a road from which there is no return."

He turned his head, stared at her for several moments, then looked back at the fire. "You need to find her, bring her here discretely, and then..." he turned to look at her with narrowed eyes, "make the problem go away, permanently."

Mingmei nodded, her face expressionless.

"Get Wang and Zhou to check all the motels, hotels, boarding houses. She's an old lady. She won't be far away."

"Yes." Mingmei dipped her head in acknowledgement.

Xie expected nothing less. She had undertaken similar tasks for him before. The lawyers were there to sort out the rest, close off the access, reclaim the property. With enough money, he could make all problems go away.

Another thought struck him. "The son." Xie frowned. "Where is he?"

Mingmei's right eye twitched, and Xie noticed.

"Well?"

"He is missing."

"He's also missing? I thought you were tracking his movements?"

Her eye twitched again. "We were. But he has... vanished."

"And when did you think it was the right time to tell me this?"

"I'm dealing with it."

Xie raised his cognac glass and stared into it. Suddenly, it didn't seem so delicious anymore. "Don't come back until you've found him," he growled.

92

Ramesh pushed away from the desk, sending his office chair rolling across the room. He swivelled as he reached the other side and picked up the polystyrene food container sitting on the bench-top, then pushed the chair back to his main terminals. With one eye on the screens, he opened the container and inhaled the fragrant steam. Ramesh had been in Dubai for the better part of ten years now, but he could not do without Indian food, in particular, Tamilian food. A lifelong vegetarian, he rarely ate anything else. Today it was mushroom biryani.

He took a spoonful of the flavoured rice, pushed the microphone on his headset out of the way, and smiled with contentment as he chewed.

His headphones had been quiet for some time, the call from John having cut out once he went underground. But there was nothing to warn him about. The Land Rover left on the hour every hour—you could almost set your watch by it—and the camera at the motel showed nothing out of the ordinary.

Ramesh switched his attention from the two screens

displaying the security camera feeds to one showing a multitude of graphs and charts. He moved closer as he took another mouthful of biryani, narrowing his eyes to study the constantly changing figures on the screen. Placing the biryani on the bench top, he reached for the keyboard and started tapping away. The yen was up ten pips against the dollar, giving him a tidy profit. Time to close out the trade.

He finished entering the commands and reached for the food again, his smug grin reflected on the monitor. It had been a profitable day.

A movement on the other monitor caught his eye, and he glanced over. Two men in suits were descending the steps from the main house. With his free hand, Ramesh moved the mouse and zoomed in on their faces. Even in the poor light, he could see it was the two Chinese bodyguards. He watched them walk over toward the parked Range Rover and climb inside. Ramesh waited to see if anyone else came from the house to join them, but when the car's lights turned on and it pulled away from the house to head down the driveway, he shrugged and picked up his biryani and resumed eating.

Biryani was always best when it was hot.

93

John struggled to get free, but the arm around his neck tightened. He kicked back with his right heel, heard a grunt, but then was pulled off balance. A boot kicked his legs out from under him, the hand releasing its hold on his mouth, and he was forced to the ground. A knee pressed with the full weight of his captor into the middle of his back, making it hard to breathe. With difficulty, he turned his face to the side; the movement knocking the headlamp from his head onto the floor. John could see nothing but a pair of black combat boots. A gloved hand pressed his face into the cold stone floor, and he felt a warm breath on his face.

"Quiet," a voice hissed in his ear. "I'm not here to hurt you. If you promise not to struggle, I'll let you go."

John saw another set of boots move closer. That's two sets of boots, plus the guy on his back. At least three men. *Fuck! Things had been going so well.*

"Do you promise to be quiet?" the voice asked again.

"Yes," John hissed. There was little point in struggling.

He was clearly outnumbered, but at the same time, he didn't want to be a pushover. "Get off me," he growled.

The gloved hand left his face, and the weight shifted from his back. He felt two pairs of hands lift him easily from the floor to his feet and then turn and push him back, gently this time, until his back was against the wall.

John's brain struggled to identify what was standing in front of him. He'd heard a human's voice, but this was something else. It stood a head taller than him and pressed him against the wall with one strong hand. Instead of a face, small round eyes protruded from its head on the end of two cylinders, and in the dim red light from his fallen head lamp, it looked like some kind of alien insect.

John gave his head a quick shake, as if doing so would clear his thoughts and change the vision in front of him.

Then the creature released its hold on his shoulder and, with the same hand, flicked the eyes upwards, away from its face.

Night vision goggles.

"I'm guessing you are John Hayes."

The voice was deep, with an accent. John had heard it before, but his brain was still muddled.

He didn't reply, instead looking over the man's shoulder. There were two more men, both large and dressed in what he now recognised as black tactical clothing. They too removed their NVGs and one bent down, picked up the headlamp from the floor, and passed it to John.

John held it in his hand, directing the red light onto his captor's face. It was hidden behind a balaclava, but he could see dark skin around slightly bloodshot eyes.

Then he remembered where he'd heard the voice before. "Joseph Tamba."

The big man chuckled, the sound coming in a low rumble.

"I see everything I've heard about you is true, John."

"What do you mean?" Even though he'd guessed correctly, John was still confused. What was Joseph Tamba doing here?

"I made some enquiries, after you called. I was told you are a determined, resourceful man, one who doesn't give up."

"Who told you that?"

Joseph chuckled again. "A mutual friend in Hong Kong." He turned and gestured to the two men behind him. "Moses and Junior."

John's frown deepened as he looked over Joseph's shoulder. One man stepped forward and offered a gloved hand. "Moses."

John shook it, returning the greeting. "John."

Moses gestured to the third man and grinned. "Junior doesn't speak much. He's shy."

Junior raised a hand and nodded. Joseph and Moses were both over six feet tall and well built, but Junior made the two men look short and thin. John couldn't imagine how he'd made it through the tunnel.

He turned to look at Joseph. "How the hell did you find me?"

94

"We spotted you crossing the fields."

"Oh." That explained the tingling on the back of his neck, but he still had so many questions. "But..."

"Why are we here?" Joseph removed his balaclava and tucked it into his tactical vest. His skin was as dark as the balaclava he'd worn, with high cheekbones and hair cropped close to his skull. He looked younger than he sounded, and when he grinned he flashed perfect white teeth, looking more like a Ralph Lauren model than an army officer. "I couldn't let you have all the fun, could I?"

His grin faded, and he glanced over at Moses. "But seriously, we've had enough of our country being exploited. First the Europeans, and now the Chinese. My father wants what's best for his people. He doesn't need..." he jerked his head toward the house above them, "Xie telling him what to do so he can loot the country."

John nodded slowly, his brows still knitted together. "So why now? Your father could have said no to him before."

"He did, but..." Joseph bowed his head, "my father is not perfect. He..."

John reached out a hand and placed it on Joseph's arm. "I know. It's okay. We all have our demons."

Joseph nodded once, but wouldn't meet John's eye.

"So, you decided to do something about it. Put an end to the blackmail."

"Yes." Joseph took a deep breath and raised his head. He studied John's face before continuing. "When you called, it got me thinking. I did my research, took a gamble you might do something soon, and thought I should take advantage if an opportunity presented itself. We were doing a recce when we spotted you."

John nodded slowly. "And you came in through the tunnel behind me?" His eyes flicked toward Junior.

The grin reappeared on Joseph's face. "Don't let Junior's size fool you. He moves like a cat."

John glanced again at Junior, who was suddenly finding the floor very interesting.

"Moses and Junior are here at my father's request. To ensure my safety while I'm here in this dangerous country." Joseph winked.

"Safety? Aren't you at Sandhurst?"

"My father worries a lot." Joseph shrugged. "But anyway, after tonight, I won't be returning."

"Why?" John asked with raised eyebrows.

Joseph exchanged a look with Moses. "We have a plan. We're going to make sure Xie won't be a problem for my father anymore." Looking back at John, his expression turned serious. "Or you."

John studied his face for a moment, then looked down at the weapon hanging on Joseph's sling. He wasn't an expert, and it was dark, but it looked like they were carrying MP-5s.

"Okay, but as much as I want to get rid of Xie, a shootout on his estate was not what I had in mind."

"Nor us." Joseph patted the weapon. "These are more for... how do I say it... persuasion?"

John exhaled with relief. "Good, because right now he's holding my father hostage."

"Really?" Joseph frowned, turned and muttered something in a language John had never heard before. Moses replied, and then there was a brief discussion between the two men. Finally, Junior spoke for the first time, just three words, but the two men nodded agreement.

Joseph turned back to John. "We'll help you, John. We'll ensure your father is safe."

John nodded, then looked at each man in turn. "Thank you."

"Now maybe you can brief us on what's waiting upstairs."

95

John spent the next few minutes explaining the layout of the house and the Estate, as well as the number of men to expect.

"There are two Chinese bodyguards who spend most of their time near Xie. I expect them to be in the main house. The rest of the security is either in the stable block or patrolling the Estate."

"We spotted them. Two men in a Land Rover. There's one at the main gate too. Sloppy, not well trained."

John hoped Joseph was right. "But they're armed. I've seen handguns."

Joseph shrugged. "We'll deal with that as we come to it. So we have at least two in the house, three outside in the Estate..."

"And three more, I think. Either resting or in the stables. I've only ever seen six on the cameras."

Joseph looked up. "Cameras?"

"I... we hacked into the security system. I've been watching the camera feeds."

Joseph said something in his language again, and his two companions smiled.

Moses spoke up, "Can you shut the cameras down?"

"There's no need... we've recorded a loop which," John turned his wrist and looked at his watch, "should be playing on their system instead of the live feed."

All three men chuckled this time.

"You said we?" Joseph asked.

"My computer guy. Don't worry, I trust him with my life."

"Ok," Joseph removed the balaclava from his vest and shook it out. "John, I know you'll want to get to your father as soon as possible, but we'll clear the house first and secure Xie. Without the boss, his men won't know what to do. After that, we'll find your father."

John nodded reluctantly. He didn't like to leave his father there any longer than necessary, but Joseph made sense.

Joseph removed a handgun from his side holster and held it out butt first to John. "Do you know how to use one of these?"

John took it and held it closer to the light. A Glock 17. He popped the magazine and checked it was full, then pulled the slide back and ensured the chamber was clear. Satisfied the weapon was safe, he re-seated the magazine.

"I guess you do." Joseph smiled. "But try not to use it. Our MP-5s are suppressed. That isn't."

96

Junior led the way up the steps, stopping two short of the door, his head already touching the roof of the basement. Moses was immediately behind him, followed by Joseph and John.

The door was a larger version of the one at the entrance to the tunnel. Solid wood with large iron hinges and a sturdy lock. Junior whispered something, which Joseph translated. "He thinks he can pick the lock."

"Wait," John whispered in reply, and passed forward the can of WD40. Junior examined it for a second, then sprayed it liberally on the hinges and into the lock. He then removed a small bundle from his vest, unfolded it, and removed several tools. He swung his weapon behind him, knelt on the top step, and fiddled with the lock for several moments. There was a click, which sounded way too loud in the confined space, and they froze. They listened and waited, and then, when satisfied no-one had heard them, Junior eased the door open. A thin bar of light from between the door and the frame lit up the steps.

John reached up and turned off his headlamp as Junior

got to his feet, stowed his lock picking kit, and raised his weapon to his shoulder. He glanced back, checked everyone was ready, then, with his left hand, opened the door and stepped through. Moses followed immediately after and a moment later John heard a whispered, "Clear."

John followed Joseph up the steps into a storeroom lit by moonlight from a small window set high in the wall. Sacks of rice were stacked against one wall and shelves stocked with cans, vegetables, and jars of preserves lined the other. Moses crouched with his ear to the door at the other side of the room, a hand held up in caution. The hand changed to a thumbs up, and the two men stood, Moses easing the door open and Junior slipping through. Moses followed, then Joseph and John.

They had entered an empty kitchen, but concealed lighting beneath the overhead cupboards lit up a pot simmering on the stove.

John walked over and lifted the pot lid. "It's some sort of Chinese stew," he whispered. "Which means Xie is here. One sec..."

John pulled out his phone, checked for a signal, then dialled Ramesh.

He answered immediately, "All okay?"

"I'm in the house. All clear?" John whispered.

"The two Chinese guys left in the Range Rover about half an hour ago, but apart from that, I've seen nothing out of the ordinary. I'm playing the recorded footage on their system."

"Do you know how many are in the house?"

"I can't tell from here, but I've not seen Xie leave, just the bodyguards."

"Good, I'm leaving the line open. Keep me posted." John moved closer to Joseph and his men. "The Chinese bodyguards aren't here. There may be others in the house... I don't know. But I say, let's make the most of it and go now."

"Agree." Joseph replied and the other two men nodded.

John heard Ramesh's voice in his ear. "There's someone else with you?"

John held up his finger, indicating that Joseph should wait, then turned slightly to show he wasn't talking to them. "Yes, it's a long story, but I have three men with me. All in black and armed, in case you see them on the camera."

"Oh. Okay. Understood. I want details later, though."

"Yup." John turned back to Joseph and gave a thumbs up. "Let's go."

97

Moses and Junior moved out of the kitchen into the service corridor, one turning left, the other right, and John followed closely after. He immediately ran into the back of Junior, who was pointing his weapon at a frightened looking Chinese man in a white chef's jacket and checkered pants. John stepped around Junior, held his finger to his lips, and gestured to the cook to kneel. The cook was confused at first, his eyes darting from John to Junior and back again, before kneeling down and placing his hands behind his head. John stepped behind him, shrugged off his backpack, and removed a roll of duct tape and some cable ties. He first secured the man's wrists behind his back, then whispered in his ear. "Do you speak English?"

The cook nodded.

"Who else is in the house?"

The cook hesitated and Junior stepped closer, the barrel of his weapon just inches from the cook's face. The man trembled, and he started babbling in Mandarin. John wrapped his arm around the cook's neck, putting him in a sleeper hold, and began applying pressure. He growled into the man's ear. "I told you to be quiet. Do you want to stay alive?"

The cook nodded, and John eased off the pressure on his neck.

"How many people are in the house?"

"W...w... wu."

John tightened the neck hold and growled, "English."

"F... five. Five."

"Including you?"

The cook nodded.

"Who and where?"

"Two maids upstairs, one guard in the corridor, and..."

John encouraged him to continue with another squeeze on his neck.

"Mr Xie."

"Where is he?"

"He was working, but I called him to the dining room for dinner."

"The Chinese woman?"

"In her office."

"In the stables?"

The cook nodded eagerly, perhaps hoping that if he helped John, he wouldn't be harmed.

"Good." John let go of the cook, then wrapped a strip of duct tape around his head, covering his mouth. The cook gave no protest, still staring wide eyed at the barrel of Junior's MP-5. John looped an arm through the cook's, pulled him to his feet, then pushed him past Junior and Joseph and into the kitchen. Once there, he pushed him to the floor and cable tied his ankles together.

"Keep quiet and stay here," John growled as sternly as he

could. The cook nodded, a large wet patch spreading across the front of his pants.

Back out in the corridor, John paused to look at the photo of the floor plan he'd saved on his phone. "This way."

The service corridor was narrow, the floor grimy, the walls battered from centuries of use. The money Xie had spent on renovation obviously hadn't touched the service areas. John stopped outside a door. If the plan was correct, the door led directly into the dining room in the owner's part of the house.

John pointed at the door and whispered, "The dining room. Xie is in here."

Moses eased him aside, held three fingers up, gave a visual countdown to one, then opened the door. Junior moved through the doorway and a moment later muttered, "Clear."

A long, highly polished wooden table filled most of the wood panelled room. At the far end, facing the floor to ceiling windows that overlooked the grounds, was a place setting for one. The cook had told the truth, but there was no sign of Xie.

John pointed to a door at the end of the room. "That way."

Moses eased the door open, and Junior peered through the gap. He held one arm out with the thumb pointed down.

John had seen enough war films to know what that meant. Enemy.

Junior stepped back from the door, unclipped his MP-5 from its sling, and handed it to Joseph. From his belt he removed a wicked-looking commando knife, the blade flashing in the light from the dining room chandelier.

John was about to protest, but before he could, Junior had gone. John moved closer and shifted position so he could see through the partially open door and down the hallway.

Diagonally opposite, outside a closed door, a heavily built man leaned against the door frame, with his back to them. He held a cell phone in his hand and, judging by the flickering light from the screen, was watching a video.

Junior moved swiftly down the corridor toward him, silent and graceful like a cat, his soft soled combat boots soundless on the stone floor.

There was a grunt, and the cell phone fell to the floor as the guard struggled to get free. The knife blade pressed against his throat didn't seem to deter him, but when Junior turned him and he saw Moses advancing with his MP-5 pointed at his head, all the fight went out of him.

John immediately taped the guard's mouth shut while Junior held him still, then secured his wrists and ankles with cable ties.

Junior pushed the guard onto the floor, and John crouched beside him. Searching him, he removed a Glock from the guard's shoulder holster, then pointed toward the door. "Xie?"

The guard's eyes moved from John to the armed men behind him, then, deciding he wasn't paid enough, nodded.

98

Xie rose to his feet and shuffled closer to the fire. Pulling a poker iron from the rack on the side of the hearth, he jabbed at the burning logs, sending sparks and then flames into the air. He shoved the poker back into the rack and held his hands toward the heat. Was he getting soft? When he'd been a child in Shanxi, it had been much colder than this. All the time he'd spent in Africa must have thinned out his blood. As soon as the deal with Tamba was signed, he would take a trip to Nkuru. Get some warmth back in his veins.

Reaching back for his cognac, he took a sip while staring into the flames. The conversation with Mingmei had irritated him. Even the cognac had lost its taste. Damn her for spoiling his mood.

He heard the door open, and he clenched his jaw, tightening his grip on the glass. "I told you to knock, you Russian oaf," he snarled.

Turning to glare at the guard, he froze as two black-clad figures entered the room. He was about to shout for his guards, then remembered they'd been sent out to find the old woman. The glass in his hand shook as a mixture of fear and indignation coursed through his body.

Who would dare to enter his house like this?

Anger won the battle with fear and he brought his other hand up to steady the glass, narrowed his eyes, and watched the two men move silently to opposite sides of the room. Which of his enemies would have the balls to stand up against him? Balaclavas masked their faces, so he studied their equipment, trying to find clues. Black tactical webbing, no insignia, MP-5s. *The British SAS? Did they still use MP-5s? What had he done to the British?*

Two more men entered the room, the first dressed like the others, but the second man looked different. He was smaller than the others and had no tactical gear, just dark clothing. He held a firearm in one hand and his face was smeared with black paint. But there was something familiar about him.

"Xie," the man snarled.

His name on the other man's lips sounded like a curse.

"Who are you, and what are you doing in my house?"

The man walked over, prised the glass from his hands and tossed it into the fireplace. Xie flinched as the glass shattered and the cognac exploded in a ball of flame singeing the back of his neck. Before he had time to recover, he felt a stinging blow to the side of his face, knocking him sideways. He lost his balance, bounced off the side of the armchair, and fell to the floor. Stunned, he lay with his face in the carpet, eyes watering from the blow.

Who...? What...?

Then a hand grabbed the hair on the back of his head, yanking it backwards, and he felt the hot breath of his attacker in his ear. "That's for burning down my parent's house, you fucking bastard."

The son.

99

John pressed down on Xie's head as he stood up, forcing his face into the carpet. He stepped away, then paused, before turning around and looking back down at the pathetic, overweight, balding little man who had ruined his parents' life. His lip curled.

"Fuck you," he cursed, pulled his boot back and kicked Xie in the groin.

Xie shrieked, then curled into a ball, and began to sob.

John was about to kick him again, then with an extreme force of will, stopped himself. There was something more important to do.

"He's all yours. I'm going to find my dad."

Joseph nodded. "Moses, you know what to do. Junior, come with me and John."

John crossed the room, stopped in the doorway, and looked back. Moses was wrapping Xie's head in duct tape, leaving only a small hole for his nostrils. He then removed a black cloth from his load vest. He bent down and pulled the black cloth, a hood, over Xie's head, cinching it tight around his neck. John exchanged a look with Joseph, opened his mouth to say something, then decided against it. "Let's find my dad."

Junior led the way into the hallway, and John glanced down at the guard who had manoeuvred himself to sit with his back against the wall, his legs stretched out in front of him.

"What do you want to do with him?" Joseph asked.

John frowned. "I don't know." His only thought had been for his father's safety, but now there were too many other decisions. He hesitated a moment longer, then said, "Leave him. He can't go anywhere." *Father first, others later.* Then he remembered something. "Shit, we forgot the maids upstairs."

Joseph stepped back into the room and said something in his language before stepping out again. "Moses will deal with it."

John hesitated again and Joseph continued, "Don't worry, he won't hurt them."

John nodded. He couldn't worry about everyone else while his father was a prisoner. "Okay, follow me."

He led the way down the hall toward the rear of the house, passing large, luxuriously furnished rooms on each side. Using his memory of the floor plan, John located another door that led into the service area corridors. He paused with his ear pressed to the door. After a moment, unable to hear anything, he eased the door open, and leading with his Glock, stepped into the corridor, turning left, Joseph immediately behind him turning right. The corridor was empty.

"This way." John led the way along the corridor, then turned right into another short hallway that ended in a mudroom. Jackets and hats hung on hooks on both sides, and boots and shoes were lined up neatly along the wall. At the end, a door led to the outside.

"About eighty metres in that direction," John pointed at a forty-five degree angle to the door, "is the stable block. Between here and there is the parking lot."

"Any cover?"

John shook his head. "Nothing. It's open ground from the house to the stables."

Joseph shook his head slowly and glanced back at Junior. John watched as the two men looked at each other as if communicating telepathically. Junior shrugged, his shoulders brushing against the coats hanging on the hooks.

The movement gave John an idea.

He pulled a waxed Barbour jacket off the hook and held it up, checking the size. "Here," he tossed it to Joseph, who caught it in mid-air. "Put this on over your gear. The guards all dress like this... and remove your balaclava." John turned back to the hooks and grabbed a tweed Stornoway cap. "Stick that on too."

He looked at Junior, sizing him up, then searched through the coats, finding the largest one and tossing it to Junior. "That's the biggest one."

Junior held it up, the coat looking like a child's jacket in his hands, and shook his head.

"No," John agreed. "Okay. Joseph and I will lead. You follow afterwards once we've cleared the way."

Junior nodded, and John selected a jacket for himself, pulling it on over his dark clothing, and adding a flat cap to complete the look. He held the Glock with his right hand in the jacket pocket, then reached for the door handle with his left. Looking over his shoulder, he asked, "Ready?"

Joseph nodded and followed his nod with a broad grin. He appeared confident and relaxed, as if they weren't in any danger.

Feeling much less confident, John took a deep breath, then opened the door.

100

Ramesh leaned back in his chair, interlaced his fingers and stretched his arms over his head, hearing the satisfying pop and click of his vertebrae. It had been a long day... a long couple of days... with little sleep. But John depended on him and he wasn't going to let him down because he was feeling tired.

Ramesh admired John. He did things he couldn't imagine doing himself. Ramesh wasn't physically strong... wasn't brave... avoided direct confrontation where possible, and felt uncomfortable out in the real world. But here in the darkness, in front of his monitors, things were different. Here, he was confident, highly skilled... brave even. He was a version of John Hayes that he could never be in the physical world.

Ramesh shrugged. There was a role for everyone in the world, and this one happened to be his.

His eyes roamed the screens, but there wasn't much happening. He couldn't see John, but could hear him occasionally in his earpiece.

Who were the men with him and where had they come

from? They spoke perfect, if slightly accented, English, but their pronunciation was too good to be Englishmen.

Ramesh grinned.

The English spoke the worst of all nowadays, with their slang, dropped 't's and lazy pronunciation. The men with John spoke the "Queen's English" of a well educated Indian, but the names he had heard suggested otherwise.

Joseph, Moses.

Most likely African.

But if they were African, who were they, and why were they helping John?

A movement on the screen interrupted his thoughts, and he sat forward and with the mouse zoomed in on the camera feed from the rear of the house. Two men dressed like farmers stepped out of the back door. Judging by what he'd just heard in his earpiece, it had to be John and the other guy... what was his name...? Joseph. Ramesh zoomed in on Joseph and smiled. He had guessed right. African. Zooming out again, to give him a wide view of the area behind the house, he watched them walk casually across the gravel area toward the stables.

Another movement in the corner of his eye caught his attention, and he dragged his eyes away to view the monitor showing the security feed from the motel.

A dark Range Rover had pulled into the forecourt. It parked and the two front doors opened almost simultaneously. He frowned and zoomed in.

"Shit!"

He heard John's voice in his ear. "What is it, Ramesh?"

"Nothing, nothing," Ramesh replied hurriedly and muted his microphone. John had enough to worry about already. Ramesh picked up another phone and dialled Will, his eyes still on the screen as he waited for him to pick up.

The two men walked from the Range Rover toward the motel reception.

"Come on, pick up, pick up," he muttered, his fingers tapping a nervous rhythm on the desktop.

"Hello?"

"Will, it's Ramesh. Get out of there now. Xie's bodyguards have found you."

"Shit!"

"Yeah, they've just entered the office."

"Ok."

The line went dead and Ramesh slid the phone onto the desktop, his eyes glued to the screen. There were two feeds. One from a camera in the reception, and the other on the forecourt. In the reception, one bodyguard stood by the door while the other spoke to the receptionist. On the outside feed he saw the door to one of the motel rooms open, and a man, presumably Will, peered out before stepping outside. He was followed by someone wrapped in what looked like a bedcover. The gait, posture, and size suggested it was an elderly woman.

John's mother.

They moved slowly away from the room—too slowly—and he urged them on, "Hurry up, hurry up."

At that moment, a voice in his ear caught his attention.

101

Will ended the call and moved the net curtain aside just enough to see out. He spotted the black Range Rover parked four spaces down from his Pajero and saw the door to the reception closing behind someone.

"We have to go."

"What's the matter?"

Will turned back to look at the tiny, frail old lady sitting in the armchair, the light from the television flickering across her face.

Will had to protect her. "They've found us." Crossing the room, he grabbed his jacket and pulled it on. He took the bedspread, helped Carole to her feet, and wrapped it around her shoulders.

"Who's found us?"

"The bad guys, come on, we have to get out of here."

Will turned off the television, guided her to the door, then stepped in front, opened the door a crack and peered out. The coast was clear. He stepped outside, grabbed Carole by the arm, and pulled her out. She stumbled, and he moved to support her, but she didn't complain.

With another glance toward the reception, he led her to the Pajero and helped her into the passenger seat, then hurried around to the driver's side. As he slipped into the seat and pulled the door shut, he saw the door to the reception open and someone step out.

"Shit," he cursed, then remembered who was beside him. "Sorry." What should he do? If he drove off, they would see him. He was about to curse again when he got an idea.

"Sorry about this," he said as he reached across Carole, fumbled for the recline lever and dropped the seat back until Carole was lying flat on her back. He did the same with his own and whispered, "Don't say a word."

She didn't reply, and he looked over to make sure she had heard. Her lips trembled as she stared wide eyed up at the roof of the Pajero.

"It will be okay," he whispered, more to reassure himself than her.

Turning back, he raised his head just enough to see over the dashboard. The two men were outside John's room. Will ducked down, waited for a moment, and then raised his head again. The men were gone, but the door was open.

"W... what's happening?" Carole whispered.

"They're in the room."

Shifting his weight to the left, he removed the phone from his pocket and, keeping the screen angled down to hide the light, sent a text to Ramesh. *Where are they?*

A moment later, the phone buzzed with a reply. *In the room. Stay where you are.*

Will lay back on the seat, his heart racing, and he took several slow breaths to calm himself. He hated being caged in the car like this, but hadn't been able to think of an alternative plan in the little time he had. Carefully, so as not to rock the vehicle, he searched his pockets for the keys, then inserted the key in the ignition. At least if they had to make a quick getaway, he would be ready.

He risked taking another peek over the dashboard, but there was still no sign of the men, and the door remained open. Will checked the phone. No new message. He scrolled to the call log. Ramesh had called only five minutes earlier. Five minutes? It felt like they had been in the car for much longer.

As if hearing his thoughts, Carole whispered, "Are they still in there?"

"I think so. Ramesh will tell me when it's safe."

"What if they check your car?"

Will had been thinking about that. He reached up and pressed the central locking button on the door. The sound of the doors locking seemed ten times louder than usual, and he held his breath, hoping the sound had gone unnoticed.

His phone buzzed again. *They're coming out.*

Will tensed, expecting at any moment to be discovered. What would he do? Start the car and reverse out of the parking as quickly as possible? The Pajero couldn't possibly outrun the Range Rover, but if he drove into the city, toward the nearest police station, perhaps that would dissuade his pursuers from doing anything?

The phone buzzed again. *They're walking towards their car.*

Will exhaled and slowly raised his head. One of the men tossed John's laptop and a roll of plans onto the back seat of the Range Rover and climbed in. The headlights came on and as the vehicle backed out of the carpark, the headlights swept over the Pajero. Will ducked down and heard the deep rumble of the powerful Range Rover V8 as it rolled past. Sitting up, he looked over his shoulder at the red taillights disappearing up the road. They were safe.

"Can I get some help here?"

Will turned back to see Carole struggling to sit upright. "I'm sorry."

He jumped out of the vehicle and ran around to her side, opened the door and brought her seat upright. "It's okay, they've gone. We're safe."

"And John? My husband?"

Will looked back up the road. He fumbled for his phone and called Ramesh. Turning away from the car so Carole couldn't hear, he spoke as soon as Ramesh answered, "They took his laptop and plans."

"I saw."

Will heard Ramesh typing and muttering something.

"Is everything okay? Is John in danger?"

"It's okay, Will. I'm monitoring everything. John is safe."

"But they'll find his escape route."

"Don't worry, I'll warn him, but... he has some help there."

Will frowned. "Help?"

"I'll explain later. Just keep his mum safe. Got to go."

The phone went dead.

Something was going on, Will was sure of it, but what could he do? He'd promised to look after John's mother, and that's what he must do. He took a breath, relaxed his face, and turned back to the Pajero.

Carole Hayes was out of the vehicle, standing with her hands on her hips, oblivious to the cold.

Will smiled. "Ramesh said John's okay. We should wait until he comes back."

She thrust her chin forward. "Don't lie to me, young man."

The smile slipped from Will's face as he looked down at the woman, twice his age and half his size.

"I have a feeling he's in trouble."

"No, no—" Will protested, but Carole cut him off.

"He needs our help, Will."

Will opened his mouth to say something, but stopped when she held out her hand.

"Give me your keys."

"Keys?"

"Well, I'm not sitting around here, young man. You can either drive me, or I'll take the car myself. That's my son out there."

Will hesitated, scratched his head, then nodded. "Okay, but I'm driving."

Carole smiled. "Good. Because it's been twenty years since I last sat behind the wheel."

102

John and Joseph were halfway across the parking area when a door opened in the stable block, a shaft of light spilling out across the gravel. A man stepped out, an unlit cigarette in his mouth. He cupped his hands around his mouth, lit the cigarette with a lighter, then took a long puff, tilting his head upwards as he exhaled a plume of smoke. It was only then that he noticed John and Joseph walking towards him.

He took another puff while he watched them approach and John pulled the peak of his cap lower, keeping his face in shadow.

"Who are you?"

John kept walking, his head angled downwards. "We're the new guys." He remembered the name of the security company he'd seen on the alarm box. "From CSS. Mr. Xie asked for more men."

"Huh." The man coughed, a rasping smoker's cough. "No-one tells us anything."

John was just a few metres away now, and he pulled his right hand from his jacket pocket.

The guard, preparing to shake hands, transferred the cigarette to his left, and held out his right, then stared wide eyed at the Glock in John's hand.

Joseph stepped past John, grabbed the man by the front of his jacket and pushed him back against the wall with one hand, covering his mouth with the other.

The guard flinched as John jammed the barrel of the Glock into his temple, and a whimper escaped from behind Joseph's gloved hand.

"Not a sound. Do you understand?"

The man nodded, his eyes wide and darting around in panic.

"We don't want to hurt you, but I won't hesitate to put a bullet through your head if you try anything."

The man nodded again.

"Good." With his left hand, John felt inside the man's jacket and removed a handgun from his shoulder holster, slipping it into his jacket pocket. "Any other weapons?"

The man shook his head.

John reached down into the side pocket of his cargo pants, removed a bundle of cable ties, and passed them to Joseph. Joseph turned the man with ease, pinning his face into the stone wall of the stable block, and quickly secured the man's wrists together. He did the same with his ankles. John stepped closer and pressed the muzzle into the man's temple again.

"Don't kill me, please. I have a wife and kids."

John leaned in and growled in the man's ear. "Then if you want to see them again, you know what to do. How many of you inside?"

"Three."

"Including the Chinese woman?"

He nodded.

"And where's the prisoner? The old man?"

"Th... th... that's nothing to do with me. I told them not to take him."

John passed harder with the gun barrel. "Where is he?"

"The room at the end."

John heard the rattle of an old diesel engine approaching, and his heart skipped a beat.

Shit!

He'd forgotten the patrol.

103

The Land Rover pulled into the parking lot, its tyres crunching on the gravel, the headlights sweeping across the stable block and stopping on John, Joseph, and the security guard.

Before John could think, Joseph had spun around, swinging the MP-5 from underneath his jacket to his shoulder. The suppressed weapon coughed twice, there was the tinkle of breaking glass, and the headlights went out.

"Help!" the guard cried out and John pushed him back against the wall with his hand around the man's throat. "Quiet," he snarled, then reversed the Glock in his hand, and brought the butt down on the guard's temple. His eyes rolled back and his legs gave way. John stepped back, pushed him to the ground, then turned back to deal with the Land Rover.

Joseph had already moved sideways, away from John, and was advancing toward the Land Rover, weapon at his shoulder.

The engine revved, and John heard the clunk of the ageing gearbox as the driver selected reverse. The rear

The Neighbor

wheels spun in the gravel and the Land Rover leaped backwards.

Joseph's weapon coughed again, a double tap, and the rear tyre burst. He continued firing as he advanced, sparks flying off the front wheel, followed by a hiss of air as the tyre exploded.

John moved right, his Glock held in both hands, pointed at the windscreen. He didn't want to fire unless absolutely necessary.

The vehicle continued to move backwards, but slower, the wheel rims grinding on the gravel underneath, the engine revving in protest.

John heard the cough of a suppressed MP-5 again, but this time, the muzzle flash was on the other side of the vehicle, as Junior advanced from the other side.

There were repeated clangs and pings, then the pop of tyres and the Land Rover ground to a halt.

John advanced toward the stationary vehicle, still aiming at the driver's side of the windscreen, as Joseph and Junior approached the doors. Both doors opened, and the driver and passenger thrust their raised hands through the gaps.

John jogged forward and pulled the door fully open while Joseph stood back, covering the driver.

"Get out," John growled, reaching in with his left hand and grabbing hold of the driver's jacket. He was half out the door when there was a gunshot and an explosion of sparks as a bullet ricocheted off the door frame beside John's head. Instinctively, he dropped to the ground, pulling the driver with him as bullets pinged and thudded around him.

"Get behind the vehicle," Joseph yelled as he dropped to one knee and returned fire.

John rose to a crouch and, pulling the driver with him, scrambled around to the opposite side. The other guard already lay flat in the gravel, his arms covering his head while Junior rested his elbows on the hood, his MP-5 firing rapidly, bullet casings raining down on the windscreen and bouncing off the hood. Joseph too had moved back, and was using the rear of the Land Rover as cover.

John peered underneath the chassis and saw two guards retreating inside the stable block, pulling the door closed behind them.

The firing stopped, and John heard clicks as Joseph and Junior inserted fresh magazines.

There was a voice in John's ear.

Ramesh.

"John, are you okay?"

"Y... y... yeah, I think so," he panted as he took stock. His hands trembled with adrenaline, there was a persistent ringing in his ears and his heart was pounding in his chest. But he wasn't injured.

"Shit," he said, more for himself than anyone else.

Over at the stable block, the first guard was crying, "don't leave me here. Somebody help me."

Joseph fired two rounds into the wall above his head, the brickwork splintering and showering the man with fragments. The guard shrieked, then went quiet. John could see him pressing himself into the base of the wall, trying to appear as small as possible.

Joseph looked over. "Okay, my friend?"

"Yeah. You?"

"All good. We need to move fast, John. Someone will have heard the gunfire."

John grimaced. So much for the element of surprise. He heard Ramesh speaking, and he pressed the earbud deeper into his ear to try to counteract the tinnitus.

"I'll shut down the internet, and the main phone line,

but I don't know about the cell phones. I'll see what I can do. Give me a sec."

"Okay," John looked over at Joseph, "My guy is trying to shut off the phones, but no guarantees."

Joseph nodded and said something to Junior, the big man grunting a reply. He was shaking his head and didn't look happy.

"I can't leave my dad there," John interrupted.

"We know," Joseph sighed. He studied the stables for a moment, then looked back at John. "Okay. Secure these two. Can your guy turn off the power?"

"No," Ramesh replied in the earpiece.

"He says no."

Joseph spoke to Junior again and this time he nodded while replying—'okay' being the only word John understood.

"I can shut the power off." The voice came from the ground.

John looked down at the guard who had turned his face so John could see him.

"Admir."

"Yes... John." Admir shifted slightly in the gravel, raising himself onto his elbows. "I know where the main power supply comes in and also where the new generator is."

"And why would you help us?"

"They killed my dog."

John nodded slowly, remembering the gunshot he'd heard the day they had kicked him off the Estate.

"Can you do it quickly?"

"I think so." He jerked his head toward the stable block. "The generator and the main junction box are behind the stable."

John nodded slowly again. Could he trust the man he'd

met only briefly a few days ago? There was no way of knowing for sure, but what were the other options? "Okay. Are you armed?"

"Yes." Admir shifted his weight onto one elbow and opened his jacket with the other hand, exposing a shoulder holster.

John reached over and removed the weapon, adding it to the two already in his jacket pockets.

"Go on then."

Admir pushed himself to his knees, glanced at Junior, then back at John, and nodded. "Give me two minutes."

He crawled toward the front end of the Land Rover. Hesitating, he glanced up at Junior, who was still leaning on the hood, his MP-5 aimed at the stables. "If they shoot at me, shoot back."

Junior grunted, but didn't take his eyes off the stables.

John heard Admir take a deep breath, then watched him leap out from behind the Land Rover, bent double as he ran for the far end of the stable block.

"Fucking Albanians," the driver grumbled from the gravel and John nudged him with the toe of his boot.

"Shut the fuck up."

Admir had made it halfway when there was a shout from the stables, and a shot rang out. Junior replied with a couple of rounds through the window, shattering the glass, and the firing stopped.

Admir reached the corner of the stable block and disappeared from sight.

"Can we trust him?" asked Joseph.

John shrugged. "They killed his dog."

104

Will had guessed correctly that the Range Rover would cut through town before taking the country roads toward the Atwell Estate and it hadn't taken him long to catch up; the driver keeping well under the speed limit. Now Will hung back, keeping the vehicle just in sight, but not close enough for them to suspect they were being followed. He had no idea what he would do when they reached the Estate, but John's mum had been right. They couldn't hang around and do nothing while John was in trouble.

He had been following for about ten minutes when the Range Rover accelerated away from them, the red taillights disappearing into the darkness. Will frowned. Had they spotted him? He didn't think so, and they were taking a risk driving that fast through a residential area. The speed limit was only fifty kilometres per hour, and they had to have been doing double that.

He passed his phone to Carole, "Can you redial the last number and put it on speaker? Do you know how to do that?"

She gave him a look, then did as he asked. "I may be old, but I'm not dumb."

Will chuckled and increased his speed while the call connected.

"Hello?"

"Ramesh, Will here. I'm following the Chinese guys. They've just taken off at high speed. Is everything okay?"

Will could hear rapid typing and muttering.

"Ramesh?"

"Yeah, look..." Ramesh sounded exasperated. "Ah..." more typing and then something in a language Will didn't understand, but it sounded like a curse.

"Ramesh, this is John's mother, Carole. Is John in trouble?"

The typing stopped, and there was silence for a moment. Then Will heard Ramesh clearing his throat.

"Yes ma'am, I mean sorry ma'am. Pleased to meet you. Um... John is having some difficulty right now, but nothing for you to worry about."

"Don't lie to me, young man."

"Yes, ma'am. I mean, no... I won't lie. Ummm Will are you still there?"

"Yes."

"Do whatever you can to stop the Chinese guys from reaching the Estate. That will help a lot."

The line went dead and Will shot a worried glance at Carole. She looked straight ahead, the still glowing phone in her hand, her brow furrowed. Will stamped on the accelerator, then flashed his lights as he pulled out to overtake a slow-moving vehicle. The driver honked in disgust as he passed at almost twice the speed limit.

He stole another look at Carole. She was looking down at the phone and tapping in a number.

"Who are you calling?"

She raised the phone to her ear while holding up a finger, signalling him to be quiet.

Almost immediately, she started speaking. "Police please." Her voice was different, no longer the forceful, confident voice that had questioned Ramesh. Now it sounded flustered, shaky...

"Yes, t... t... two men just threatened me with a gun. They p... p... pointed it at me through the window. I almost crashed... yes, umm... black Range Rover... just turned onto the Stockbridge road... umm I'm passing the Roebuck Inn now... please hurry, they're driving very fast... they might kill someone."

She ended the call, placed the phone on her lap and winked at Will. "That should fix them."

About a kilometre past the Harestock Road junction, on the outskirts of Winchester, flashes of blue light filled the sky and Will rounded a bend and braked heavily, almost running into the back of a line of stopped cars. Ahead were several police cars blocking the road and in between them was the black Range Rover.

He grinned at Carole.

"Well done."

She nodded once. "Now don't waste time here. We have to help John."

105

John had just finished securing the driver's hands and feet when they were plunged into darkness.

"He did it."

There was no reply, just the sound of rapid footsteps across the gravel parking area.

John stood up and, as his eyes adjusted, he could just make out the two dark forms of Joseph and Junior sprinting toward the stable block. He pulled the Glock from his jacket pocket, stepped over the body of the guard, and ran after them.

By the time he reached the stables, Joseph and Junior were formed up on either side of the entrance door, their night vision googles pulled down over their faces.

"Wait here, John." Joseph pushed John back against the wall.

"No, my dad's in there." John fought back against Joseph's hand.

Joseph sighed loudly. "Okay, but hang back. It's going to get loud." He removed an object from his webbing. "Close your eyes and cover your ears."

John hesitated, but then saw Junior kick the door open and realised what was about to happen. Just in time, he turned away, covering his ears and screwed his eyes shut. There was a loud bang and a flash visible from behind his closed eyelids. When he opened his eyes, the two men were gone.

The ringing in his ears had intensified, but he could hear screaming and shouting and his heart sank. "Dad!"

He stepped through the doorway, almost immediately stumbling over an object on the floor. It was soft and groaned when he kicked it.

"Secure him, John," came a command from the darkness. "Secure them both."

"My dad?" John protested, scanning the room, his eyes slowly getting used to the darkness of the interior. "Where is he?" John stepped over the body. "Dad!" he called out. There was no answer, and he felt a hand grasp his leg.

He tried shaking his leg free, but the hand was joined by another one, clutching at his pant leg. He gave up fighting and stamped down with his other leg. He heard the exhalation of air and a groan.

He could now make out the figure of the guard on the floor, and he pulled his leg back and kicked him in the side, the man grunting and curling into a foetal position, his arms wrapped around his head.

John removed the cable ties from his pocket, knelt down, and yanked the man's arms behind him, securing his wrists together. He did the same with his ankles, then stood and moved across the room and out into the corridor. A figure rose from the floor and staggered blindly toward him, hands held out, feeling for the walls. John braced himself, legs slightly apart, weight evenly distributed. His parents' house had been destroyed, his father kidnapped, and he had been shot at. He channelled all the rage and frustration into the right cross that struck the man's jaw, knocking him sideways into the wall. He followed immediately with a kick to the side of the man's knee. There was an audible crack followed by a scream of pain, and the guard slid down the wall onto the floor.

"Fuck you," John spat, adrenaline coursing through his system.

He dropped to his knees, flipping the man over and made quick work of securing his wrists and ankles, while the man whimpered with pain.

Voices carried from further inside the stable block, then a shout, and he jumped to his feet. "Dad? It's John..."

The man at his feet groaned, "Fuck you, mother..."

John cut him off in mid-sentence with a kick to his injured knee, and the man screamed.

"Serves you fucking right!" John stepped over him and moved on, deeper into the stable block, Glock held at the ready. Glass from the shattered windows crunched underfoot as diagonal shafts of moonlight lanced through the lingering smoke from the flash bang.

So far, they had captured four men. There was Admir, and one guard manning the gate. That made six. He had only ever counted six, but that didn't mean he hadn't made a mistake.

As if hearing his thoughts, the hair on the back of his neck tingled, and he spun round, raising the Glock, his finger curling around the trigger. A powerful hand grabbed his wrist, pushing his hand upwards, and John reflexively pulled the trigger. In the confined space, the gunshot was deafening and fragments of plaster showered down on him from the hole in the false ceiling.

"Careful, John," rumbled a deep voice. Moses.

The big man pushed past, and John flinched as another figure appeared behind him. He pointed the Glock, but hesitated as the man held up his hands.

"It's me, Admir,"

John gulped and relaxed his grip on the weapon. "Admir, turn the bloody power back on. I almost shot you."

Without waiting for a reply, John turned around and followed after Moses.

He had to find his father.

106

Carole Hayes took a deep breath and applied the brakes. It had been a long time since she had driven a car, let alone a vehicle as large as Will's Pajero.

Fortunately, it was an automatic, and she didn't have to worry about gears and a clutch pedal.

She turned slowly into the entrance of the Atwell Estate, stopping in front of the closed wrought-iron gates. The Pajero's headlights lit up the road inside, falling on the guard standing in the middle of the road. He was looking toward the house with a radio in his hand. He turned at the sound of the Pajero arriving, and Carole flicked the headlights into full beam, blinding him. She honked and wound down the window. The guard shielded his eyes with his arm and took a tentative step toward the gate.

She honked again, and the man took another step toward her.

"Turn those bloody lights down," he shouted.

"Oh, I'm sorry," Carole called out, and the sound of a female voice seemed to put the guard at ease. He walked toward the gate, but Carole waited until he was at the gate before she turned the lights off, plunging the gate into darkness. The guard, his night vision ruined, fumbled with the gate latch, and called out, "Who are you? What do you want?"

"Young man, I seem to be lost. Is this Fanshaw Manor?"

The guard opened the gate and stepped through, moving around to the driver's side of the vehicle. He stared at Carole, then peered inside the vehicle.

Carole gave him her biggest smile and said, "I've got very confused in the dark, young man."

The guard stopped frowning and opened his mouth to reply, when a large arm wrapped around his neck. The man's eyes widened as he struggled to get free, grasping at the arm as it tightened around his neck. Around ten seconds later, he went limp and Will relaxed his hold; the guard slumping unconscious in his arms.

"Throw him in the back, William. We don't have time to waste."

Will grinned. "Yes, Ma'am."

107

"Dad!" John called out again, throwing all caution to the wind. There were now three highly trained soldiers ahead of him to deal with any threat, and John's sole focus was finding his father.

"Down here, John. Last room." Joseph's deep voice came out of the darkness.

John hurried forward, stumbling over debris on the floor, almost losing his balance. He put an arm out to the wall to steady himself as the beam of a flashlight flickered through the open doorway of the last room.

John stepped through the doorway just as the lights came back on. He stopped, temporarily blinded, and blinked rapidly until he could see clearly.

David Hayes sat in a chair in the middle of the otherwise unfurnished room, blinking furiously against the sudden bright light. Junior knelt behind the chair, cutting the duct tape holding David's arms and legs, and to one side Moses was speaking quietly into Joseph's ear.

David's eyes came into focus and he stared back at John, his mouth hanging open in shock. His eyes went from John's face to the Glock in his hand, then back again. He then seemed to notice Moses and Joseph for the first time, and his eyes widened.

John hurried forward, slipping the Glock back into his jacket pocket, and knelt down in front of his father. "Dad, are you okay?"

David's eyes searched John's face, as if checking he was real, then he gulped and nodded. His arms fell forward as they came free, and he winced as the blood rushed back into his hands.

John grabbed them, rubbing them between his, warming them and increasing the circulation. There was a bruise on the side of his father's face, and his lower lip was split. His tie was loose and out of place, and patches of blood stained his shirt.

"Are you okay, Dad? What did they do to you?"

His father shook his head, then spoke for the first time, his voice faint and uncertain. "N... n... no, nothing." He swallowed and when he spoke again, his voice sounded more normal. "I'm okay." He glanced over at the three men in black, Junior having joined the others, then back at John.

"Who... who are they?"

John smiled. "Friends."

"You... you did this?"

John shrugged, "It doesn't matter, Dad. You're safe now."

Joseph cleared his throat, tapped his watch, then jerked his head toward the door. John nodded.

He stood up and, taking hold of his father's arm, helped him to his feet. "Let's get you out of here."

David's legs buckled, John catching him in time, but then he found his footing, shifting from one foot to the other until he was steady.

As he led his father up the corridor, John glanced into

the rooms he had passed in the darkness on the way in. There were several offices, a storeroom, and a room full of bunk beds, which had obviously served as accommodation for the guards. Six beds, six guards. He'd been right. But...

"Hey," he called out. "The Chinese woman. Where is she?"

Joseph stopped and looked back. "There's no-one else here. We cleared all the rooms."

"Shit! She has to be here somewhere. The house?"

"I cleared the house," Moses replied. "Only the two maids."

"Then where the hell is she?"

Joseph shrugged. "I don't know, but we have to move, John. We can't stay here."

John frowned, and half turned to look back down the corridor. Where did she go?

"John, the police will be here soon."

John hesitated, then felt a tug on his arm.

"Is something wrong?"

John turned back and looked down at his father. He suddenly looked very old and fragile.

John smiled. "No, Dad. It's okay."

Joseph was right. It was better for all if they weren't there when the police arrived.

At the entrance, Joseph and his men ignored the two men on the floor, stepping over them and out into the carpark. But his father stopped.

"Wait." He had turned his head to one side and was studying the guards' faces. "This is the one."

In the light, John recognised the guard with the injured knee. Broken Nose. He was still groaning, and flinched as John stepped closer. "What do you mean?"

"He hit me."

"Really?" John stepped back, raised his boot and stamped down on the guard's injured knee. An anguished scream filled the room, followed by sobbing.

"Good." David Hayes nodded. He looked up at John, straightened his back, and puffed his chest out. "Let's go, son. Your mum must be worried sick."

108

Joseph and his men stood in a tight huddle in the parking area. Moses held a satellite phone to his ear, and there were several large canvas bags piled up beside them.

Joseph noticed John looking at them and grinned. "Information."

John shrugged. He wasn't sure what Joseph meant and didn't really care. He had what he needed.

One of the bags, longer than the others, moved and John frowned. Did he imagine it? When it moved again, John realised what it was.

"Is that...?"

"It is." Joseph nodded. "He won't be bothering your parents anymore."

"What are...?" John stopped mid-sentence, looking past Joseph toward the entrance to the Estate.

The three men had heard it too, and they scattered, sprinting to the edges of the carpark and taking up defensive positions in the shadows.

John was too slow to react, so he stayed where he was,

dropping to the ground, pulling his father down with him. He pressed him flat into the gravel with his left hand, while drawing the Glock from his pocket with the right. Headlights appeared from beneath the trees lining the driveway as a vehicle approached at high speed.

John caught sight of the vehicle as it passed under the light at the front of the house, before sweeping into the gravelled parking area and sliding to a stop.

"Hold your fire, hold your fire!" John jumped to his feet and shouted. "It's a friend."

Joseph and his men emerged from the shadows and advanced toward the vehicle. They still had their weapons trained on the Pajero, but thankfully held their fire.

A pair of hands emerged from the passenger door, and then Will's voice, "Don't shoot, it's me, Will."

John blinked in surprise. Then who was driving? He moved forward, keeping the Glock trained on the windscreen, but the light reflecting off the glass prevented him from seeing inside.

Will climbed out, but instead of coming toward John, he hurried around to the driver's side and opened the door.

A moment later, John recognised his mother, grinning as Will helped her out.

"Mum?" He lowered the Glock. "What... what are you doing here?"

Carole Hayes chuckled, "I thought you might need some help." There was a light in her eyes, and she looked twenty years younger.

John glared at Will. "I thought I asked you to keep her safe?"

"Yeah." Will shrugged. "She's a hard woman to say no to."

"Carole, honey."

John's father was getting to his feet, and he rushed over to help him up. He shook off John's hand and, ignoring those around him, hurried over to his wife and embraced her.

"You silly old goat."

"Me?" came Carole's muffled reply, her face pressed into his shoulder. "You're the one who got caught."

John couldn't make out his father's reply, but he didn't care. They were both safe now.

He nodded at Will. "Thank you, Will."

Will winked, then raised an eyebrow at Joseph and his men. "Who are they?"

"I'll explain later, but right now, can you get Mum and Dad out of here?"

"You're not coming?"

"I'll meet you back at the motel. I've got some unfinished business here."

109

John helped his mother back into the Pajero and closed the door behind her. "I'll see you soon, Mum," he said through the open window.

"Be careful."

John smiled, "Always."

"Son?"

John looked over his mum's shoulder at his father, who sat on the floor in the rear of the van.

"Thank you. I... I'm... proud of you."

John felt moisture forming in his eyes, and he blinked. He opened his mouth to reply but couldn't find the words, so he nodded, slapped the roof of the Pajero twice and stepped back as Will pulled away. He watched it take a wide circle before heading back down the main driveway toward the front entrance to the Estate, leaving the body of the captured guard lying in the gravel next to John's feet.

As the engine noise faded away, John heard something else... another engine... but it wasn't a car. He glanced back toward Joseph and his men, but they didn't seem concerned.

He jogged over. "Can you hear that?"

Joseph grinned. "It's our ride."

"Your ride?"

The noise grew louder until suddenly a dark shape appeared low over the trees, circled once, then settled into a hover over the middle of the car park. John instinctively crouched down, turning his back on the unlit aircraft, the rotor wash sending stones and leaves flying as it dropped to the ground.

Moses hoisted the bag containing Xie over his shoulder as if it was empty, then grabbed another large canvas bag in his spare hand before running effortlessly toward the helicopter. Junior grabbed two more and followed after him.

John leaned toward Joseph and shouted to make himself heard over the roar of the engine, "Where are you taking him?"

"To meet my father." Joseph's teeth flashed in a wide grin.

John nodded. "What's in the bags?"

"Computer hard drives, files, cell phones. It's the end of Xie's company."

"Good." John looked back at the helicopter. It was a Eurocopter, the type used by emergency services and military all over Europe, but this one had no markings on the silver fuselage, and apart from a black stripe running along the side was unidentifiable. Even the tail number had been masked over with black tape. "Are you coming back?"

Joseph shook his head. "No." He held out his hand. "Thank you, John. For saving my father and... in a way, our people."

John took Joseph's hand in both of his. "Well, I couldn't have done it without you, Joseph. You saved my father, too. I'll always be grateful."

"So will I." Joseph winked. "You know where to find me. Keep in touch."

John gave Joseph's hand one more shake, then let go, and Joseph picked up the remaining two bags and stood up. He took two steps, then turned back. Leaning close so John could hear, he shouted, "I forgot to tell you, Moses said there's a lot of cash in the safe." He winked, "spoils of war," then set off at a run toward the waiting helicopter.

John watched him toss the bags in and as soon as Joseph put one boot on the skids, the helicopter rose into the air.

110

As the helicopter disappeared into the darkness, John turned and faced the stable block. Admir stood hesitantly by the corner of the stables, and John beckoned him over.

The Albanian approached slowly, his hands held away from his body, palms forward, stopping just short of John.

"It's okay, Admir. My fight is not with you."

Admir nodded slowly and some of the stiffness went out of his posture. He gestured with his head toward the departed helicopter and asked, "Who...?"

"Friends," John replied. The less people knew, the better. "Can I trust you, Admir?"

Admir shrugged.

John studied him a moment longer than went with his gut. "Come with me." He turned away and set off for the main house at a jog, skirting the bullet-pocked Land Rover.

"Hey, don't leave me here," the driver called out, but John ignored him, looking back only once to check if Admir was following.

Once in the house, he made his way to Xie's office,

where two young Filipinas huddled together on the sofa, their hands bound behind their backs, faces streaked with tears.

John held up his hands as he walked across the room. "It's okay. I'm not going to hurt you."

Xie's desk had been turned over on its side, the computer monitor smashed on the floor, and behind it, on the wall, the tattered remains of a large oil painting hinged away from the wall, exposing an open safe behind it. The edges of the safe were blackened, as if something had blown the door open.

John approached the safe and looked inside. There were several empty manila folders, a jewellery box, and bricks of cash in multiple currencies, held together with rubber bands.

John heard a low whistle behind him and muttered words in what he assumed was Albanian.

John reached in, pulled out the jewellery box, and flipped open the lid. He counted twelve gold coins and five small gold bars, each weighing around 50 grams. He snapped the lid shut, turned, and tossed it to Admir. "All yours."

Admir caught it easily, opened it, and his mouth fell open. He closed it and quickly tucked it into his waistband.

John looked around, then picked up a cushion from the floor and pulled off the cushion cover. Removing the bundles of cash from the safe, he stuffed them into the makeshift bag until the safe was empty, then crossed over to the sofa. The two women pulled their knees up and cowered away from him.

"It's okay." John smiled and crouched down so his face was at the same level as theirs. Holding out one of the cash bundles, he said, "I'm going to let you go, and give you this on one condition. You don't talk about what happened tonight to anyone. Do you understand?"

The two women nodded hesitantly.

"Do you give me your word?"

"Yes, sir," they replied in unison

"Good." John tossed the bundle onto the sofa and removed his phone. "But to make sure, I'm taking your photo, and if you ever tell anyone... my friends, the men you saw earlier, they'll come and find you."

The women gulped. "W... we won't say anything, s... s... sir."

John pretended to take their photo, then smiled again. "Good. Now you should get out of here before the police arrive."

Removing a Swiss Army knife from his pocket, he levered open the blade, stood up, and leaning over the women, cut the cable ties securing their wrists and ankles.

"Not a word," he warned, then with a nod to Admir, left the room with the cash-filled bag under his arm.

Outside in the hallway, he waited for Admir to join him, then moved him away, out of earshot of the guard sitting on the floor.

"Admir, I trust you, but what about the others?"

Admir wrinkled his brow, unsure of what John wanted.

"What I mean, Admir, is you're free to go." He nodded at the jewellery box in Admir's waistband. "Take that and get out of here, because once the government finds out what happened, you'll all be in trouble. Kidnapping, extortion, arson... I'm sure there's more."

Admir made to protest, and John stopped him. "I know it wasn't you, but the police won't know that."

Admir gulped.

"So, the others, what should we do?"

Admir took a deep breath and exhaled slowly. He glanced at the man on the floor. "Sergei, he is a good man, and Lorik also. The others..." he made a shape with his mouth and shrugged, "so, so... but one of them killed my dog."

"Who burnt down my parent's house?"

"Gerry." Admir pointed to his nose.

"The broken nose?"

Admir nodded.

John narrowed his eyes. The man was lucky John had only broken his knee.

He held out the bag of cash. "Divide this amongst you, however you see fit."

"I'm not giving any to Gerry."

"I don't care. To be honest, if he was never seen again, I wouldn't be upset."

Admir nodded slowly, the trace of a smile in the corners of his mouth.

"I'll leave it up to you how you do it, but tell them, my friends are powerful people. They've taken all the computer records. They have your names, addresses, passport copies, everything. They'll hunt you down if you utter a word of this."

Admir's smile had vanished.

"My advice is to get away as soon as you can. You don't want to be answering tough questions."

"I understand."

John stared back at him for a moment and then, satisfied he had scared him enough, reached out and gripped the man's shoulder. "Thank you, Admir. Now, go home to your family."

111

John jogged along the hedgerow marking the edge of the field, no longer worried about being seen. Half of his attention was on the ground underfoot and the other half on the voice in his ear.

"So I've inserted a virus into the security company's system to corrupt their files. No-one will ever find a record of what happened."

"Good," John panted as he dodged a patch of uneven ground. He slowed to a fast walk, taking a moment to catch his breath. "Ramesh, can you do the same with the motel footage?"

"Already done it."

"Thanks, Ramesh. I owe you big time."

"Don't mention it, John. I was glad of the excitement. It was like watching one of those LiveLeak videos. Who were those guys?"

"I'll explain when I see you. I'll be back in Dubai soon."

"I can't wait."

"Thanks again, Ramesh. Get some rest."

"You too, John."

The line went dead and John removed the ear bud from his ear, tucking it away in his pocket. Nearing a pond, John slowed, then stopped by the water's edge.

Nothing moved. There was no breeze, no sound, and the surface of the pond was a sheet of polished obsidian dotted with pinpricks of light. High above, the clouds had cleared again, exposing the heavens, and the new moon lent just enough light to bathe the countryside in a silver luminescence.

John suddenly felt very small and insignificant.

He took a deep breath, and as he exhaled slowly, scanned his body. There was a lingering tinnitus in his ears, his lower back ached, and the bones in his right hand throbbed with the memory of the guard's jaw.

He shifted position and felt the confiscated Glocks weighing down his jacket.

Covering his hand with his sleeve, he removed the weapons from his pockets, and using the front of his shirt, wiped them free of fingerprints. Then he hurled them one by one into the middle of the pond.

He watched the ripples spread out, disturbing the reflected night sky, and waited until it smoothed out and became like glass again.

No, he wasn't insignificant.

Xie was gone, and his parents were safe. He had achieved everything he had set out to achieve. Perhaps not as planned... John smiled... what plan? But the result was one he was happy with.

So far, he hadn't heard any sirens, and John doubted the guards would call the police. There had been a lot of money in the safe, enough to keep them all quiet, and money always trumped morals.

There was no record of John being on the property and

if it came to it, John would say he'd been in the motel all night. His parents and Will would back him up.

The only issue was the Chinese woman. She had vanished into thin air, but John didn't want to worry about it and spoil his mood. One thing he could be certain of, though. She wouldn't go to the police.

A frog gave a tentative croak from amongst the reeds, then another replied from the opposite side of the pond. John took another deep breath and finally allowed himself to relax.

As the frogs broke into a rhythmic chorus, he angled his head back and gazed up at the billions of distant worlds twinkling their light upon him.

Once again, despite all the odds, everything had turned out okay.

He smiled and whispered, "Thank you."

Far in the distance, a fox yelped a reply.

John chuckled, and he turned away from the pond for the last stretch across the fields toward the hidden van.

He was mentally and physically exhausted, and longing for his bed, but he drove slowly, carefully, keeping to the speed limit, obeying all the traffic rules. The last thing he wanted was to be pulled over by the police when everything had gone so well.

He kept himself alert by thinking about what needed to be done next. An insurance claim would have to be filed for his parents' house, and they would need somewhere nice to live while the house was rebuilt.

Perhaps Philip Symonds could help with the design? It should match the original, but John could add some improvements, make the house more comfortable and easier for his parents to maintain.

In the end, maybe the fire was a blessing in disguise?

He thought back to his father's parting words, *I'm proud of you,* and he smiled.

Maybe everything that happened was a blessing?

With that thought, John pulled into the motel forecourt and parked in the space outside his room. The door opened immediately, and he saw his father standing silhouetted in the doorway.

John turned off the engine as his father was joined by his mum, then Will, his frame blocking the light from behind them, allowing John to see his parents' clearly.

Apart from Adriana, his entire world stood in that doorway. A warmth filled his body, and a lump formed in his throat.

Come on John, you're getting sentimental!

He took a moment to compose himself and was about to open the door and step out when his phone buzzed in his pocket. Frowning, he pulled it out and looked at the screen. Who would message him at this time of the night?

Number withheld

John shrugged. Probably a spam message. He reached for the door handle while tapping on the screen with his thumb, then froze.

It was a photo.

A photo of a Chinese Feng Shui cat, its paw raised in a wave.

John Hayes will return in The Chinese Cat: John Hayes #10

NOTES

Chapter 2

1. See Vengeance: John Hayes #1
2. See Faith: John Hayes #8

Chapter 39

1. See A Million Reasons: John Hayes #2
2. See A New Beginning: John Hayes #3
3. See Payback: John Hayes #6
4. Payback: John Hayes #6

Chapter 41

1. See A Million Reasons: John Hayes #2

Chapter 46

1. A Million Reasons: John Hayes #2

Chapter 70

1. See Disruption: The Hong Kong Series #1

ALSO BY MARK DAVID ABBOTT

The John Hayes Series

Vengeance: John Hayes #1

A Million Reasons: John Hayes #2

A New Beginning: John Hayes #3

No Escape: John Hayes #4

Reprisal: John Hayes #5

Payback: John Hayes #6

The Guru: John Hayes #7

Faith: John Hayes #8

The Neighbour: John Hayes #9

The Chinese Cat: John Hayes #10

The John Hayes Box Sets

The John Hayes Thrillers Boxset : Books 1-3

The John Hayes Thrillers Boxset : Books 4-6 (Save 33 %)

The Hong Kong Series

Disruption: Hong Kong #1

Conflict: Hong Kong #2

Freedom: Hong Kong #3

The Hong Kong Series Boxset :Books 1-3 (Save 33%)

The Devil Inside

The Devil Inside

Flipped

The Devil Inside : Boxset (Save 33%)

As M D Abbott

Once Upon A Time In Sri Lanka

READY FOR THE NEXT ADVENTURE?

The next book is currently being written, but if you sign up for my VIP newsletter I will let you know as soon as it is released.

Your email will be kept 100% private and you can unsubscribe at any time.

If you are interested, please join here:

www.markdavidabbott.com
(No Spam. Ever.)

ENJOYED THIS BOOK? YOU CAN MAKE A BIG DIFFERENCE.

First of all thank you so much for taking the time to read my work. If you enjoyed it, then I would be extremely grateful if you would consider leaving a short review for me on the store where you purchased the book. A good review means so much to every writer but especially to self-published writers like myself. It helps new readers discover my books and allows me more time to create stories for you to enjoy.

ABOUT THE AUTHOR

Mark can be found online at:
www.markdavidabbott.com

on Facebook
www.facebook.com/markdavidabbottauthor

on Instagram
www.instagram.com/markdavidabbottauthor

or on email at:
www.markdavidabbott.com/contact